ALL I WANT

A. D. JUSTICE

BLURB

Right time. Right place. Right woman.

I was blowing off steam when a guys' trip led to a hot fling.
She was exactly what I needed for our ten days together.

I said I'd never fall in love.
I said I'd never get attached.
We were never supposed to see each other again.
We were never supposed to be anything more.

But when she comes back into my life, I remind myself of one
thing: *Wrong place. Wrong time. Wrong man.*

**All I Want is book one in the compelling *All of Me* duet
series.**

CHAPTER ONE

Rod
The Past

Ten months out of the year, I'm nine years older than my sister, Juliana. But for two months, our numerical age aligns perfectly at ten years apart.

Who would have ever believed those two months could end up being a "make us or break us" deal?

"How is she?" Dad asked from Juliana's doorway, keeping his voice low so he wouldn't wake her. He leaned his shoulder against the doorframe with his arms folded across his chest and a worried expression on his face.

"She's had a rough day, but she seems to be resting easier now." My gaze drifted back to my little sister and a swell of protectiveness filled my chest. Unlike other older siblings who resented not being the only child, I welcomed her into the family with open arms when she was born. Being an only child sucked, and I wanted to be a big brother.

"She needs her medicine refilled tonight. If she wakes up sick again, we can't let her get dehydrated. Do we have the money to afford it?" Mom moved to stand beside Dad, but she'd fixed her worried eyes on Juliana.

"We don't have a choice, Debbie. If our bills have to wait, they'll just be late. Don't stress over that, babe. Give me a few minutes and I'll go to the twenty-four-hour pharmacy." Dad turned his head and watched Mom for several long seconds. I remember the scene like it was yesterday because it struck me as so odd. His daughter was the one he should be focused on, yet he stared at Mom as if it he was seeing her for the first time.

"Thank you, Chris. I know you've already had a long day at work. I can go if you'd rather stay home."

"No, babe, I'm okay. I have a feeling your day has been worse than mine." He leaned down and kissed her on the cheek, then disappeared into the other room for several minutes.

Mom took his place holding up the doorframe. That's when bits and pieces of adult conversations I'd heard over the past couple of years started to make sense. Mom was still relatively young, only in her early thirties. She'd married and had me when she was still a teenager. Then Juliana came along ten years later as a big surprise. The strain of holding our little family together was beginning to show in her face.

"I'm leaving now," Dad announced when he reappeared. "I love you." He stroked Mom's face with his fingertips and she instinctively leaned into his touch.

"I love you too, Chris."

Then he walked over to me and motioned for me to stand. When I complied, he wrapped his arms around me and embraced me in a tight hug. "If I haven't told you lately, I just want you to know what a wonderful son you are, Rod. You've had to grow up way before your time, but I'm proud of the man you've become. I love you, son."

"Love you too, Dad."

Careful not to wake her, he leaned over Juliana and placed light kisses on her cheek and forehead. "I love you, my little precious girl." He straightened and turned his attention back to Mom. "She feels warm again. I think her fever is returning."

"We may end up in the emergency room tonight. I'm doing everything I can to avoid it." Mom scraped her hand over her face, fighting the anxiety of a potential hospital bill we couldn't afford to pay.

"Some things can't be helped, Debbie. We all do the best we can." Dad shrugged, but the heavy weight on his shoulders only amplified the effort that simple move took.

When he moved toward the door, Mom sent him out with her usual request. "Be careful, honey, and drive safely."

Dad looked over his shoulder. He wore a forlorn expression and forced a smile as he nodded.

When he didn't return home within the hour, Mom started to worry about him. She began running through the telltale signs of wringing her hands and looking out the window every few minutes for headlights. At hour number two, she called all the emergency rooms around Atlanta, one after the other, asking about a man who might fit his description. But her search was in vain. After a few hours with no word, she called his buddies, profusely apologizing for waking up the ones who answered.

Despite her efforts, she had no luck finding him anywhere. I kept my vigil beside Juliana's bed the entire night, holding a wet washcloth to her head to help bring her fever down. I wiped her mouth when the little fluid she had in her came back up and held her hand to reassure her she wouldn't die on my watch.

Sometime very early the next morning, I fell asleep in the sentinel position beside her bed in case she needed me again. Mom didn't get one wink of sleep, though. She paced the floor until small streams of sunlight broke through the blinds, shedding light on the dining room table. That's when she saw it, the note Dad had left in a place where he knew we wouldn't find it right away.

What lower-middle-class family ate their meals in a formal dining room?

Some people call it a "Dear John" letter. I call it the coward's way out.

Dear Debbie,

I'm sorry, but the life you want is not the life I want.

Please don't look for me.

I just can't do this anymore.

Chris

This was his family.

This was his wife, his son, and his daughter.

He deserted us, knowing Juliana desperately needed that medicine to get well. He did this, knowing Mom needed her husband and his kids needed their father. But *this* meant nothing to him in the end. The life he wanted was out there somewhere, in a place where we weren't. Whatever he was searching for was obviously better than we were. Something waited for him that was more exciting. He had something new that made him want to get up in the morning and come home at night.

We never knew what we did wrong to make him walk out and leave. None of us had a clue. The coward left that bullshit note and didn't bother to even send us a fucking postcard in all the years that followed. I was only fourteen when I was left to help pick up the pieces of our tattered lives. He destroyed everything when he chose the absolute worst time to have a midlife crisis.

As for his whereabouts, I don't know if Mom ever looked for him after she found that note. I sure as hell didn't look for him either. Our grandparents on his side of the family were devastated by his actions. He was still their son, and they loved him just the same, though. Truthfully, that only made me more bitter about the entire situation because that was a direct insult to my worth. That resentment emerged every time they tried to bring up the subject.

Juliana and I went to visit them one weekend when I was sixteen and she was six. Even at her tender age, she understood what Chris had done to us as a family, although she wasn't as aggressive about his betrayal as I was. When Grandma brought him up around me, it always resulted in a showdown.

"Chris is your father, Rod. You should call and talk to him." She felt it was her place to push us back together, always hoping for a family reconciliation. "A growing boy needs to spend time with his dad."

"Are you talking about the loser who left to go buy medicine for a sick little girl then never came back home? Didn't call. Didn't send money. Didn't care if we had food on the table, clothes to wear, or if we were even still alive. Is that who you're calling my father?" I loosely crossed my arms and gave her a disinterested glare.

Her eyes teared up, and she put her hand over her heart, maybe trying to keep it from breaking in two, but my response ended the conversation. At least she never tried to justify his actions. That would've sent me over the edge and she wouldn't have seen me again. When he left, my heart turned to stone. Fitting, since that's also my last name.

Still, Grandma and Grandpa tried to give us hints or some other small clue as to his whereabouts, hoping Juliana and I would contact him on our own. But neither of us took the bait. By that time, he was dead to me anyway, and I didn't want him to come back or try to make amends for anything. Watching Mom wear herself out to feed, clothe, and keep a roof over our heads during those years had sealed Chris's fate with me.

During the four years after he left us, I did everything I could to help Mom keep us alive. When she worked extra shifts at the carpet mill, I played with Juliana, read her books, cooked her meals with what little food we had, and made sure she took her bath every night. When Mom came home after spending eighteen to twenty hours on her feet, working in a hot warehouse-style building, she somehow still made time to ask about our days, our grades, and our friends. We never felt as though we were a burden or that we came last to her.

Grandma and Grandpa tried to pick up some of his slack. They knew Christmas and birthday presents were luxury items our pitiful little family couldn't afford to waste wishes on, much less spend money to buy. They made sure the major holidays and milestones were covered. On my sixteenth birthday, an old beater car appeared in our driveway and mysteriously never had an unpaid car insurance bill. Then, there was the Dell laptop and printer they insisted I needed so I could do my homework and get into a good college.

While Mom worked and Juliana slept, I studied every computer language book I could find until I could code new programs in my sleep. Technology was growing by leaps and bounds and only seemed to be more promising in the future. That's where I set my sights from an early age. Fueled by vengeance, but determined, nonetheless, I vowed our little family would never struggle again.

CHAPTER TWO

Rod

"When you're right, you're right. I'm glad you talked me into taking off work and starting our boys' trip a few days early. This is exactly what I needed. The first day of October in the Caribbean does not suck at all." I'm talking to my best friend, Kevin, but my eyes are glued to a hot brunette's ass as she passes by. "Damn, would you look at that? Her ass looks like a volleyball—hard and plump. Makes me want to sink my teeth into it."

"Man, she's fine, all right. She keeps glancing over her shoulder at you, Rod. *Annnnd* she's slowing down now. Are you going over there to talk to her or what?"

"Or what. The ladies come to me, dude. I'm not chasing tail for the two weeks we're here. Tail chases me."

"My bad, my bad. I keep forgetting what a catch you are."

"Was that sarcasm I detected? That's no way to treat your wingman."

He chuckles and takes another swig of his beer. "After all the shit you gave me over picking this destination for our getaway, you deserve worse."

This "destination" is a singles resort in Punta Cana. There's clear blue ocean, white sand beaches, and sexy, half-naked ladies as far as the eye can see in every direction. It's not exactly Hedonism II for singles, but it's pretty damn close. Since they celebrate Halloween for the entire month, they've also planned a couple of costume parties during the time we're here to further nurture the party atmosphere.

After several minutes of eye-fucking the brunette with the nice ass from behind my shades, giving her every opportunity to proposition me to no avail, I turn my attention elsewhere. If she's not bold enough to make a move and accept my open invitation, she's not bold enough for the bedroom antics I have in mind. Our other two friends, Hunter and Jace, rejoin us at our spot poolside with four ice buckets full of bottled beer.

"Man, that bartender is the woman of my dreams. I've used every line in the damn book to get her attention, but that nut ain't cracking." Hunter turns his gaze toward the poolside tiki bar and shakes his head. "I would rock her world if she gave me half a chance."

"Hunter, the chick works here, man. She's heard more lines than you could ever dream up. She's nice to you because it's her job and she's dressed to kill for the tips. Besides, that girl is so far out of your league, you'd have to be an astronaut to reach her." Jace grabs a beer from his bucket and takes off after a girl who catches his eye, not giving Hunter a chance to rebut.

"Will he score this time? Let's analyze his approach. He's confident but approachable. He's showing his best smile and bleached-white teeth. There's the subtle touch, ladies and gents. He went for the simple tactic of stroking her long hair between his fingers and letting it flow across his palm—innocent but suggestive. Watch how his knuckles graze across the exposed skin of her chest. It worked! She steps closer to him, looking up at him from under her eyelashes and smiling sweetly.

"Wait. What's happening? Her expression changed suddenly, and she's looking to her friends for advice. Jace pours on the charm, trying to sway the estrogen pack in his favor. Will he be able to close the deal this time, or will he be shot down once again? The suspense is killing me."

Kevin and I stare at Hunter, who is completely oblivious to our silence during his monologue. Even though I want to tear my eyes away and check on Jace, I can't figure out if Hunter is jealous or impressed. Maybe both? Or neither?

"No fucking way."

Kevin and I simultaneously jerk our heads toward Jace in time to see him wrap his arms around the shoulders of all three ladies at once. He glances toward us, with a satisfied smirk on his face before the four of them disappear inside the luxury resort together.

"You know what this means, boys?" I lift my beer to my lips and take a long pull from the plastic bottle.

"What?" Kevin replies, but his attention is definitely elsewhere.

"We have to up our game exponentially. Jace just went up

to the room with three girls. We've been here three full days without a decent score. The next ten days will be hell on earth if we don't find a way to show him up."

"Oh, fuck. You're right, Rod. We'll have to listen to him bragging every fucking day for the rest of our lives. Any chance there's a penthouse orgy we can get invited to? Rod, you're loaded, you know people. Get us on the list, man." Hunter swipes the sunglasses off his face and stares at me expectantly.

"I don't know what the hell you think I'm involved in when you're not around, but I don't belong to a secret society of swingers."

"But you have one-night stands all the time. You have to meet them somewhere."

"Yeah, on my own. I've never been to a sex club. Sorry to disappoint." I shrug and finish my beer while it's still cold in this heat and humidity. "Not that I wouldn't visit one if the right person invited me. I'd have to scope it out first."

"I'm going to mingle. Catch you losers later." Hunter saunters off and joins a group of ladies in the pool.

"Want to put money on how long it'll take before one of them tries to drown him?" Kevin nods toward the disappearing smiles and open scowls directed at Hunter.

"Too easy. He's already down to mere seconds to live now." We chuckle at first, then burst out in a horse laugh when one girl splashes water directly in Hunter's face. "Oh, shot down. He just doesn't have the touch."

"No, he doesn't. Bet he'll be touching himself again tonight, though."

We raise our beers in the air and cheer Hunter on from the sidelines. He responds by raising the middle fingers on both hands, which only makes us laugh harder. He retakes his seat, still soaking wet from the encounter, and scoffs loudly. "The only explanation is Jace paid those girls. They had to be hired by the hour."

"Give it a rest, Hunter. We have plenty of time left on the island to trump Jace. I'm more worried about Kevin. He's the one who insisted on coming to this singles resort, but he hasn't even attempted to hook up with anyone yet. What gives, man?"

"Nothing gives. All three of you are missing the point of this place. I'm not here to have one giant fuckfest."

"So, there *is* one. Is the location printed on the brochure somewhere?" Hunter tips his bottle back but can't hide his smile.

"Every one of you complains about how you can't find a decent girl to date for any length of time. This one wants your money. That one wants to marry the first guy who asks her out. Another one has baggage you don't want to be saddled with for life. You have a chance to meet someone here, but you're looking for the resort's orgy room instead." Kevin leans his head back against the lounge chair and closes his eyes.

"Working on your tan? You are a little pale," I quip.

"Fuck off, Rod. You're just jealous because you didn't work on your tan before our flight left, so you're basically Casper the pale white ghost out here. On the other hand, I can simply lie here in my natural olive-skinned awesomeness and attract the ladies who venture out of their basements and into the sunlight." He doesn't bother to open his eyes when he answers.

"That was a good burn, man." Hunter high-fives Kevin and they chuckle at my expense.

"Excuse me. I don't mean to interrupt, but I wondered if you could help me open this bottle. My hands are so slick with suntan oil." The brunette with the volleyball ass finally worked up the nerve to approach.

"Here, let me help you with that." Hunter is at her side in half a second. He slides his hand along hers before taking the bottle and twisting the top off with ease.

"Thank you. My hands are just so slippery from rubbing oil all over my skin." She giggles for additional emphasis.

"I think you missed a spot. Better let me fix that for you so you don't burn. The sun is very strong today."

"Are you sure you don't mind?" She bats her eyelashes at him. I thought that only happened in a cheesy romance novel.

"Not at all. What's your name, beautiful?" Hunter places his hand on her lower back and steers her away from my chair. They walk in the general direction where I saw her earlier, but they veer off course at the last second, disappearing inside the resort.

"She came over here fishing for you. Why didn't you bite?" Kevin's eyebrows nearly touch his hairline.

"Eh, she's not what I'm fishing for today. I'd have to throw her back."

He pulls his shades down to show me his bullshit detected glare. "Yeah? A few minutes ago, you were ready to eat her alive."

"One, her approach was lame. Two, she hadn't even tried to open that bottle. If it was slick with oil, Hunter would've wiped it off first. Three, I can find her type all over Atlanta. I don't need a tropical island to score an easy lay. I'm not looking for Mrs. Rod Stone, but meeting someone who's the complete opposite from all the others would be nice for a change."

"Don't wait too long to find Mrs. Right. You're not exactly a spring chicken anymore."

"What the hell, man? I'm only thirty-five."

"Exactly. The average life expectancy for American males is seventy-two. You're basically middle-aged right now. You've already passed your prime, my friend. It's all downhill from here."

"That's depressing as hell. What the fuck, man?"

"Someone has to be straight with you. Find someone you'd want to settle down with soon, or you'll soon have to settle for whoever you can get."

"You're one to talk. We're the same age and you're still single too. Where did this all this shit come from, anyway? This doesn't sound like you at all."

He shrugs one shoulder. "My parents just celebrated their anniversary and something my dad said really made me think. He and Mom married young, and they struggled for a long time. Their friends said they were crazy, they'd end up divorced before they were twenty-one, and they were ruining their lives.

"He attributes a lot of their early troubles to being young and stupid, letting those words create a self-fulling prophecy. Then he almost lost Mom, and that woke him up. He realized she was never his ball-and-chain, weighing him down. She lifted him up. His life wasn't ruined because of his love for her —it was made complete. He didn't regret one day he spent with her. He wished they'd never had a day apart.

"I've realized I want what my parents have. The single life doesn't appeal to me anymore, but finding someone I can share my life with does. That's why I'm not interested in a one-night stand with a different girl every night anymore."

"Hmm … and you think you'll find the love of your life, the woman of your dreams, here? Among all the drunken misfit Barbie wannabes?"

"That's just the thing, Rod. You never know who you'll meet or where you'll meet her." He turns toward me and a slow smile crawls across his face. The one that's usually reserved for complete and utter mischief. It seems out of place in this serious conversation.

"All right, enough of the girl talk. You're in danger of losing your man card. If you start talking about waxing body parts, I'm out of here."

"That's all right. You'll grow up one day, whether or not you like it."

He's not wrong about his parents. Their marriage is the stuff movies are made of and others can only hope to have one day, if they're lucky. If they win the spouse lottery. If they're in the right place, at the right time, and have the right set of circumstances to meet the perfect person.

I've never found luck to be on my side.

Everything I have comes from my blood, sweat, tears, and long nights of hard work to make it happen. Nothing was freely given to me. I scraped and fought for every inch I've gained in life. The notion of randomly happening upon the perfect mate, one who could make me want to be monogamous, is about as real to me as a fairy tale. The problem is, those tall tales are the exact ones that automatically set up relationships for failure because that level of perfection is impossible to achieve.

It's a recipe for instant disappointment and certain heartbreak.

Been there, done that, and I bought the T-shirt as a permanent reminder I'll never be that vulnerable or that pathetic again.

CHAPTER THREE

Daisy

"I feel so guilty about taking this trip. Maybe I should cancel and stay home instead. You can get someone else to go with you." I glance around my new house and take in the unpacked boxes and general mess from my recent move.

"Maybe you should take the ten-day vacation we've looked forward to for months and enjoy yourself for once. Let your hair down and have some fun. Meet some hot guy and let him do all those things you read about in your steamy romance books. Make sure he's a billionaire badass biker with a secret big heart who's looking for everlasting love, though." I can always count on my best friend, Tracy, for stellar life advice.

"Look at this place, Tracy. I'm nowhere near finished unpacking, and I start a new job soon after I get back. If I go, I won't have enough time to finish unpacking and get caught

"

up on the past and future lesson plans for my class. The timing is just off. Maybe next year will be better."

"Nope. Next year you'll have an entirely different set of excuses to avoid going. A new reason to avoid facing the real reason you're hiding. You're avoiding your own life, Daisy. How do you ever expect to find happiness when you hide from the very things you say you want?" Tracy pins me with that no-nonsense stare of hers that makes me squirm.

She knows she's right.

She knows I know she's right.

There's no getting around it.

"Fine. You win, I'll go. I just won't get any sleep after we get back and before I start my job. Happy now?"

"Not entirely, but that's better. Don't plan on getting much sleep during the trip, either. We have ten days in the Caribbean—sun, sand, surf, hot guys, bad decisions, and an unlimited drink package. Don't you even think about wimping out on me, Daisy Nash."

"You're going to be this bossy during the entire trip, aren't you?"

She cuts her eyes at me with her brows drawn down and a bewildered expression on her face. "Of course. That's why we're going together, so I can be your voice of reason."

That makes me laugh out loud. "If you're the voice of reason in this relationship, we are in deep shit on this trip."

"Don't be a spoilsport. You've already given all the emergency contact information to your sister. Your parents probably even have the resort manager's name. You're hitting the best beaches, in the most luxurious resort, with the hottest guys, and the best friend slash partner in crime you've ever had. We will have the time of our lives together. Trust me."

"You know I trust you with my life. That's not even a question."

"You just don't trust my judgment regarding your hoo-ha. You're not fooling me." She hits the button on the blender, mixes our pre-flight piña coladas, and passes a glass to me. "To our trip. We leave tomorrow, so you'd better get busy finding your itty-bitty-polka-dot-bikini in all this mess, or you'll be the talk of the resort in no time."

With my drink in hand, I sip the frozen concoction through the straw while I find the box with my summer clothes in it. Before Tracy leaves my new place, we pack my suitcase, make sure my passport is in my purse, and finish off the bottle of Captain Morgan, so he's not left here alone while we're vacationing in the Caribbean. I'm not sure what I'll find in my suitcase tomorrow when we board the plane, but I'm feeling too good to worry about it in the least tonight.

"Why did I let you talk me into drinking so much last night?" I glance over my shoulder at Tracy as we stand in line for security.

Here I am, hanging on to an ounce of energy by a single thread, and she's perfectly put together as if she didn't stay up all night with me. It's not fair, really, and should be against the girl code. If I look and feel like shit, the best friend solidarity rule should apply and be strictly enforced. Sensing my glare, she has the nerve to flash her bright-eyed and bushy-tailed smile at me. The laugh isn't there, but it's definitely implied.

"You needed all the rum last night to loosen your sphincter muscle so you can breathe a little."

"One has nothing to do with the other. I don't know what science class you took or how your mother explained *anything* to you, but your sphincter muscle doesn't help you breathe. At all. That's your diaphragm."

"That's exactly what I mean. You're too damn anal to just relax and breathe. Let whatever is going to happen unfold on its own. You don't need every moment of your life planned. Nothing has gone according to plan so far anyway, so we're doing this vacation my way."

"If you say so." I'm not so sure about her plan of not having a plan.

"All I want is for you to have fun without worrying about tomorrow or next week or next year. Live in the moment and be happy—truly happy—for once." She means well, but she obviously doesn't know me as well as she thinks she does.

Planning gives me a sense of security. Not planning makes me nervous because I don't know what's coming around the bend.

When I don't respond, she lowers her brows and narrows her eyes. "I know exactly what you're thinking, Daisy Nash. Not having your every moment scheduled will be liberating, not frightening."

Well, perhaps she knows me a little better than I initially thought, but that doesn't change my stance. But for her sake, I'll try to go with the flow and see what happens. Worst-case scenario, she's forced to acknowledge I can't function the same way she does. Best-case scenario, I learn I can. We both win either way.

At least, that's what I'm trying to convince myself anyway.

"Okay, I'll try this your way. Don't make me regret it. What do you want to do first when we get there?"

"Grab a couple of drinks and check out every amenity the place offers. After you've had enough liquid courage, we can walk around and find you a delicious man. Out of all the guys who will be there, there has to be at least one you'll like."

One thing Tracy has given me an earful about is how picky I am about who I will and won't date. I've had plenty of offers, but my response is almost always a "no, thank you." I can't help it, though. I have standards I expect them to live up to immediately, and when they fall short before they've even suggested a date, I can't lower my expectations for a free meal and a movie.

My standards are simple: no players, man-whores, or any man who takes longer to get ready than I do.

Going by those three principles alone, I don't think I'll find "the one" at a singles resort, despite Tracy's insistence that I shut up about it and just have a marvelous time. Let whatever happens happen. Throw caution to the wind and let it all hang out.

I'm not so confident I can do that. But I'm determined to have fun with my bestie, so I'll fake my way through the awkward moments until we're back in Atlanta and back in our comfortable routines.

We board our three-and-a-half-hour flight and take our seats in first class. The flight attendants spoil us, bringing drinks and high-end snacks until the pilot lowers the wheels for landing. We exit down the stairs and walk straight into a separate line for immigration and customs. Our all-inclusive resort thought of everything, including our transportation via the Mercedes van, with a hotel concierge onboard to check us in so we can avoid the line in the lobby. I rarely splurge for myself, but I couldn't resist doing it for this trip. This is the first time I've been away on a vacation like this in my entire life. I don't expect to find the love of my life on this trip, but I do want to meet someone and have fun, despite Tracy's doubts otherwise.

When we arrive at our hotel, we're met by the resort's greeting staff, trays of tropical umbrella drinks, and porters who take our luggage to our rooms. With our drinks in hand, we walk through the lobby with our mouths hanging open and giddiness building inside with our every step. Tracy takes my hand and pulls me up the grand staircase and through the doors to the expansive patio overlooking the vibrant blue sea below.

The wind blows across our face, and we have the best views of the clear Caribbean Sea. We settle against the railing, sip our drinks, and leave all our cares behind. For the next ten days, we're two single ladies on an elegant island oasis, complete with pools, restaurants, bars, casinos, spas, and costume parties, on a warm southern island in the Caribbean Sea.

With my eyes closed for a moment, I inhale the salty air and envision the day ahead of us. We have what's left of the day and all night to explore the expansive resort. Then tomorrow night, we have a late-night costume party to kick off the festivities in a big way. Focusing on the here and now helps calm my mind and tamp down the anxiety lying just under the surface, agitating all my nerves at once.

My life is splendid now, and this trip will only reinforce that fact in my mind.

"Drink up. Another round is coming." Tracy interrupts my Zen moment with her demand, but I'm picking my battles.

Having another drink on a tropical island isn't on my list of worries.

When my glass is empty, she replaces it with a fresh one before we stroll along the pathway to the other side. "I already feel more relaxed. This was an excellent idea. Thanks for making me come with you."

"Of course. I'll always be your wing-girl, and you'll be mine wherever we go. Someone has to make sure you have a little fun in your life. You can't always be the responsible one."

Her words strike a chord deep inside me, immediately conjuring memories I'd rather forget, but can't. Instead of dwelling on them yet again, I intentionally turn my mind's eye to the positive. "One of us has to be. We'd end up in the local jail for most of our trip if I rely on you to be the adult."

Before she can hit me with her typical sarcastic comeback, two handsome men walk through the door behind us. The one in front is tall, obviously works out and takes care of himself, and has the most gorgeous blue eyes I've ever seen in person. The gold flecks around the center sparkle in the sun. His black hair is purposely messy on top and short on the sides, tempting any woman with a pulse to run her fingers through it.

The moment his gaze lands on me, his eyes darken, becoming more gray than blue, as I watch in awe. I've read about this happening but never experienced it firsthand. The reason behind the instant attraction I feel is apparent. This guy is all man and no boy, with a devastatingly handsome face and an air surrounding him that quietly, but undeniably exudes his powerful essence. With his perfectly pressed designer clothes, expensive watch, and name-brand shoes, I'd automatically say he's a player, visiting a singles resort to add several more notches to his bedpost.

The worn bird pendant on the strand of leather around his neck is at odds with the rest of his attire and makes me think there's more to him than what meets the eye. That worthless piece of jewelry conveys a story contrary to the rest of his clothes and demeanor combined. The sentimental value outweighs the importance he places on the more expensive material things, even if he hides it from the rest of the world.

None of that explains the way my soul recognizes his, or why I know instantly that somehow, he and I are kindred spirits, without even knowing his name or hearing his voice.

"Hello, ladies. Hope we're not crashing a private party." His voice matches his face—masculine and oozing sex appeal.

My reaction to him is entirely out of character for me. I'm not an inexperienced little girl who falls in love with the first guy who pays attention to her. I'm a grown woman who has lived through events that would cripple lesser people. My real-life experiences made me grow up, whether or not I wanted to. Being tongue tied in front of any man is not in my DNA.

And yet… I can't speak.

"Not at all, guys. We're just enjoying these amazing views. Can you believe this place? This is Daisy, and I'm Tracy." She extends her hand to the second handsome man, not at all affected by their presence, while I want to wipe my hand on my clothes in case it's sweaty and clammy. But I can't because that would be too obvious with how close we are.

All I can think of is how to get out of shaking hands.

I wrap both hands around my frosty glass that's still full of my frozen concoction, for just a couple of seconds, as I move it to my left hand. That's all the excuse I need. Thank God for condensation. After I quickly dry my hand on my shorts, I extend it toward my soul mate and give him a smile that's not too awkward.

"Nice to meet you."

"It's very nice to meet you too, Daisy. My name's Rod, and this is Kevin. But you don't have to remember his name—only mine." He steps around Tracy to move directly in front of me.

The blush starts at the base of my neck and slowly creeps toward my face. I feel the heat increase with every blink. The way my name rolled off his tongue felt like a lover's caress, filled with so many naughty promises whispered in the dark. When his hand slides into mine and his fingers curl around my skin, I feel the electric current flash through my veins and strike the center of my chest.

"Rod? I've never met anyone with that name, though I am a huge Rod Stewart fan." I don't know why I said that. Are there any holes around I can crawl into?

"I've never met a Daisy either. It's obvious we're both one of a kind." His comfortable laugh puts me at ease. I appreciate a man who knows how to cover up a gaffe, rather than make fun of it.

"Oh, yes. You're exactly right." I laugh with him, and we forget the stupid comment, just like that.

"Have you seen the pool area yet?"

"Only on their website. We just got here, so this is as far as we've made it on our tour of the grounds. I bet the pool is more unbelievable in person."

"They really went all out to make it a paradise oasis. Shall we?" His hands are in his pockets, but he extends an elbow toward me.

"Sure. Why not?" I wrap my hand around his arm, and we fall in step together. Tracy and Kevin follow several yards behind us, lost in their own conversation.

"Kevin and I arrived a few days ago with two other friends, Hunter and Jace. They're around here somewhere. We've spent most of our time around the pool, listening to music and drinking beer by the bucket."

"That sounds fun. You're not dressed for the pool today, though."

"No, Kevin and I went into Punta Cana to check out what it has to offer. We decided the resort has everything we need, so we came back. We were just talking about grabbing some dinner soon."

"The reviews for the formal dining restaurant said it's out of this world. I think Tracy already confirmed our reservations tonight. You should try it out." Suggesting he should go to the same restaurant feels a little forward for me, but I'm enjoying his company.

This man would break my heart if I let him, I can tell by a single glance. And yet, I can't make myself walk away from him just yet. There's a kindness in his eyes that draws me in, compelling me to get to know him better. There's a familiar air about him that encourages me to spend time with him, exploring his mind and finding out everything there is to know about him. Under his confident exterior and name-brand clothing, he's a different man. I'm sure of it.

We reach the pool area, and the encompassing scene shocks me speechless. From the waterfall surrounded by palm trees, to the zero-entry pool that I'd swear was an actual beach, to the tiki hut bars with the massive sound system, this area is a tropical paradise. A group of women walk by, wearing thin pieces of floss for bathing suits, and I instantly feel inferior and self-conscious. I'll never be one of them, walking with confidence and pride while wearing next to nothing. Judging by Rod's handsomeness, I can't help but think he'd prefer one of these beauties over me. When I chance a glance at him, his eyes are glued blatantly to the ass of one girl who just passed us.

"Well, thanks for the tour. We should see if our room is ready now." I extract my arm from his and put a little distance between us. His ass-trance breaks, and he immediately notices my obvious move away from him.

"You know, you look so familiar. I'd swear I know you from somewhere. Do you work at Subway by any chance?"

"Um, no, I don't." I'm more focused on making my retreat than his ridiculous question.

"That's funny because you just gave me a foot-long. What do you say to sharing it with me?"

He did not just say that out loud. Why did he have to ruin every-thing with his gawking and idiotic pickup line?

"What do I say?" I hide my disgust long enough to throw him off his game. Then I grab the waistband of his designer shorts, pull it toward me as far as it'll go, and pour my icy drink on his crotch. "I say you need to cool your engines before you blow a gasket, Hot Rod."

Tracy openly gapes at me for a few seconds, unblinking and unable to make any sound. Then she simultaneously bends at the waist and releases the loudest laugh I've ever heard. It echoes all around us. I can imagine it floating on the wind, being carried to the rest of the resort so everyone else can join in on the fun.

Hot Rod jumps around on his tiptoes, trying to get the

thick blended ice off his junk before he suffers from frostbite while yelling, "what the fuck," repeatedly. The crowd around us breaks out into fits of laughter at his expense.

"Come on, Daisy, I'll buy you another drink. You deserve one after that move. That was the funniest shit I've seen in a long time." Tracy throws her arm around my shoulders and guides me past Rod and Kevin.

CHAPTER FOUR

Rod

"Did it freeze and fall off? Are you a eunuch now?" Kevin asks from outside the bathroom door. The fucker isn't even trying to hide his laughter.

"You worry about your own cock and balls, and I'll take care of mine. I don't need your help." I drop my wet, sticky shorts on the floor and jerk my shirt over my head before stepping into the shower.

Kevin opens the bathroom door so he can continue to razz me about my blatant strike out with the first girl I approached on the island. "Are you that rusty, man?"

"What are you talking about now?"

"That lame pickup line you used on that girl. That was terrible." He bursts out in uncontained laughter again. "I mean, you're lucky she only doused you with a cold drink.

She could've kneed you in the balls and put you out of commission for the entire trip. That would really suck."

I sigh and shake my head, the droplets of water flying in every direction. He's right. It was a stupid line to use on her. Despite my obvious humiliation, I think of imaginative ways to run into her again, accidentally on purpose. "Yeah, I should've known better than to say that. It was supposed to be funny, like an icebreaker to move out of the friend zone, but it didn't have that effect on her."

"Uh, no, not at all. They bill this place as a chance to meet someone you can have a genuine connection with and possibly explore a long-term relationship. But we both know what can sometimes happen when men and women meet on an exotic vacation. They lose inhibitions. They throw normal standards out the window. But with a classy lady like her, that probably wouldn't happen before you've taken her to dinner, though."

"Dude, I had to wait forever in soaked, sticky shorts with wet, sticky junk before our maid finished cleaning our room. I'm not in the mood to be made fun of the rest of the day." I turn off the water and run a towel across my wet skin.

"You're exaggerating again. The maid wasn't in here that long. Just be glad Jace and Hunter weren't around to witness that."

"Don't you fucking dare tell them either." I pin him with my don't-fuck-with-me glare.

"Your secret's safe with me." He holds up his hands in mock surrender. "They won't even be back in their room tonight."

"Are they still with the same girls they met yesterday?"

"Yeah. Can you believe it? Jace sent me a text saying he's officially in love."

"After one night together? Come on."

"Hey. When you know, you know."

"Man, I barely believe love exists, so there's no way love at first sight is real."

"Is that right? Then why are you taking so long to get dressed for dinner? Hoping you'll run into Daisy again to change that shitty first impression you made?"

"Nope." *Yes.*

After I dress, we head out to grab some dinner. Daisy confirmed my suspicion that she's the formal dining type, so the dress slacks and button-down shirt I packed came in handy for the on-site four-star restaurant.

Why am I even looking for her after the disaster earlier? I don't have a solid answer for that question, but there's no way in hell I'll let Kevin know I want to see her again. She's gorgeous and spirited and plucky. That's a combination I haven't encountered before in any woman I've met and one I'd like to get to know better.

We head to the resort's more formal dining room and find our assigned seats for the evening. The resort switches the seats every night to encourage mingling and meeting other people.

While glancing over the menu, I take a moment to peer around the room. Since I first laid eyes on Daisy, I haven't been able to think of much else. Okay, so I screwed up with my asinine comment, but I'm more than willing to make up for that blunder. I'm close to giving up on seeing her at dinner when she walks through the door wearing a black shift dress that hits mid-thigh and drapes off one shoulder. Those strappy black high heels she's wearing make her legs look sexy as hell—tanned, toned, and flawless.

I wait until she and her friend find their table, then I approach the maître d' with a hefty tip to reassign my table to be beside wherever she's sitting for the rest of the trip. Thankfully, the party that occupies the table beside them tonight hasn't arrived yet, so swapping our seats doesn't cause much of a disruption. At least not until Daisy looks up and realizes Kevin and I are appropriating the table immediately next to hers.

"What the hell do you think you're doing?" She pierces me with those deep blue eyes. Anger mixed with intrigue swirls in the depths.

"I'm here to have dinner. What are you doing?" I keep my tone friendly, no hint of being bothered by the earlier altercation. I'm fascinated by how she takes me to task without losing her cool.

"Well, I was about to enjoy dinner, but maybe I should order room service instead." She moves to push her chair back from the table, but I reach over and gently wrap my fingers around her wrist, stopping her in place.

"Give me just a minute to apologize. My earlier comment was way out of line and disrespectful. I was trying to be funny and charming and memorable, but I failed miserably. If I'd heard some guy use that line on my little sister, I would've beaten his ass for it. You don't deserve any less respect. I'm sorry, Daisy. Can we start over?"

She stares me down for several seconds, weighing her options and considering her next move. "You achieved memorable, just not in the way you intended. Apology accepted. But, for the record, I'm not interested in a one-night stand with you, so don't even try. Got it? You're sitting beside us for dinner tonight, and there's nothing I can do about your table. But I can just as easily tip the staff to change my table."

You try to convince yourself of that, love. Your body gives me very different vibes—from the way you look at me to how your pulse jumps when I'm near. Two sixty-second meetings in one day tell me more than your words ever could. Now all I have to do is earn your trust.

"I'm only trying to apologize and have a friendly dinner. I'll leave you alone now. You won't be bothered by me anymore."

Tracy cuts her eyes over to me and hides a knowing grin behind her glass of water. "That's very thoughtful of you, Rod, to apologize like that. You didn't have to go to the trouble of changing tables just to say that, though. Maybe there's more to you than just a well-dressed douchebag."

So, the best friend is an excellent judge of character and can read people at first glance. Her tone and smile are playful, telling me she means no offense by her insulting jab. It's no worse than what the guys and I throw at each other. This dynamic should make the rest of our stay interesting, to say the least.

"Rod and I thought it would be an excellent idea to help protect you two ladies from any creeps on the grounds. We need to be close to you to be more effective." Kevin jumps into the conversation with a smile and a wink for Tracy.

She nods, a smile still playing on her lips, and continues to hold his gaze. I wonder if there's something there between them, brewing under the surface. If I fan that flame, maybe it'll help convince Daisy she should spend more time with me.

I'm even willing to try a couple of double dates while we're here, if that changes her mind.

"Well, we appreciate your concern for our safety and well-being. Don't think we can't kick your asses if we need to, though." Tracy playfully bats her eyes.

"We wouldn't dare make that mistake." Kevin leans in, giving Tracy all his attention.

It's sickeningly sweet, to be honest. The man is already whipped.

Kevin continues to flirt with Tracy, so I block them out and give Daisy my full consideration. I don't know why I'm compelled to win her over and rectify how I insulted her earlier. There are plenty of other beautiful women at this resort who have already shown an interest in me, even on the quick walk to the dining room. But Daisy is the only one who's expanding my attention span. Right beside her is exactly where I want to be... for now.

"So, what do you do for a living, Daisy?"

"Rod, I appreciate what you're doing, apologizing and being friendly now, but I think it's best if we don't share any details from our everyday lives. I'm not playing hard to get when I say *this—*," she gestures between us, "isn't going anywhere. You can drop the charade and go find someone more receptive to what you're looking for. I assure you I won't mind."

"And what is it you think I'm looking for?"

What is wrong with me? I love how she tests me and calls me out on my bullshit, but I'm not looking for anything longer than this vacation will last. That's not exactly a one-night stand, but it's not a lifetime commitment either. I think what attracts me to her the most is her self-respect.

She doesn't pretend to be something she's not to get attention.

"You're looking for a warm body to heat your sheets and bid you a quick goodbye at the end of the trip. But that's not what I want. I'm a grown woman, and I want more than just a series of short romances or one-night stands. Don't misunderstand me because I'm not judging you for it. We simply have very different expectations and standards." She shrugs nonchalantly while leaving me out in the cold.

"I'll just have to work harder to change your mind then."

"You won't, so you shouldn't even try. You can't change first impressions, Rod, and I believe what you offered earlier was exactly what you want from me—or anyone—for that matter. No more, no less."

Our waiters arrive just in time to stop me from arguing my useless point any further. I just met the girl, and it's not as if we're two souls destined to sail away in the night and spend the rest of our lives together. My solemn vows to never fall in love are written in stone, my heart of stone, as I like to say. I will never become attached to anyone. I will never marry or have kids of my own. This isn't merely a bachelor's creed. It's a survival reflex.

We'll eat, chat over a superb meal, and go our separate ways at the end of dinner. She's made that abundantly clear. But she piques my interest more than I care to admit. Daisy has a solid backbone, and when she makes up her mind, she stands by it. Beauty, brains, and brawn all in one gorgeous little package.

The ladies finish their dinner, then push away from the table to leave. Tracy looks at me, then at Kevin. "What a great first day, right? Maybe we'll see you around tomorrow, boys."

THE NEXT MORNING, KEVIN AND I ARE LOUNGING BY THE POOL when Daisy and Tracy stroll past us in their bikinis and claim two empty chairs a few spaces down from us. I can't take my eyes off Daisy, but she doesn't even spare me a glance. Tracy blows a flirty kiss at Kevin, who catches it in the air before sending one back to her.

How the hell did they get so lovey-dovey since dinner last night?

We have a full day enjoying the resort amenities before the staff's matchmaking activities begin first thing tomorrow morning. They gave us a whole itinerary of pre-planned events to help strangers meet when we checked in, but we've both ignored it until now. Kevin and I move the moment the couple beside Daisy and Tracy vacate their seats. Between the two of us, we use every excuse under the sun to strike up a conversation with them. While Tracy is talkative and open, Daisy only replies to the direct questions and doesn't elaborate on anything. After repeated attempts to get her to open up only ultimately to strike out, even after using my top-notch moves, I should be ready to give up on her.

But I love a challenge, and she definitely offers that.

A few entertainment staff members set up a karaoke machine on a small, raised stage at the end of the pool. One of the guys gets up on the stage with his clipboard and the microphone, asking everyone for their attention.

"Hello, everyone! My name is Josh, and I'm one of your activity coordinators. Throughout your stay, my partner, Alisha, and I will host several friendly competitions here in the pool area. The prizes include cash, a trip to our spa for a nice massage, and even a chance for a free return vacation. Our first event is a karaoke performance contest. Take part in our *Fantastic Fanatic Antics* to enter. Who will be our brave first contestant and belt out a song for us?"

I'm determined to break the thick layer of ice Daisy has put between us one way or another. Serenading her with a song may not be the best solution, but it's a start.

"I will." I stand and get their attention.

The crowd around the pool cheers, and several people lift their glasses toward me. At least most are already three sheets to the wind, so my lack of singing in the proper key won't be an issue.

Josh hands me a list of songs, and there's one that instantly jumps out at me. It is perfect. He laughs when I point it out to him, but he has no idea just how funny it is. When the music begins and the lyrics scroll up the screen, I turn my attention to Daisy and sing "Do Ya Think I'm Sexy" by Rod Stewart directly to her. Only her. Over the entire song.

Her face turns a scorching shade of red. She nervously glances around, but her gaze always returns to me. Tracy nudges her from the side, laughing maniacally, but I keep going. Then I realize I need to turn up the heat and get the crowd on my side. My hips slowly undulate from front to back, suggestively beckoning her to me. My chest is already bare, so I use my free hand to offer my body for her viewing pleasure. Then I turn around and shake my ass before crooking my finger at her, telling her to walk in my direction.

The catcalls and whistles from the people around the pool are deafening, but the extra encouragement works. Daisy leaves her seat at last and joins me on stage. With my arm around her waist, we finish the song together and give the audience an entertaining show. We take a bow to the clapping and cheers from our peers before rejoining our friends.

"That was awesome, Rod. The boy has talent, doesn't he, Daisy?" Tracy smiles from ear to ear.

"Yes, I have to give you credit, Rod. You sounded great up there. And a nice choice of song, too. Rod Stewart." She shakes her head in disbelief, but at least she's smiling and speaking to me now.

"That's very kind of you. I'm afraid that's the extent of my abilities, though. Don't ask me to sing anything that requires any kind of range. At all. Or a song that requires me to be on key."

"Ah, you're just modest. I bet you have all kinds of hidden talents." Tracy laughs and flags a passing waitress for another round of drinks.

While others humiliate themselves with more karaoke, the four of us drink, dance, laugh, and make small talk. I don't dare venture into any personal topics with Daisy yet. Just from our limited interaction, it's clear she's leery of strangers and isn't keen on giving second chances. She's only beginning to give me the time of day now, which is a step up from how she virtually ignored me just a few hours ago. So I'm not screwing this up by pushing the limits just yet.

On the other hand, Kevin and Tracy seem to be very chummy, and no topic is off-limits for those two. Part of me still wonders if I shouldn't give up and move on to greener pastures, since Daisy still isn't warming up to me very well. There are plenty of women surrounding us who are staring at me, just waiting for me to nod in their general direction. For the sake of group sanity, I'm on my best behavior and trying to get along with the one intent on ignoring me.

More than a few guys try to approach Daisy to get her attention, but I intercept that bullshit before they reach her. Something about her draws me in and holds me hostage. Something I've never experienced before. On one hand, I feel as though I know her. On the other, she's a complete enigma, wrapped in a mystery, and bound with a barbed wire bow.

I recognize a defense mechanism when I see one.

My attraction to her is more than physical, though I can't and won't deny that's part of it. There are aspects of her personality I can't figure out, and I'm good at sizing people up with a quick glance. Her secrets lie far beneath the surface, carefully guarded and intentionally kept. Only time will tell what they are because she's not the type of person who would bare her soul before she's ready.

After we've soaked up all the sun and rum, Daisy and Tracy get up to leave in the late afternoon hours. Tracy lingers behind Daisy before stopping in front of our chairs and pulling her shades down her nose.

"You boys try to stay out of trouble. Remember, no one will be themselves tonight."

That's an odd statement. What is she trying to tell us?

The first costume party is later tonight in the rooftop nightclub. I'm betting she will be there with little Miss Daisy Piña Colada in tow. In fact, I'm counting on it now, especially after Kevin's endless flirting with Tracy all day. I wasn't looking forward to attending the parties at first. Dressing up in a costume seems so juvenile at my age. I'm attending for one reason, and one reason only. If going incognito gives me a second chance at a first impression, I'm all for it.

The feisty little blonde with the rocking body, beautiful face, and soulful blue eyes is definitely worth getting to know better, even though she humiliated me with the drink down my shorts bit yesterday and shot down every attempt I made to convince her to give me a second chance today.

I'm obviously a glutton for punishment because her steely resolve only makes her that much sexier.

After she walks off, I cut my eyes to Kevin, and he smiles from ear to ear. "That's right. You are going to that costume party tonight, and you're wearing the one I brought for you."

Why do I have a sinking feeling in my gut?

Oh yeah, because I've left the fate of my man card in the hands of my friend… who lives to humiliate me.

CHAPTER FIVE

Rod

"I should know better than let you pick out our outfits for the costume party." I stare at the over-the-top ensemble in disbelief.

"What's wrong with you? You're over six-feet tall. Muscular. It'll fit you perfectly." Kevin has the nerve to sound offended.

"Dude. You're dressing me up as Captain America. The most straitlaced, by-the-book member of the entire gang."

"Maybe, but he's also one of most lusted after members of the gang too. Women eat that shit up. Truth, courage, heroism, that's what he stands for, so that's how they'll see you. You should make good use of the illusion while you can."

"Are you saying I'm not all those things without the costume?" I arch one eyebrow in a direct challenge.

"Are you fucking with me right now? You won't even tell

your overnight guests to leave. You still make your little sister do it for you." Kevin throws a barb back at me.

Touché.

"I can't believe you two are dressing up. Both of you are acting like a couple of little girls." Hunter leans against the doorway of our adjoining rooms.

"Envy green isn't a good color on you, bro. You're just jealous because this looks damn good on me."

"I suppose you're right. Maybe it'll help you finally get laid… at a singles resort… that's full of willing and able hot babes. But you do what you have to do, pal." Hunter and Jace laugh it up on their way out.

Their jabs don't bother me. I've never been susceptible to peer pressure, and I'm not about to start now. They're two of my closest friends, but I'd never seek their advice for money, women, or life in general. If I want to find the best watering holes or which dating app offers prime selections, I may ask their advice then. But only if I become desperate.

The Captain America outfit has one distinct advantage. The helmet covers half my face, exactly like the one in the movies. In a dimly lit nightclub, with flickering colored lights and lots of bodies moving around, maybe I can hide my true identity for a few hours. Only long enough to convince Daisy she should give me a second chance. Why? I'm not even sure. It's not as if anyone meets and falls in love within a brief span of ten days. That bullshit only happens in the sappy romance movies chicks love to watch. I've never met a woman who held my interest for more than twenty-four hours.

Given that Kevin hasn't stopped talking about Tracy since we left the pool area, I suppose I'm stuck with Daisy for the duration of the trip if I want to hang out with my best friend at all. But, if Daisy hooks up with some other guy, all bets are off. I'll revert to my typical pattern and not sweat the small stuff. Barring that, we have ten days in this tropical paradise, then we'll go our separate ways.

Spending that time with her while we're on vacation wouldn't be so bad. Ten glorious days of enjoying the Caribbean sun, lazing by the pool, and staring at her bikini-covered body from behind my mirrored shades is not a hardship. We'll have late night strolls on the beach, being anything but lazy. We'll take advantage of the resort's island excursions to get away for a while, then attend the after-hours parties where adult libations flow like water. When this trip is over and we go our separate ways, we can avoid any awkward goodbye moment, unlike my other overnight guests.

This plan suits me to a T.

"Fine. I'll wear the goody-two-shoes costume. What are you wearing?" I turn to Kevin with my full costume in place.

"Get a load of this shit." Kevin disappears into the bathroom to change so he can hide his getup from me.

For the record, any time in the past when Kevin fully reverted to his full Southern accent and muttered the words, "get a load of this shit," it has never ended well for either of us. It's his equivalent of, "hold my beer and watch this."

After I'm satisfied the helmet hides enough of my features to identify me, I glance over and find the bathroom door is still closed. "Kevin, what are you doing in there? Does your costume require you to remove all your body hair or what?"

The door swings open, and he steps in front of me in all his alter-ego glory. I'm literally stunned speechless for several moments before I burst out in laughter.

"What do you think? It's perfect, right?" He extends his

arms out in front of him, giving me a full view of his ensemble.

"Honestly, it is the best costume I've ever seen. You look exactly like Popeye, even down to your squinty eye and corncob pipe."

"I'm a sailorman. Coming into port on a tropical island. Get it?" His smile splits his face in two. He's so proud of his idea.

"Yeah, yeah. I get it, man. It's great. You know I'd tell you if it wasn't… because I wouldn't let you wear it and embarrass me."

"Man, I make Popeye look good. That suit fits you perfectly. We'll have all the ladies eating out of our palms tonight."

"There's only one lady I'm interested in palming tonight." I didn't mean to let it slip out into the open like that.

"The great Rod Stone only wants one lady. Is the world ending? Who are you, and what have you done with my best friend?"

"Let it go, Kevin. I've given it some thought. It just makes sense to hook up with one person for the entire trip. Avoid the awkwardness of running into each other around the resort. Especially since you're already attached to Tracy at the hip."

"Uh-huh." His smirk says it all. He's not buying my reasoning one bit. But I don't have time or the inclination to examine it any deeper than I already have. Thankfully, he drops it and accepts my word.

"Time to head up to the roof. The party is already in full swing, and we're late."

"Absolutely. Can't let anyone else cut in on your territory, can we?"

With a playful shove, I move him out of our suite and toward the elevators. When we walk into the nightclub on the top floor of the hotel, the lights are low, the music is thumping, and the alcoholic drinks are flowing. Two by two, bodies on the dance floor become one darkened blur. I quickly scan the area, trying to spot Daisy in the throngs of people.

The damnedest thing is, I feel her before I see her.

It's the same sensation I get during a lightning storm. The electrons in the air and the protons in the ground react inside my torso, warning of an impending strike. One million volts right to the chest, delivered by a gorgeous little lady with a disarming smile. I turn around and watch her walk through the door.

With my jaw on the floor and my tongue rolled out like a fucking red carpet. My eyes remain glued to her as she moves through the people loitering in the entryway. She's dressed as Harley Quinn, complete with short shorts, tight shirt, four-inch heels, and a plastic baseball bat. She's wearing her long blond hair in pigtails, one side colored blue and the other pink.

Before I can gather my wits enough to make my feet move, some fucker near me sets his sights on her and begins his beeline to intercept her.

Not tonight, buddy.

With swift steps, I move in sync with him and extend my foot to trip him. When he falls face first, I'm tempted to yell "timber," but think better of it. Then I stop in front of Daisy, and I forget about everyone else in the room except her.

"Captain America, I didn't know you'd be here tonight.

Are you here to arrest me?" Her playful side is so much fun. Now to keep her in an excellent mood.

She's not making it easy to behave. Now all I can picture is her in handcuffs. Fuck me, this will be a long night.

"Only if you're a naughty girl. But to be on the safe side, I should probably buy you a drink and stick close to you. Make sure you don't cause any trouble in here." I intentionally lower the timbre of my voice to add to my disguise.

A moment of hesitation flickers in her eyes, but Tracy's elbow in her side forces a reply. "A drink would be great. Thank you."

She wraps her arm around my extended elbow, and we walk toward the bar together. When we run out of space to walk side by side, I pull her in front of me and wrap my arms around her waist from behind. Walking with her back to my front, she's securely held in my grasp. Men gawk at her as we pass, but quickly avert their eyes when they catch a glimpse of the dare in my eyes and the thin line of my lips.

I've been told I have a severe case of resting asshole face that is downright scary when I'm pissed off. Color me red, because I'm pissed at every one of these fuckwads eyeballing her.

We reach the bar, and she makes no move to leave the safety of my embrace. I can't deny the slight swell of pride in my chest over such a simple gesture. I motion for the bartender, then lean down until my lips graze across the shell of her ear.

"What will it be?" Simple question. So many meanings.

Goosebumps break out on her arm, starting at the top and cascading to her forearm.

"I'll have a cosmopolitan."

"Anything you want, beautiful." I relay our order, and the bartender returns a quick nod.

She slides her hands down my arms until her fingers rest on top of mine at her waist. Simple act. So many meanings.

"Who was the genie that came in with you?"

"That's my best friend, Tracy. Doesn't she look great as a sexy genie? I love that outfit. I told her we're swapping for the next costume party."

"She does look good in it, but not nearly as good as you look. Will she mind if I keep you to myself for a little while?"

Daisy looks around the club until she finds her friend already on the dance floor, grinding with Popeye. She chuckles, her body vibrating in my arms. "I don't think she'll miss me at all. Looks like she's already found a sexy sailorman to keep her busy."

"I promise you're in expert hands. You know you can trust me. I'm Captain America, after all."

"What makes you think I need a man to take care of me? I am Harley Quinn, after all. *You* should be afraid of *me*."

No truer words have ever been spoken.

We take our drinks and move away from the crowded bar. I'm forced to let go of her and only hold her hand as we work our way through the crowd and find an empty table. I pull out her chair for her to sit first, then move the other chair as close to hers as possible. Once I'm seated, I slide my arm along the back of her seat and reestablish the body contact.

She lifts her glass to her lips and looks up at me from under her eyelashes. I purposely keep from staring directly into her eyes, just in case she recognizes anything about mine. "What brings you to this resort? I'd imagine you have men lined up a mile-long at home, waiting to make you theirs."

"Not hardly." Her self-deprecating laugh has a nervous edge to it. "But I'm actually here for Tracy. She views this as a kind of high-end matchmaking service. It's only for singles who are looking for that special someone. Only the more adventurous people will jet away to a remote location like this, and that characteristic definitely attracts her. I couldn't let her come alone."

"Does that mean you're not here looking for your soul mate?"

"I'm not sure I even believe in that anymore, to be honest. Not that I'm a cynical old spinster, but life has made me become more of a realist in that area than it has her."

Just like that, I want to know everything about her. If I can get inside her head, I can figure out what makes her tick. I want to know what she's passionate about. What she loves, what she hates, what she wants out of life. And why she doesn't believe in love anymore. Yeah, I heard what she said, but I also listened to what she didn't say.

She finishes her first drink and sets her glass down. Before she asks for another one, I want to get her on the dance floor for a little grinding of our own. When I open my mouth to ask her to dance, the music changes, and the lights dim even more. When the Righteous Brothers croon "Unchained Melody," I can't sit still any longer.

"Dance with me, Miss Quinn." I extend my hand toward her and hold my breath at the same time.

She places her soft hand in mine, and we walk to the dance floor with our fingers laced. I turn and pull her tightly against me as we sway to the soulful sounds of the best love song ever recorded. Her hands slide up my chest and wrap around my neck. Even with her heels, I have to bend to keep her from stretching too much. But that doesn't bother me since it puts me even closer to her.

When she releases the anxious breath she's been holding, her entire body relaxes, melting into mine. I slide my arms up her back, holding her possessively against me. I feel her sigh and hear the whimper she tries to hide. She's every bit as affected by me as I am by her, but she doesn't know I'm *me* me.

The DJ is reading the room and feeling the vibes from the crowd because the next song, "I'll Make Love to You" by Boyz II Men, cues up immediately. I'm glad he's paying attention because I'm not ready to let go of Daisy yet. Before I even realize I'm doing it, I softly murmur the words of the song in her ear, singing along with the music. I tell her I'll make her wishes come true. I promise not to let go until she tells me to. All the words simply flow out of me as if I penned the lyrics exclusively for her.

Just when doubts start creeping in, concerned I'm over-stepping another invisible boundary, her fingers curl into my skin through my super suit. She turns her face toward mine, and our lips are only a heartbeat away. Like a man lost in the desert, I'm dying for just a taste of her sweet lips to quench my thirst. But just as quickly as she turned toward me, she looks the other way. Second thoughts cloud her eyes in that split second, guarding her heart, body, and mind all at once. A passionate woman lies underneath the layers of caution and leeriness that govern her life.

I can't stress how fucking much I want to be there when she finally unfurls her freak flag.

Since she purposely moved her lips out of my reach, I slide mine along her jawline until I reach her ear. "Now I can't wait to see you dressed up as a genie. I already know what my three wishes will be."

"In that case, I'll make sure I look extra special for the next costume night." That little coo of hers sends all my blood rushing to my cock. Being a nice guy is killing me. "As much as I hate to say this, I'd better head back to my room. We have an early morning excursion scheduled, and this has been a long day."

"I'll walk you back so I know you arrive safely."

"You don't need to do that. We're at an exclusive resort. I'm sure it's safe."

I pull back and look at her. Thankfully, the room is still mostly dark because I hold her gaze while I speak. "It's not safe at all, beautiful. You're on an island with a bunch of single guys, most of whom are drunk. And even if it weren't a singles resort, there are still plenty of male workers and places they can hide your body until they can toss you into the ocean in the middle of the night. I won't pull any fast moves on you. You have my word. But I won't sleep at all tonight if I'm not one-hundred percent certain you're safely inside your room."

She tilts her head and narrows her eyes at me in thoughtful reflection. "All right, Cap. You can escort me to my room, but no funny business. You'll be sorry if you're lying."

"Scout's honor." I hold up three fingers to emphasize the point.

"Were you a Scout?"

"Nope, never."

She smiles and shakes her head. "At least you're honest about it. Lead the way out." She motions toward the door and tells me her room number on the way.

When we reach her room, she unlocks it and checks

behind all the doors and curtains while I stand in the open doorway, watching her every move.

"All safe and secure now. But thank you for walking me back. That was very thoughtful of you." She stops moving when we're so close our bodies are almost touching again.

Is this a test... or an invitation?

"Be safe on your excursion tomorrow. I'll be dreaming about my genie in the bottle until the next costume night."

"Are you changing costumes? How will I find you?"

"Don't even worry about that, beautiful. I'll find you. You're not slipping through my fingers."

I lean in and leave a lingering kiss on her cheek. Her soft gasp and the rush of her breath create visions of the other sounds she would make under my hand. Our faces are still touching, and her fingers brush along the scruff of my beard and along the back of my neck. With every fiber of my being, I want to capture her mouth with mine. When her quick inhale makes her lips part, I want to seize the opportunity and plunge my tongue deep inside her mouth, owning it with every moan that escapes from her. That I want to feel the velvety smoothness of her tongue gliding across mine in an erotic dance nearly breaks my resolve to keep this encounter PG-13.

When the urgency building inside her overflows, I want to know the very second the cracks and fissures form in the walls she's built around her, undermining her willpower. When that dam breaks, sending a tsunami crashing down on both of us, I will be there to save her from drowning in a pool of want and need and desire.

But tonight's intense reaction is fueled by alcohol, island

stimulation, and not knowing who I am. I can't take advantage of her state of mind like that.

"Good night, beautiful. Sleep well." I murmur the words against her mouth, our lips barely touching, because I'm nowhere near ready to leave her personal space just yet. But I force myself to do just that anyway and walk backward, away from her. "Lock that door and don't open it for anyone you don't know."

"Yes, sir." She gives me a mock salute, and I'm surprised my spandex suit isn't teepeed. She slowly closes the door, and when I hear the locks click into place, I turn and head back to my room.

Alone… with only visions of my personal Harley Quinn-sexy-genie to keep me warm tonight. Warm isn't the right word. It's more like my body catches up in flames that can't be extinguished.

Yeah, this will be a long fucking night, all right.

CHAPTER SIX

Daisy

"Change of plans for today." Tracy walks into our shared room with an enormous smile on her face.

"We're not going on the eco tour I booked?"

A disgusted expression flashes over her face. "No, Daisy, we're not. I'm not wasting my time here hiking and biking in this heat and humidity. Do you have any idea how frizzy my hair will be by the end of the day? We're here for one reason—men. Plus, there are cruise ships docking today, and they'll have those little half-sized human-things with them."

"Do you mean children?" One feature she liked best about this resort, other than the hot guys, was the "no children allowed" policy.

"Yes." She shakes her entire body as if trying to ward off any curses at the mere mention of kids.

"Did someone just walk on your grave?" I can't help but have a little fun at her expense.

"You know I love your Southernisms, but that one is just creepy. I don't have a grave, and I don't even want to think about dying yet. Are you planning to kill me or something?"

"That depends on what you signed us up for today, instead of the hiking and biking tour I wanted to do." I fold my arms across my chest and wait to make my decision.

"We are joining a group of outgoing people at a private cabana owned by the resort. It's built on top of the water and has a big water slide, a hot tub, a fully stocked bar. And–" She pauses for dramatic emphasis, "–It also comes with a chef, a butler, and a bartender. Get your bathing suit on, pack your beach bag, and let's go."

"Who are these outgoing people we're spending the day with?"

"Just a bunch of people I met in the club last night when you ditched me at the costume party, so you could hug up to Captain America on the dance floor. Don't worry, you'll like them."

"If you say so. And I didn't ditch you. You looked content in Popeye's arms. Give me a minute to change and get everything together."

"That's my girl." Tracy turns to rifle through her drawers for her bikini, ignoring my return jab.

While changing, I can't shake the feeling she's up to something, and I'm being played. But I'm going along with her plan either way. If there's one fact I'm sure of, it's that she'd never do anything intentionally to hurt me. She and I have been best friends for as long as I can remember. We graduated from the same college, then moved to the Atlanta metro area together five years ago.

From the outside, everyone thinks everything comes easily to Tracy. She is tall and beautiful, with perfectly coiffed black hair and pearly white teeth. She's one of the smartest people I know, and her sense of humor matches mine to a T, sarcastic and witty. We've been inseparable since the first day we met. She pushes me out of my comfort zone and is the sole reason I had the courage to attempt most of the daring feats I've accomplished.

I see polar opposites when I look at pictures of us together.

She's outgoing and boisterous. I'm quiet and reserved.

She's tall and perfectly poised. I'm short and awkward as hell.

She's a beautiful, strong black woman. I'm a timid blonde with longstanding self-esteem issues.

Her childhood was one tragedy after another, but she chose to rise from the ashes and make something of herself rather than let anyone drag her down to their level. Many people in our small town, including her parents, believed she should stick to her own "kind" instead of the blended and diversified friends she chose. When we were seniors in high school, she announced she was in love with a white guy and didn't care what anyone thought about it. While she wasn't bothered by their differences, her parents certainly were, and forbade her to date him. Tensions remained high in her family for weeks, then tipped over the boiling point when she brought him home for dinner one night, unannounced.

All I know for certain is a huge brawl quickly ensued, but both families were tight-lipped about the details and the aftermath. The black eyes, busted lips, and icy glares between her brother and her boyfriend in the school hallway were the only confirmation the rest of the school had that the fight happened. I was the one who tried to console her broken heart and endless tears every day when we got home.

A few months after we graduated, she walked away from what she called a toxic family atmosphere and has barely looked back since. She still refuses to visit her family for more than a few hours at a time, and she never has taken another date home to meet them. She's as stubborn as she is strong. Sometimes I have to remind myself that I have just as much strength, only in different areas. I find it harder to believe in myself than she does. In fact, she has ample faith to support both of us.

I feel her eyes burning a hole through me. When I turn my attention to her, she narrows her eyes, reads my body language, and immediately knows what's going on in my mind.

"Get those thoughts out of your head right now. You are more than good enough for anyone on this island. In fact, you're too good for ninety-nine percent of these fuckers. If you end up with anyone, he'll be lucky to have you. If you decide no one is worth your time, I'll fully support you in that too. Deal?"

"Deal." I pull my beach bag onto my shoulder, and we make our way down to the excursion departure area of the resort.

Her ability to decipher my thoughts and emotions at times goes beyond how well she knows me. At twenty-seven, I should be more comfortable in my own skin. But I'm not quite there yet. But she's right, I need to let my guard down and attempt to have a pleasurable time. Demons from my past try to cripple me and keep me locked away in an invisible cell. I've literally only had blind dates Tracy coerced me into accepting over the last several years.

The man behind the mask I met in the club felt so different from all the other men I've ever known. Maybe the real charade is his knight in shining armor act. But his concern for my safety wasn't fake. There must be women in his life he cares deeply about—maybe his mother or even the sister he mentioned. That small, chivalrous act of walking me to my room made me trust him when he never even told me his name or showed me his face.

We were so close to an actual kiss while we stood in my doorway. His lips were right there, and I turned toward them, fully intending to be the one to initiate the kiss. In one second, I was ready to be bold and go for what I wanted. In the next, there was a voice in my head asking if I knew what I was doing, what I was inviting, and what could go terribly wrong. The cynical view won that round because I turned away from his full lips before anything happened.

Then he kissed my cheek instead.

That minor act spoke more to me than all the words in the dictionary combined. He knew I was hesitant and understood I was conflicted. Rather than pressuring me, he was giving me space to decide while still showing how much he desired me.

What makes a man really are the little things.

Those little things become the big things we can't live without. They show character, define integrity, and reveal who the person really is. Anyone can pretend to be someone they're not, but the truth will always show. Eventually.

I haven't told Tracy about that encounter with him yet.

She'll think I'm crazy for being so infatuated with a stranger dressed in a Captain America costume. To be honest, I can't explain it myself. But the truth is, I don't want to try. Dissecting my feelings will only burst the bubble of giddiness I've felt since he approached me in the club. This is the first time, in a very long time, I've been excited about meeting a guy, and I'm not ready to lose that loving feeling.

Tracy and I reach the offshore excursions desk and check in for the magical outing she signed us up for without asking me first. We move to the area designated for our boat ride out to the small island just offshore and wait for the others to join us.

"Good morning, ladies. Fancy meeting you two here." The deep masculine voice resonates from behind me, and the flurry of birds in my chest takes flight all at once.

I turn my head to find Rod and Kevin approaching us, wearing swimming shorts, tank tops, sunglasses, and enormous smiles. Two more guys are right behind them, barely awake and possibly still drunk from last night. Their black shades cover their eyes and their preppy sun visors do nothing to hide their bed hair.

"Good morning, boys. Where are you headed today?" I already know the answer. I'm curious which one will confess to the charade first.

"We're just along for the free booze. I heard drinking first thing in the morning cures a hangover from the night before. Fuck, I hope that's true." The blond guy rubs his temples. The dark-haired one beside him simply nods, then immediately winces, regretting the sudden movement.

"Please ignore our obnoxious friends. We tried to sneak out of our room without them hearing us, but no such luck."

Kevin rolls his eyes. "Rod rented the private cabana on the small island today and we invited a bunch of people from the party last night to come along for the fun."

Kevin cuts his eyes to Tracy, and the intimate change in them is overt and instant.

I jerk my gaze toward her to see if she returns the sentiment. When her eyes soften, my jaw drops open before I can stop it.

She senses my stare and turns toward me. "What?"

"You and I will have a long talk. Later." She's leaving me out of the loop on this developing relationship with Kevin. She's making plans and not involving me until they're already set in stone. She's supposed to be my best friend. We're supposed to talk about all the guy stuff when they're not around.

"If you don't want to go to the cabana with a bunch of people, we won't force you." Rod pushes his sunglasses on top of his head, only improving the sexy, messy hair vibe he has. My heart sinks to my ankles, and the flurries in my chest seize in place.

He doesn't want me to go. I hate how my mind automatically goes to the worst-case scenario. That's not what he said, and I know that, but that's exactly how the words translate in my mind.

"Um, no, the cabana sounds great. Thank you for renting it and for inviting us. All I meant was my best friend in the entire world isn't telling me everything for some reason. That just caught me off guard is all."

"Let me know if you change your mind. I'm sure there are plenty of other activities to try. I read about a hiking and bike riding tour. Probably too late to get in on that one today, but we can make our own adventure, if you want."

The cocksure man from our first day here is nowhere to be found. With that comment about hiking and bike riding, I'm positive Tracy told him what I'd planned. He wouldn't have just pulled that out of thin air and offered the very activity I was looking forward to doing.

"Do you bike and hike a lot?"

"As much as I'm able. I'm only about an hour and a half from the Blue Ridge Mountains. Plenty of trails for hiking and biking up there. My sister and I used to take day trips there frequently, just to get away from the city."

"That's pleasantly surprising. You strike me as more of a GQ guy than a mountain man." I smile, letting him know I'm not attempting to insult him.

"I'm only model-perfect where my work is involved. The rest of the time, I'm as slouchy as anyone else." His smile reaches his eyes, and they change to a lighter blue right before me.

"Since you already have the cabana, let's just enjoy it with the water and beach today. Maybe they'll have a nature excursion open another day." The words just tumble out of my mouth before I realize what I've said.

Awkward.

I just insinuated I expect him to join me one of the other days we're here. Where is a deep hole when I need one to crawl in and pull the dirt over my head to hide? I didn't mean that the way it sounded, but if I try to correct it now, I'll just make an even bigger fool out of myself.

Change the subject, quick.

Dear God. For the life of me, I can't think of anything else to talk about now. He's smiling while I'm dying inside. Is this a prelude of how the entire day with Hot Rod will be?

"So, you said several others are joining us?" Finally. Something came to mind. Anything. I should've talked about the damn weather or anything else mundane eons ago.

"Yeah, they're meeting us a little later. They wanted to do some souvenir shopping first."

"That's smart. If it's half as beautiful as the pictures I've seen of the beach and the ocean, they won't want to leave the cabana once they get there. By the way, are your friends all right over there? They look like they're passed out cold." The other two guys with us broke down and sat on the floor with their backs leaned against the wall.

"Good. Let's leave them there. I was trying to get away from them for the day. I can only take Hunter and Jace in small doses… say, five minutes at a time… tops. That drops to about two minutes when they're together. They're usually better to be around than they've been on this trip."

My eyes stray to his bare arms as he speaks. The muscle striations contract and expand with his every movement. I have an overwhelming urge to run my fingers over the deep cuts and prominent ridges of his biceps. Instead, I grip the straps of my beach bag tighter until my knuckles turn white. I've made it painfully obvious I can't trust myself around him, letting my mouth run away from me. Now my fingers are plotting mutiny from obeying my brain.

Just hold it together for a few more minutes, Daisy. You can do it.

The staff saves me from any further embarrassment by calling our group to board the next boat. Thank God for small favors.

"Ladies first." Rod extends his arm, indicating for Tracy and me to take the lead.

When we reach the small boat that will serve as our water taxi, the waves pick up and make the boat rock harder. The foot or so that separates the water taxi from the dock suddenly seems very far away.

"Hang on a second, Daisy. Let me hop on first so I can help you aboard." Rod notices my hesitation and steps up without a second thought.

He jumps from the pier onto the boat with the nimble grace of a finely tuned athlete. Then he takes my bag from me and drops it on the seat before offering his hand. I slip mine into his, and he keeps me steady as I cross the great divide. When I step onto the lip of the tender, I'm face-to-face with Rod, and the boat is rocking from the waves. My fingers itch to feel the tautness of his muscles. I've never been this close to a man with such muscle definition. Under the guise of steadying myself, I grip his other bicep with my free hand, and my fingers thoroughly enjoy what they find.

Fine. The rest of me is also pleased. Sue me.

"Thank you, Rod. I appreciate the help. I'm not exactly one for swimming alone."

"If you fall, I'll fall with you."

Simple statement. So many meanings.

I'm not sure how to respond, so I keep my mouth shut for once and step down into the boat. When I take my seat, I realize Rod is right beside me, and Kevin is helping Tracy across the gap. Is it wrong that I'm a little too pleased with knowing he only helped me? He could've easily stayed there and helped my friend.

But he didn't.

He's sitting beside me, not leaving a space for Tracy on our bench. He wants to be close to me, to talk to me, to spend time with me.

This man will break your heart, Daisy. You know it's coming.

Let it come. I plan to enjoy the ride as long as I can. There will come a time when we'll part, my logical brain knows that. But I'll cross that bridge when I reach it and not let that knowledge ruin anything between now and then.

CHAPTER SEVEN

Rod

Our private cabana is better than I could've imagined, even after seeing the pictures of it. We have the entire beach and clear, aqua blue water of the Caribbean Sea to ourselves since the area surrounding it is secluded. We're fortunate the staff is attentive without being overbearing. They had already made a tray of tropical drinks and delicious snacks to greet us the moment we arrived.

Kevin invited a group of people he met last night, but they won't be here for a while, which is fine with me. Now that we're here, I don't want to share Daisy with anyone else, so I'm regretting going along with this plan somewhat. This is my time to get to know her as myself, with no masks, no subterfuge, and no audience.

Just a man, standing on a wooden pier, asking a girl to give him a second chance to prove he's not a complete self-absorbed dick.

Lounging by the pool with her yesterday was nice, but there were too many people crowding our space. Other men were trying to get her attention, and other women were vying for mine, despite the overt clues that showed I wasn't interested. Daisy watched with mild amusement every time some other woman tried to catch my eye. I'd never admit this to anyone, but her lack of jealousy or possessiveness over me was a little insulting. She doesn't know this, but I quietly told more than a few guys to fuck off when they tried to approach her.

I suppose that means I need to up my game, show her what a catch I am.

What is she supposed to do with you when she catches you, Rod?

Shut up. My rational brain and my emotional side aren't on the same wavelengths at the moment.

Daisy drops her bag on one of the lounge chairs and pulls her cover-up over her head. With the rays of sun shining directly on her blond hair, she leans her head back with a smile playing on her lips and basks in the warmth. She's wearing a tiny bikini that shows off her perfect form.

"This is pure heaven. I can't imagine anything that could feel better than this. Soaking in the sun with the surf lapping at my toes. Friends surrounding me in a place that's heaven on earth. Name one thing that could top this feeling." Daisy's smile is contagious, because I've broken out in one just watching her.

"Multiple orgasms." Tracy drops her bag and removes her cover-up, oblivious to the images she just conjured in my mind. Not of her, though. They're all of Daisy … screaming my name.

"Hmm … good call. Too bad I can't help you with that." Daisy giggles at their friendly banter. "Can I offer you some sunshine instead? It feels damn good on my skin." She runs her fingertips along her arm to demonstrate.

My lips twitch on their own, hungry to feel every inch of her. My tongue darts out, longing to taste every inch of skin she's showing. My hands ball into tight fists, aching to throw her over my shoulder and carry her somewhere far away from prying eyes. This petite lady is getting to me in ways I never imagined.

A vision of her meeting my sister Juliana pops into my mind, as clear as the ocean water before me.

This is only a vacation fling. Remember what that is, Rod? You can't even wish for more.

I'll only admit to myself that a five-foot-two beauty captured my mind and is worming her way into my heart with every awkward encounter we have. I am powerless to stop this speeding train while I'm around her. When the trip is over, I'll go back home and only remember the enjoyable times. I will repress anything more than that in the recesses of my memories, along with everything else I'd rather forget.

I don't know what Kevin has done to me. He chose one woman to stay with for the duration of the trip, and I followed suit. By definition, my predicament is his fault, and he deserves a good ass-kicking for it. But for today, I'm pushing my own commitment issues aside and enjoying the company of an intriguing woman.

"What can I interest you in first?" I approach her with a

fruity tropical drink in hand, complete with one of those little umbrellas all girls love for some reason.

She accepts the proffered glass from me, takes a long drink, and peers up to my six-foot-one frame from under her lashes. "I'm ready for that swim now if you are. The water is too perfect not to jump in right away."

"I'm absolutely ready. Thought you'd never ask." I grab the back of my tank top and pull it over my head. My chest swells with pride when her eyes bug out and her lips part as she stares at my bare chest.

Yes, I work out and take care of myself. But it's still nice to witness that level of appreciation.

She takes another long pull from the straw, and half her drink disappears. "Let's check out the slide."

Liquid courage, but courage, nonetheless.

"Do you want me to go first so I'll be down there to catch you?" I toss my shirt on the same chair as her bag and walk toward the back of the cabana.

"That's very sweet of you to offer, but I think I can take it from here." She laughs as she climbs up to sit on the top of the slide. "But you'd better be right behind me."

"I won't leave you hanging."

Despite my encouragement, she still hesitates at the top of the slide. She's afraid, but she faces her fears and tries to garner enough courage to overcome it on her own.

"Do you want me to go down from behind you?" I honestly didn't mean that the way it sounds, but the words are already out in the universe. And now that's all I can think about. Thankfully, she didn't catch the double entendre of my offer, because I'm more than willing to help her with that too.

"Would you mind?" She looks over her shoulder at me, a little fear and a little embarrassment in her eyes.

Someone has made her feel ashamed of being afraid or asking for help. What I wouldn't give to get my hands on that fucker right now.

"I don't mind at all." I join her on the slide and position my legs on either side of her. Then I wrap my arms around her waist, much like I did last night when she didn't know I was dressed as Cap. "Ready to go for a swim?"

"Let's go."

I push us off, and we fly down the tall slide, rushing toward the clear water below with her squeals of delight echoing in the air. When we hit the water, I don't release her. For whatever reason, I can't seem to make my fingers let her go, so I push her to the surface and join her immediately after.

She turns in my arms to face me and throws her arms around my neck. Her embrace is merely one of pure innocence. The sole reason behind it is genuine gratitude, I *know* this. But that doesn't stop me from pulling her tighter against my chest. The desire to shelter and protect her only grows with every second I'm near her. Touching her makes it damn near impossible to separate. She feels so good in my arms.

So right.

"Thank you so much for doing that, Rod. I know you probably think I'm such an enormous baby, scared of everything. Maybe I am. But thank you for not pointing that out and embarrassing me, especially when it was my idea to go down the slide."

There's a motherfucker out there somewhere I need to kill. I feel it with every cell in my body.

"I'd never do that to you, Daisy. I'll go down that slide with you all fucking day, if that's what you want."

She stares at me in disbelief for a second, weighing the odds that I'm about to laugh in her face and shame her. When she realizes my offer is sincere, she shocks the shit out of me by pressing her lips against mine. Her hands slide around my neck to hold my face as I get lost in her kiss.

"I've never met anyone like you before. I didn't think there were still kindhearted men out there. I'm thankful we met, and I'm glad I came on this excursion with you. Thank you, for everything." Her eyes dart between mine as she speaks, emphasizing her message with the intensity in those beautiful blues.

She called me a kindhearted man, but I'm not so sure most of the other women in my life would agree with her assessment. But from Daisy, I'll accept it.

"You're welcome. But believe me, it's my pleasure. I wanted to spend the day with you to make up for our first meeting and get to know you better. One-on-one."

"You've more than made up for that comment, Rod. Don't even think about it anymore. I don't, so quit beating yourself up. You'll look back on it and laugh about it before long. Why not start doing that today?"

"We'll laugh about it together then."

"You've got a deal. Ready to go down behind me again?"

Simple question. So many meanings.

I physically have to hold back a groan. "More than ready."

After a few more trips down the slide, Kevin and Tracy join us for a swim. The staff manning the cabana provides us with masks and snorkels, so the four of us spend a couple of hours swimming the shallow waters. Daisy shows me every new fish she finds, and her excitement is contagious. I'd like to know her story, every last detail. On the one hand, she doesn't seem like she gets out much. On the other, she's very shrewd and intuitive. She has a backbone when needed but seems almost shy the rest of the time.

Yeah, I'd really enjoy peeling back the layers of this sweet onion.

We finally take a time-out and sit on the beach, letting the water lap at our feet and the sun drench our bodies in its warmth.

"This was exactly what I needed today. This place is paradise. If only I could win the lottery and have an island of my own." Daisy lies back on the sand and stretches her arms out, not trying to hide the grin that's splitting her face in two.

"Money isn't all it's cracked up to be. You can have tons of it and still not find happiness." I know from experience.

"That's true. Money can't buy true love or happiness, but it sure can take away a lot of worries."

She's not wrong. My fortune eliminated many of the worries that used to plague me. How would I feed and clothe my sister? How would I keep a roof over our heads? How would I ever be able to send her to college? But for the most part, we still live like we did before the money. I have a sizeable house and a nice car, and Juliana and Isabelle are set for life, but that's the extent of my extravagant lifestyle.

I wonder what Daisy worries about, but I don't want to ask right now and change the mood she's in. She's finally relaxed and having fun.

"Looks like our other friends are finally here. Just in time for lunch, too. The chef is keeping our food warm. Let's go eat, boys and girls." Tracy exits the water with Kevin close behind her.

I stand then help Daisy up, and we walk together toward the cabana. We keep several paces behind Tracy and Kevin, walking in sync with our arms wrapped around each other as if it's the most natural position for us. With every step, we move slower, extending our time alone as long as we can before joining the noisy crowd already congregated on the lanai.

We're so comfortable together, it's as if we've known each other for years.

"Kevin mentioned you and Tracy already have plans for a girls' day tomorrow. Do you want to go with me on a long hike the day after tomorrow? The island has beautiful mountains and forests we can explore. There are freshwater streams to swim in and waterfalls along the trails. We'll leave Tracy and Kevin behind and create our own expedition." I realize it's a stretch to ask her to join me in the woods, alone, in a foreign country, when she barely knows me. The thing is, even though she's having a blast so far today, the party scene just doesn't seem to be her first choice.

She stops walking and focuses her attention on the large open deck of the cabana. A dozen or so people are drinking and laughing. The music is blaring, and several couples are taking advantage of the dancing space. The bartender is hopping, mixing drink after drink. The chef plates the food, and the butler delivers the dishes to the extended dining table.

Then she turns her attention back to me, and the music fades away. The laughing and loud talking from the crowd of people evaporates on the breeze. All that's left is Daisy and me in our own little world.

"That sounds like the perfect getaway. Count me in."

Color me shocked, but more than a little pleased.

We join the others and make introductions all around. I don't know who any of these people are. Kevin met them last night while I was with Daisy. Thankfully, no one has mentioned my absence. I hope they're just acting polite because they don't know whose face was behind the masks last night.

We pass the usual "get to know you" questions around the group in general conversation starters. Daisy mentions she's also from Georgia, but doesn't name a city. Just as well, though. That'll keep me from making a colossal mistake and hunting her down when we return home.

"What do you do for a living, Tracy?"

"I'm in public relations." She purposely avoids naming her employer and only gives a vague job title. "Public relations" is one of those ambiguous terms that can mean so many things. I recognize the tactics and ploys used to maintain anonymity. I've used them all myself.

Much like the maneuver I'm using by not giving my last name nor asking for Daisy's. That just makes a clean break all the easier in the end. There's no way to social media stalk someone without a full name. A minor part of me occasionally wishes I could be different, but I know this is the best way.

Others may describe me as a douche, among other things, but at least remaining a bachelor ensures I'll never be the man who abandons my family.

"Rod, what kind of job do you have?" One of our unnamed party crashers attempts to invade my privacy.

"I'm a hacker. I ruin people's lives for fun."

Everyone laughs, knowing I'm exaggerating and kidding at the same time, and we move on to other topics. The conversation flows smoothly between all of us from that point on.

We finish our excursion with more drinks, food, and dancing than should be allowed in one day, but every minute is worth it. Daisy smiles, laughs, and is more animated than ever. Seeing her come to life is a beautiful thing, almost as enticing as seeing her in that tiny bathing suit.

When we're back on the resort grounds, she turns to me and stops. "Will I see you at dinner this evening?"

"Absolutely."

And... you'll hopefully see me eat until my heart's content for many, many hours after dinner, too.

Old habits die hard.

CHAPTER EIGHT

Daisy

Tracy and I are on our fourth day of our trip and becoming more spoiled than we care to admit. Today, she and I had a girls' day out on the island and picked a couple of activities we've always wanted to do, such as swimming with dolphins and feeding the stingrays. When we returned to the hotel, we took our place by the pool and basked in the sun.

Though I have to admit, it felt strange not having Rod and Kevin with us on our day trip. I found myself looking for Rod and hoping he'd show up out of the blue, wanting to spend time with me. I also couldn't help but wonder if he'd found someone else at the resort today, since I've repeatedly shot down his previous advances. So many women have had him in their sights, and I've been ready to scrap with them every single time. Nothing in my head makes sense where he's concerned. I have spent an enormous amount of willpower biting my tongue to avoid a catfight confrontation.

Now that we're back on the resort grounds, I look forward to seeing him again.

"Did you ladies have fun today?" Rod moves an empty lounge chair next to Tracy and motions for her to move to it. She jumps at the chance to sit next to Kevin, and I try to hide my eagerness to be close to Rod.

"Yes, we did. It was definitely unforgettable." I smile up at him as he stands at the end of Tracy's vacated seat.

"Would you like a drink before I get comfortable? I'm going to grab a beer."

"Sure. A piña colada would hit the spot. Thank you."

"I won't end up wearing it again, will I? Because I almost lost my favorite parts of my body from frostbite last time."

I can't help but laugh. "No, I promise not to waste this one."

When Rod walks away to stand in line at the outdoor bar, I glance over at Kevin and Tracy. There's no doubt they're completely into each other. I'm a little envious, for a few reasons. I wish I could be as carefree and throw caution to the wind the way she does. Part of me wants to believe Rod is more than the ladies' man he seems, but that's wishful thinking. I've met too many men exactly like him, and it never ends well.

But, as far as the rest of the trip is concerned, I suppose I could find worse company.

Over the past few days of being here, I've noticed several people have already paired off into couples, finding the one they want to spend the rest of the trip with and making the most of the time we have left. I'm not quite ready to throw in the towel and agree to be a late night booty call, just because we're on vacation at a singles resort, with buff guys all around us. Every minute spent with Rod chips away at my self-control, though. Every night when he walks me to my door, I'm tempted to invite him into my room.

"Hi there, gorgeous. I've watched you nearly all day because I can't seem to tear my eyes away from you. I also couldn't help but notice you're still single and you've been alone most of the day. On behalf of the entire male population in this place, I'd like to rectify that appalling lapse in judgment. You, my beautiful new friend, should've been the first lady who updated her relationship status on social media."

A strange man appears from out of nowhere, his face right beside my ear when he speaks, startling me and making me jump nearly out of my seat. I didn't hear him walk up behind me because Rod has invaded my thoughts to the point of distraction.

"Oh, hello. To be honest, I'm not sure if I should be flattered or freaked out by your admission of watching me all day. That feels a little creepy."

He laughs with no sign of discomfort in his demeanor. "You say exactly what you think. I love it. Too many people are afraid to speak their minds and go after what they really want. Do you mind if I sit here?" He motions toward Rod's chair.

"Sorry, but that seat is taken. My friend just went to get our drinks from the bar, but he'll be right back."

"Yeah, actually I know. That's why I came over here." He sits in Rod's seat anyway, and I instantly feel protective over it. "Hear me out, then I'll leave if you still want me to. Listen, I don't know that guy, but I've seen him around the hotel a lot.

He's with a different woman every night, and he was with someone else earlier today. You seem like a sweet person who trusts people too easily. I'd hate to see you hurt over a loser like him. The objective of this trip is to help single men and women find someone special, not to be a revolving door meat market. I'm not trying to tell you what to do, but I'd dump him if I were you."

Over the last several years, I've become an expert at hiding my thoughts and feelings. When it comes to allowing myself to be vulnerable to someone else, I shut down rather than deal with the messiness of relationships. This conversation is headed in a dangerous direction. I'm not ready to assess why I'm inwardly jealous over Rod, or why I feel the need to defend him to this stranger.

Time to deflect.

"All right. Well, I appreciate your concern, but I'm a grown woman and I can take care of myself. Not to be rude, but I don't even know your name, much less anything else about you. However, I *have* spent quite a bit of time with Rod, so I'm not sure why you assumed your word would be enough for me to turn against him."

"My name is Thomas Flint. I'm sorry to be the bearer of bad news, and I don't mean to embarrass you. I'm honestly just trying to warn you about him. Whether or not you realize it, that guy is a total player and not worth another minute of your time."

"Tom, is it?" The gruff masculine voice at my feet immediately grabs my attention. "I don't know what your fucking game is, but I'm clearly not the player in this scenario. Now get the fuck out of my seat before they send you back home with every bone in your body broken and no fucking teeth."

Thomas looks over his shoulder at Rod. "This beauty been alone all day, while you were chatting up some busty chick at the bar earlier. Then you disappeared with her. You're just out looking for a fuck wherever you can get it, flirting with all the women who even look your way. If you had a clue about women, you'd know at first glance this beautiful little lady isn't your type. Why don't you step on, buddy, and find your next conquest?"

The nagging fear in the back of my mind that has been there since the day I met Rod takes front and center. Was Rod flirting with someone else? I mean, I know I don't have any claim on him, so I have no right to question him about it. But after all the attention he's given me and time we've spent together over the last few days, anyone in my place would've thought he wanted more than one night.

Apparently, I'm just a fool. Again.

"First of all, you don't even know me, so there's no chance in hell you know what I've been doing. Second, I've had plenty of chances to hook up with random women, if that's what I wanted. But I haven't even spared them a second glance, much less flirted with them. Third, *she* hasn't been alone all day. She hasn't even been out here on the deck until now, so you don't know what the hell she's been doing. Furthermore, you don't even know her name, so you haven't been paying too much attention." Rod moves between us and sets our drinks down on the chairside table. "Last chance to get out of my seat before I knock you out of it."

Thomas stands up and stands toe to toe with Rod before moving to his side. Then he looks down at me. "You come find me when you want a real man, sweetheart. I'll show you how you should be treated." He rattles off his room number before he saunters off.

"He's lying, Daisy. I don't know why he's trying to start shit with us, but everything he said is a complete lie." Rod sounds so sincere, but I've been wrong and trusted the wrong guy before. I can't afford to be that gullible again.

My reply is a simple nod, but I can't hold his gaze. I drop my eyes to my lap, pick at invisible lint, and brush out the wrinkles in the towel underneath me. The change in the air surrounding us is immediate. One stranger planted a seed of doubt in my mind, and it's working hard to take root, despite the objections I raised to Thomas.

I want to believe Rod, but I don't know if I should.

When I finally pluck up the courage to face Rod again, I'm shocked by his appearance. He looks as if he's mad enough to spit nails. When his hands curl into fists, I follow his gaze across the deck to Thomas, who's making hand gestures toward Rod as if to say he's watching him.

"I'm going to kick that guy's ass." Rod takes several steps before I catch up with him.

"No, don't do that. You'll get kicked out of the resort for fighting. He's not worth it, Rod."

"He's definitely not worth it, but defending my honor is. He came over here, uninvited, just to start shit with you out of the fucking blue. I want to know why he did that and what he's planning next. I'll make sure he gets the message to stay the fuck away from you if he values his balls remaining attached to his body."

Thomas stands and walks inside, leaving his friends behind beside the pool. Rod storms off after him with murderous intent in his every step. For a moment, I'm frozen in place and unsure of what I should do. While I don't want Rod to fight him, I also don't want Thomas starting anything else with me. With us.

"Kevin, I need your help with Rod." After I fill him in on the situation, he jumps up and trots in the direction Rod went. Tracy and I are hot on Kevin's heels.

When we walk through the sliding doors into the main hallway, the scene in front of me stops me in my tracks and steals the breath from my chest.

Rod has a buxom blonde backed up against the wall, his body leaning into hers. Her fingers on one hand grip the side of his shorts and the other hand is wrapped around the back of his neck. His lips are a breath away from hers. Her D cups spill over her bikini top. The tiny spaghetti straps are under tremendous strain from the weight of her breasts, the same ones scraping across Rod's bare chest.

I'm close enough to hear what she's saying to him, though she's not trying to hide it, anyway.

"Rod, you're so fucking sexy when you're mad. What do you say we go back to my room and you can work off all that frustration with me? You know I can take excellent care of your every need, my lover."

Bile rises from my stomach and burns my throat as tears sting my eyes. When a cross between a cough and a gag breaks free from my chest, Rod turns his attention to me and jumps back from his friend. He lifts his hands in the air in mock surrender and turns fully to face me.

"Fuck. Daisy, wait!"

Before he can spew his lies, I hold up my hand to stop him. "I don't want to hear it, Rod. I stood up for you when Thomas tried to warn me about what you've been doing all along. You made me look like a fool. Don't come near me again."

The woman sneers at me, enjoying the pain she's causing me and relishing being the winner in this tug-of-war over a man. With my head held high, I march toward the pair of losers and snatch her bikini top off her body as I swiftly walk past. It's still in my hand when I turn the corner and head toward the bank of elevators, and her shrieks fill the hall behind me until the doors slide shut.

I barely make it to the room before the surge of tears flows over my cheeks. The hot and salty mixture leaves tracks over my face, but I don't waste the energy it takes to wipe them away. I'm embarrassed, I'm irrationally hurt, and seeing those two just affirmed my secret fears.

There are no decent men out there. None I can trust with my heart or my body. None who will truly love me. I mean, Rod couldn't even *like* me and not fuck around for a week and a half, tops. How can I ever hope to find true love when life keeps showing me it's nothing more than an unattainable dream?

My intense reaction makes little sense. I've pushed him away and stressed nothing could happen between us. So why would I expect him not to seek company elsewhere? I told him to do just that two nights ago at dinner. So why am I reacting like a jilted lover all of a sudden?

I walk into the bathroom and splash cold water on my face. If a cold shower would work better to wake me up from my irrational reaction, I'd gladly take one. When I finish drying my face and calming my frayed nerves, there's a knock at the door.

I know who it is without looking. I really don't want to face him right now.

Then I remember what I did to the other woman in the hallway, and I groan in embarrassment. "What have I done?"

"Daisy, it's me. Open the door. We need to talk."

Shit.

"Daisy, I'm not leaving until we talk. If I have to sleep in the hallway propped up against your door all night, that's what I'll do. You have to open it sometime." He bangs on the door again for extra measure.

Might as well get it over with.

When I jerk the door open, I find three long faces staring at me. I step back and motion for them to enter.

"This really isn't necessary. You don't owe me any explanations, Rod. You're free to do whatever you want with whoever you want, whenever you want."

"Then why do I feel sick to my stomach because you think I had anything to do with that woman? I swear on my life, I've never even met her before, much less laid a hand on her. I don't know her name, or anything about her."

"He's telling the truth, Daisy. I hung around after you tore her bikini top off her to have a few words of my own with her. She finally admitted it was all a lie to get Rod away from you, and she paid that Thomas guy to help her." Tracy wouldn't lie to me, that much I know without a doubt.

"Why would she do that?"

"Rod owns his own highly successful company, and it's well known in certain circles. She came up with a plan to entrap him and did her best to execute it. She just didn't count on how forceful you can be when it counts." Tracy shrugs, but she's clearly proud of me.

"Yeah, I can't tell you how sorry I am about that embarrassing scene I caused, Rod. I had no right in doing what I did, whether or not she was lying. I overreacted and made a fool out of myself." I put my hand over my eyes to shield my insanity from him.

"Made a fool out of yourself? Are you crazy? That was hot as hell. I've never had a woman fight for me before. Now I'm even more determined to convince you to change your mind about me." His proud smile and the mischievous gleam in his eyes verify he's not simply being nice. I can't help but smile in return.

"Fine. If I'm being completely honest, it felt fantastic to snatch that top off her. She was enjoying my torment way too much." The trio laughs with me and it dispels most of the awkwardness.

"Rod has been my best friend since high school, Daisy. I'm not the least bit hesitant to put my good name on the line here. He hasn't been with another woman for one minute. He's only been interested in spending time with you. With that said, Tracy and I are going back up to the pool area for the afternoon activities and to give you two some time to talk alone."

Kevin takes Tracy's hand, and they leave together. My best friend clearly mouths "make-up sex" to me as she closes the door on her way out.

"I know this sounds like a cheap line, but I've truly enjoyed spending time with you these last couple of days. Part of why I was so mad at Thomas was because I could tell he made you doubt me, even if you didn't fully believe him. I didn't want you to ditch me. We both know I don't need any help in the one step forward two steps back category." Rod's confident smile belies the vulnerability in his eyes.

I know what he's asking, even though he didn't speak the words.

Can I move past my own issues and let whatever this is between us resume?

Because despite my earlier protests, there *is* something there. We both feel it and we both know it, though neither of us wants it. I'm under no delusions about falling in love or finding the perfect man. But I've enjoyed his companionship and even came to look forward to it, so in that respect, I'm not keen on ditching him.

"I've enjoyed spending time with you too, Rod. And because I don't want anything to feel awkward between us now, I think I should explain why my reaction was so extreme." I tell him to have a seat on the couch before sitting beside him.

"You have my undivided attention."

"When you asked me if I was here looking for my soul mate, I told you I didn't know if I even believed in that anymore. The truth is, I want to believe in two people loving each other for their entire lives. I want to believe there's one man out there meant only for me. When all of this happened today, it was like a hard slap in the face that woke me up and made me accept it's not in the cards for me. At all.

"Anyway, I know you enjoyed having two women fight over you, but I'm afraid my reaction was more about me and the death of something I've always wanted to believe in than it was about you and some bimbo in the hallway."

"Just so I'm clear, none of your reaction was because you felt jealous or territorial over me?" His question is meant in jest, I know that, but there's a modicum of earnest curiosity in it too.

"I can neither confirm nor deny there was any jealousy involved. But if I hike my leg and mark my territory on you later tonight, I need you to overlook it. Let it happen without commentary. Chalk it up to me having a bad day."

His roar of laughter is exactly what I need to hear after my surge of adrenaline mixed with other hormones.

"I'll do my best not to be offended by it. If it makes you feel any better, I was very jealous when I saw that jackass, Thomas, talking to you. I was ready to kick his ass before I heard what he was saying. Maybe I'm selfish, but I don't want to share you with anyone else. What if you left me because you decided you liked him better?"

Rod and I just crossed a line we never intended to traverse. There's a lot more truth behind that question than there is jest.

"That's not something you have to worry about with me, Rod. Unfortunately for you, once you become my friend, you're stuck with me for life, no matter what happens. Just ask Tracy. She's been trying to get rid of me for years, but I haven't taken the hint yet."

CHAPTER NINE

Daisy

"We had a great talk after you and Kevin left. We've kept things superficial until now. It seems as if we've turned a corner and are sharing more personal information with each other. But do you think that's such a smart thing to do? I mean, we only have a few more days together, then I'll never see him again. Not weeks. Days." I turn to Tracy, waiting for her to impart her wisdom and tell me what I should do about these damn feelings I have for Rod.

"Of course I think it's the right thing to do. Share all your feelings. Squeeze his out of him. Lay it all out on the line. How else will I get you laid? You won't give any other guy a chance to get to know you. You're brave, gorgeous, and strong. I want to add happy to that list." She waits for my argument, ready with her next countermove.

"There's an enormous problem with this scenario. Two, actually."

"And what are these two enormous problems?"

"One, I really like him. I don't want to like him because I know how it'll all end. And two, I don't know much more about him other than his first name and that he's a software developer. He's withholding information on purpose. I won't ever see him again once we get back to Atlanta. I'm not interested in a vacation fling. I thought I made that crystal clear before we booked this trip."

"Yes, you certainly did. Every damn day from the time we booked it until this very minute. But here's what you're not considering, you need to lighten up and have some fun while you're still young. So what if it's a vacation fling? It'll be the fling of a lifetime. The memories will be great and will linger awhile. The second thing, you like him, stop that shit right now. He's a means to an end, and it will end. Stop putting your heart on the line."

"You know me, Trace. You know I'm not a casual sex kind of woman. I don't take those kinds of chances. And as far as my heart, I didn't say I was in love with him. I don't even believe in falling in love anymore. Besides, I just met him, for crying out loud, so it's not as if I'm planning our wedding or anything. But his personality is almost impossible to resist. He's a different person when we're alone than when the crowd is watching."

"There's only one way to fix that, my dear. *Stop resisting.* Ride him like you're a jockey trying to win the Kentucky Derby and get him out of your system. It's the angsty buildup that's making your mind all mushy. Get that out of the way and you'll feel much better." She shrugs and sheds all her clothes on the way to the shower.

"Thanks for the pep talk. Glad I can always count on you to give me the best advice."

Only her hand emerges from the bathroom, with her middle finger standing tall and proud, in a special best friend message meant only for me.

I fling myself back on the bed and replay our conversation in my mind. Before I realize it, my thoughts drift back to Hot Rod and the day we spent at the cabana. After we rejoined the others and finished the luscious meal, everyone wanted to take a turn on the slide. Not wanting to be the oddball out, I got in line and waited my turn. Rod slipped in front of me just before I reached the ladder.

When he leaned down to brush a kiss across my cheek, he murmured words of encouragement in my ear. "You have nothing to worry about. I'll be right there to catch you."

And he was.

Not that I'd ever admit this to Tracy because she'd use every word of it against me, but once I got over my initial anxiety of the unknown, I loved the ride so much I couldn't stay off the slide. The feeling of soaring through the air, the thrill of picking up speed, and the sensation of my stomach dropping in that split second between leaving the slide and hitting the water below became addicting.

That experience is a lot like how I feel when Rod acts chivalrous and attentive. Somewhere in the back of my mind, a little voice keeps reminding me this is nothing more than infatuation. I've dreamed about a man who is thoughtful and devoted to me for so long, I've projected those feelings onto Rod and made my mold of the perfect man fit him.

But maybe Tracy is on to something with the whole building memories idea. After examining the last several years of my life, I have to face the cold, hard truth.

I haven't really been living at all.

I've been existing, moving through one day to the next without making many remarkable memories along the way.

Simply marking the days off the calendar isn't making my mark on the world.

"Tracy, I'm raiding your clothes for my dinner outfit tonight," I announce on my way to her side of the closet.

She pokes her head out of the bathroom. "Are you fucking with me right now? Just messing with me to try to psych me out?"

"Yep, I sure am. I'm totally fucking with you and messing with your head." I pick up her white mermaid dress. It's backless with spaghetti straps and a long slit in the front. It's perfect. Even though she's taller than me, I can pair it with my heels and make it work.

Then I step in front of the full-length mirror and hold it up in front of me. The silky material will perfectly cling to every curve. I can't wait to walk into the formal dining room wearing this baby.

"You look different." Tracy steps out of the bathroom to watch me. Her head tilts to the side and her expression is softer than normal. "You're *happy*."

"Why do you sound so surprised about that?"

Her eyebrows draw down, but not in anger. At this point, I think I'd prefer angry Tracy, because the look she's giving me now is one of pain. "Because I haven't seen you truly happy in a really long time."

"That's not true. I'm always happy."

"No, you're not. You enjoy making others happy, but your happiness always takes a back seat. What you're doing right now is all for you, and it looks good on you." She wraps her arm around my shoulders, and we stare at each other in the mirror. "There will come a time tonight when your fears try to take over. They'll attempt to convince you to change clothes, to hide away in the room, or something else equally dumb. Don't let them steal your joy, Daisy. You deserve to have fun, whatever that means to you."

"Rod asked me to go on a hike in the mountains with him tomorrow. I said I'll go. Just the two of us, alone, in the woods."

"That sounds fantastic. I'm happy for you. Trust me when I say, you will make it back here in one piece and completely unharmed, or Rod will never see the light of day again." She kisses me on the cheek. "You know I love you and I'd never encourage you to do anything that would end up hurting you."

"I do know that, and I love you too." I lay the dress on the bed while she grabs her makeup bag out of the bathroom and begins her routine. "You and Kevin seem to be all cute and cozy. What's going on with you two?"

"Just a little vacation fun. He's a nice guy and so good looking. And he does this crazy thing with his tongue that I can't get enough of."

"Stop. Stop it right now. There is no way this story can end with me ever looking him in the eye again. Considering I'll see him at dinner in a little while, I don't need that visual stuck in my head."

Tracy shrugs. "Your loss. I'm just trying to help so you can tell Rod how to do it."

"Tracy—seriously—stop right now." She cackles with her

evil laugh behind me as I walk toward the bathroom for my shower.

Great. Now I'm thinking about Rod, his tongue, and whether he's taught it any freaky moves. Dinner tonight won't be awkward at all. Then after dinner, when we go for a stroll on deck or dancing in the nightclub, all my thoughts will gravitate to that one question. I'll have a permanent blush on my face.

I'm blaming it on the sun today.

After showering, shaving, and setting my makeup, Tracy and I slip into our little robes and enjoy some quiet time on our balcony. Watching the waves wash ashore as the sun sets is relaxing, and not anything I get to see living in the Atlanta area.

"When we get home, I want you to promise me you'll have more fun and be happy. I'm just warning you now, so you'll have plenty of time to get your mind settled." She doesn't bother looking at me as she relates her directive. I know she means well, so I give her a pass.

"You have my word." My instant agreement surprises her at first.

"Remember this moment, Daisy, because I'm holding you to this agreement." The devious smile on her face worries me. That's usually reserved for the most heinous situations. "Time to get dressed for dinner. I can't wait to see Rod's tongue fall out of his mouth when he sees you in that dress."

Rod's tongue will fall out his mouth.

Perfect.

Someone help me.

After I slide the slinky dress over my head and step into my heels, I move in front of the mirror. I'm shocked by what I see in the reflection. If I didn't know better, I'd think she was a beautiful, confident woman who had everything going for her.

"Forget Rod. My fucking tongue is on the floor. You look so fucking hot. Too bad we're both heterosexual, huh?"

"Yeah, that's too bad." I laugh with her. "Thank you, though. I appreciate the confidence booster."

"Did you bring that other dress for formal night like I said?" She arches one brow at me.

"Yes, ma'am. I wasn't planning on actually wearing it until now, though. I only brought it so I could say I did." I smile sweetly at her to prevent her wrath.

"Just be glad you changed your mind when you did. It's in a few nights and we're going all out for it. Spa treatments, getting our hair done, and adding some new jewelry from the resort's shopping center. I can't wait." Tracy rarely gets excited over anything like this, so I know she's put a lot of thought into this.

"I'll be right beside you, with bells on. Well, maybe not bells, but a beautiful formal gown and whatever new jewelry you pick out for me."

We purposely wait several minutes past the official formal dining time to avoid the lengthy lines. Everyone else is seated already, so we're able to walk through the double doors without waiting behind anyone. It feels like the vacation equivalent of being fashionably late for a red-carpet event. When we approach our prearranged table, Rod looks up from the evening menu. His bottom jaw drops to his chest and his eyes bulge out of their sockets. I may have imagined a slightly exaggerated cartoon version of him, but that's my story and I'm sticking to it.

However, the heat level in his eyes that's nearing the flash point of spontaneous combustion is very real. I feel their searing caress as he inhales deeply and lets his gaze flow over my skin. He doesn't try to hide his obvious reaction, and it serves as an aphrodisiac for me. Being desired and feeling desirable is a heady combination.

Then he licks his lips.

My mind goes right there. To his tongue, and all the tricks it may or may not know.

The blush starts at my chest and flames up my neck to my face. With his attention solely on me, he notices it immediately. I drop my gaze from his to focus on the floor directly in front of me, but I can't stop the corners of my mouth from lifting. When I finally meet his intense stare again, there's no doubt his mind-reading skills rival Tracy's. I also detect a fair amount of pride in his realization that he's the cause of my current state, even if he doesn't know exactly why.

"You look absolutely amazing, Daisy. I mean, I've drooled over you in a bikini all day already, so I never thought putting on *more* clothes could make you even sexier. I'm not sure what to do with myself now. It's as if everything I ever believed in was a lie." He steps over to my table and pulls my chair out for me. Then he takes my hand in his and kisses the back of it.

I've always wanted someone to do that. How I wish this guy was real and not only a vacation version of himself.

"Thank you. You look very handsome tonight yourself, Rod."

Before we finish our meals, we combine our tables into one instead of talking across the aisle. We get more than a few side eyes from the others for laughing a little too loudly in the more formal dining area of the hotel. When we've eaten our fill and annoyed the other vacationers enough, we decide to take our private party to the exclusive beach and enjoy some fresh night air. The moment we step outside, Kevin and Tracy ditch us in favor of taking a stroll meant for two.

Rod smiles and extends his hand. "How about a drink, a short walk, and a comfy lounge chair with a view?"

"Just one chair?" I think I know what he means, but I'm a little rusty at this whole dating thing, or fake dating, or vacation flinging, whatever we're doing, I'm rusty at it.

"One chair. You lying in my arms under the stars with no one else around. Is that okay with you?"

"That sounds like heaven on the beach to my ears." It really does.

"Perfect. What do you want to drink?"

"A cosmopolitan. It's my all-time favorite."

We stop at the poolside bar and he orders our drinks. Then we leave our shoes on the boardwalk and stroll barefoot through the sand to the more secluded area. I hold his drink while he drags the lounge chair closer to the water. Once Rod settles in the lounger, I sit between his legs and lean my back against his chest. The warm air gusts over my skin, but the man behind me causes the goosebumps covering my body.

"Are you cold?" Before I have a chance to answer, he sets his beer bottle in the sand, raises up, and removes his jacket. Then he leans back, pulling me with him, and covers me.

Now his scent really is all over me. It's a masculine scent I wouldn't mind bathing in, spicy and woodsy, mixed with an intoxicating aroma that's so unique to Rod I'd recognize blindfolded. I sip on my drink from under his coat, though I don't need it. The gesture has my head spinning. I'm wrapped in the warmth of Rod from all sides.

Lying in his arms is the stuff dreams are made of, or at least the kind of dreams my escape into steamy romance novels gives me. I'm not sure he'd meet Tracy's minimum qualifications of a billionaire badass biker who secretly wants to fall in love, but I do think he has an enormous heart he tries to hide from the world. The brief mentions of his sister were with a distinct tenderness in his expression.

When I finish my drink, he takes the glass from me and places it in the sand beside the chair. Then his arms snake under his jacket, glide across the silky material of my dress, and brand my skin with his touch.

"Part of me wants to take you to the nightclub on the rooftop and dance the night away. Another part wants to keep you right here, where it's quiet and we're all alone. But I'll do whichever you'd prefer without complaint." His lips brush against my ear as he speaks. But he doesn't move while he waits for my choice.

He's right there. I could turn my head with very little effort and kiss him. The quick one I planted on him in the ocean was a spur of the moment decision, prompted by the circumstances, and it was a couple of days ago. In this intimate setting, I'd send a very different signal, one I'm not sure I'm ready to follow through on just yet.

The mere thought of it conjured it into being because here I am, turning toward him, and pressing my lips against his. He responds by turning so we're lying side by side. I push his jacket off me and caress his cheek with my fingertips. His eyes search mine for a moment and a flash of uncertainty lights in them, but I don't know what question he's asking me. He slowly shakes his head before capturing my mouth with his.

What starts as a slow burning candle quickly morphs into

a fully involved inferno. His tongue glides across the crease of my lips, asking for entrance, and I instantly comply. He threads his fingers through my hair and grips the roots, tugging just enough to make the pain and pleasure mix deliciously. The urgency in his kiss isn't demanding or aggressive, it's empowering to me. The way he's mastered the art of kissing should come with a warning label.

He leaves my lips and moves his mouth along my jawline toward my ear, then down my neck. The light nips, warm licks, and soft caresses he leaves have my body churned up like the ocean in a ship's wake.

"Damn, Daisy, you taste so fucking good. I've thought about your lips on mine all fucking day." His hungry growl reverberates against my skin, effectively erasing any mental capacity I have to reply.

He moves lower, sliding down my body until his tongue flicks against the skin between my breasts exposed by the deep V in my dress. "I would love to eat you alive. You smell so fucking good."

When he runs his tongue along the middle swell of my cleavage, I nearly come undone in his arms. My fingers curl into his shoulder of their own accord in response to his intense assault on my libido. I'm at the tipping point, ready to tell him to take me to his room, my room, or take me right here on this chair.

But he lifts his face and returns to his original spot. "I want nothing more right now than to bury myself as deep inside you as I can get, all fucking night long, until the entire island knows my full name and they give me a star in the resort's hall of fame. But I don't want you to make a heat of the moment decision tonight that you'll regret the second you wake tomorrow morning."

I'm shocked beyond words. All I can do is openly gape at him, literally. My eyes are as wide open as my mouth is. Yet I can't produce even an opposing grunt. If I'm in physical pain, then I know he has to be too. I mean, his balls must've passed regular blue a long time ago and moved into the midnight blue spectrum.

He rolls off the side of the lounger to stand and looks down at me. "Come on. I'll take you dancing, and we'll have a few more drinks before we call it a night."

Rod

The perplexed expression on her face was adorable. But that's the only part of ending our impromptu make-out session I remotely enjoyed. Taking her to the night-club to dance the night away, instead of back to my room to explore every single inch of her naked body, was one of the hardest things I've done. It's definitely the most chivalrous I've ever been toward a woman who's only supposed to be a pleasurable pastime for the short term.

But my damn conscience kept nagging at me, cautioning me against pushing her further than she was ready to go. She may have thought she was ready to punch her wild card, but she got caught up in the moment. For some reason, it bothers me to think she'd wake up tomorrow and regret her decision to give herself to me tonight. When she's ready, and not just momentarily worked into a frenzy, we'll both know the time is right. For now, I'm trying to be the decent guy and save her from herself, and from me.

But no good deed goes unpunished, as I'm finding out firsthand. She'd never admit it outright, but she's grinding against my crotch over the entirety of every single song just to punish and torture me.

Fast song? Grind on me.

Slow song? Slow grind on me.

At this point, I'm looking for a piña colada to pour down my own pants. A simple cold shower won't be able to touch this raging hard-on. I need an hour-long soak in nothing but ice cubes.

"Time for a drink, Miss Daisy. Are you thirsty?"

"I'm definitely parched. It's hot in here with so many people. There are more guests tonight than the other night." I wrap my arm around her to keep her close to my side as we wind through people to reach the bar.

"You came up here before tonight?"

"Of course. I was here for the first costume party. Weren't you?"

Thankfully, we reach the bar just in time that I don't have to answer, and I don't have to lie. The bartender jerks his chin up toward me, his nonverbal way of asking for our order.

"Another cosmo for you?" I look down at Daisy and wait for her confirmation before relaying the order. "Have you tried anything else? You know, besides frozen coconut concoctions and girlie drinks."

"I have, but since my drink has more alcohol content than most others, it takes fewer drinks to get that feel-good buzz. But don't worry, I never drink enough to get sloppy drunk or anything like that. I just like the taste of it better than anything else."

"Fair enough." The bartender passes our drinks across the bar and we find a deserted table in the corner to sit until we've finished them. "So, I know you like swimming, slides, and hiking. What else do you like to do?"

A pensive expression crosses her features before she quickly pulls the mask back over her face. "As boring as this sounds, I don't do much else besides work. I love my job, but one thing I've realized over the past couple of days is I need to find more hobbies when I get home."

"What is your job? What do you love so much?"

"I'm a teacher, early childhood education. I love working with kids, so that takes most of my time and energy, but I don't mind. The benefits far outweigh any drawbacks."

"That's great. I can tell how dedicated you are from the change in your tone. There's nothing wrong with loving your job and being good at it." *A teacher, huh? She can teach me anything she wants, anytime she pleases.* "Do you take summers off?"

"I do. One perk of the job. I have one passion outside of my job, a charity organization I run every summer."

"I'm not trying to pry, but it's October. Don't you have a class to teach now?"

"That's not prying. There were cuts in my district and they combined classes. I moved to a different school system a few days before this trip. My job there doesn't start for a couple more weeks, though. I'm replacing a teacher who's going out on maternity leave soon. She doesn't plan to return after the baby's born. What about your job? You mentioned once about developing software. Do you like it?"

"It's not as interesting as molding and shaping young minds all day, but I enjoy creating new toys for others to play with. It pays the bills." I realize I'm playing down the significance of my company, but my financial situation isn't something I share with many people. One mention of the name of the company I own will give it all away.

"I'm impressed. It's fascinating to me. Most users never get to see how programs run behind the scenes, and you're the one who codes them to make them work." She takes the last sip from her glass.

"Want another one?"

"No, thank you. That's my limit for tonight. I'm looking forward to our trek in the mountains tomorrow. But you should know that Tracy will watch for my return. She's a force to be reckoned with, so don't think you'll get away with dumping my body in a ravine and leaving me there."

"I've already told you once, if you fall, I fall with you. I believe I proved that to you during our outing at the cabana." I reach over and cover her hand with mine, giving her more reassurance. Her comments don't offend me. I'd expect my sister to be just as careful in her interactions with a strange man on an island, or next door.

"About that, I can't tell you how much I appreciate everything you did. Renting the cabana was a wonderful idea. The slide was so much fun, and I went down it fifty times in a row because of you." She turns her hand and laces our fingers together. "Thank you."

"Believe me, it was all my pleasure. I think I had more fun than you did."

"That's not possible."

We chuckle lightly together, but our eyes linger a little too long. Her skin is so soft, her small hand fits perfectly in mine, and the memory of how soft her lips are is a little too tempting. My superpower to remain a respectful guy is waning under the alluring way she's looking at me. If she pushes the issue, I won't take the high road again. I'll take her to places she's only read about.

"Speaking of our lengthy walk in the dark, secluded woods, where no one can hear you scream for help or come to rescue you from me, I should get you back to your room. No excuses of being too tired to keep up with me tomorrow."

"You think I can't keep up just because my legs are shorter than yours, don't you? Just wait. I'll show you, Hot Rod."

"I'll never admit to saying this, but I like it when you call me that. I consider it as a compliment, like a tribute to my sexiness."

"That's absolutely what it is. What else could it mean? It's definitely not that you think you're more charming that you actually are." The teasing gleam in her eye reveals an additional aspect of her personality. She's growing more comfortable with me and more confident in herself.

"Come on, wiseass. It's past your bedtime."

When we reach the door to her room, she stops and turns to me. The question is on the tip of her tongue.

Do I want to come in?

Yes. Fuck yes, I do.

"Thanks for walking me back to my room. Your alibi is solid now since you're on camera, showing what a thoughtful date you are." She smiles and her eyes dance with humor.

"There are cameras on us right now? That just makes me want to give them something worth watching."

She gasps and I take full advantage of the situation. Before she can reply, my lips are on hers, my tongue dives deep into her mouth, and my fingers wind around her hair. I hold her head in the exact position I want her—the one that gives me the best access to deepen the kiss even further. Her hands flatten against my chest and slide up my body, then she changes her mind and changes direction.

When her fingers graze the outline of my swollen cock through my pants, she freezes, unsure of what to do next. My hips involuntarily push it harder into her hand, seeking the attention my erection so desperately craves. The momentum drives her back against the door, and I lean into her front, never breaking the kiss that's consuming us both.

"Rod." My name escapes from her throat in a desperate plea.

We're both on the edge of a precipice, waiting for the ground to give way under our feet so we have an excuse for falling.

After slowing our pace and ending the feverish kiss, I lean my forehead against hers and focus on breathing until my racing heart slows to a manageable speed. "Sorry. I'm obviously having an extremely difficult time controlling myself around you. You're a terrible influence on me."

My tone is teasing, and she knows I mean no harm to her in the least. She releases a sarcastic snicker. "That's funny, because I was just thinking the same thing."

"That you're a bad influence on me?"

"Yes, exactly that part." She rolls her eyes at me. "No, Hot Rod, that I can't control myself around you."

"Is it terrible that I'm relieved I'm not alone in this?"

"You're not alone at all. We're both suffering and driving each other crazy at the same time."

"Then we both know we have something explosive and mind-altering to look forward to... as soon as humanly possible. Let's go with that for now." I grasp her face in my hands and place a long, lingering kiss on her scrumptious lips. "Good night. I'll see you bright and early in the morning."

Before either of us change our mind, I take her key card, open the door, and gently push her inside. "Make sure no one else is in your room while I wait right here."

"All clear," she says after a minute. "Good night, Rod. Sweet dreams." She doesn't mean that at all. There's zero conviction in her voice.

"They will be. They'll be of you, all night long." I close the door and make sure it latches before heading back to my room. Alone. Again.

This fucking trip feels like we've already been on it for weeks.

When I walk into our room, Kevin is kicked back on his bed, watching TV with an overtly satisfied expression on his face. He gawks at me as I unbutton my shirt.

"Where's your jacket?"

"Well, shit. Daisy is still wearing it. She got chilled out on the beach, so I covered her with it. She wore it in the nightclub too. I just forgot to get it back from her."

"Holy shit." He sits up and turns to put his feet on the floor. "You still haven't fucked her, have you?"

"Fuck off, man."

"*And* you won't even tell me. You like her. Admit it."

"Kevin, you are my best friend, but I will only say this once. I don't talk to you about anything remotely related to feelings, dating, girls, or advice of any kind, really. We've had this discussion before."

"You don't talk about feelings because you deny having any. But you've spent four days and nights with this girl, and you haven't sealed the deal. Either something is wrong with you, which is okay because it happens to every man now and then. We'll get you in to see a doctor. Or, you like her more than you'll say, and you don't want to use your evil powers against her. So, which is it? Do you need a doctor or an exorcism?"

I don't know how long I stand here, staring at Kevin with no expression on my face. I'm trying to decide if I should call the doctor for him and wondering if it's safe for me to close my eyes with him in the same room. "I refuse to dignify that question with a response, other than this one." I give him the middle finger salute before climbing into my bed.

"Tracy talks about Daisy a lot. They've been best friends for years. From what Tracy's told me, what you see is exactly what you get. She's not the type to use people or care about status. She wouldn't tell me what happened, but someone screwed her over horribly a while back. That's why she's so reserved."

I think back over my interactions with her, from the costume party the other night all the way through the moment I left her door just minutes ago. She was reserved at first, but she's letting me inside her closed bubble little by little. That should worry me, along with the realization that I care whether she lets me all the way in. I care what she thinks about me. I care what the end of the trip will do to her.

I shouldn't care.

Kevin is still blabbering on beside me, but my mind has latched on to Daisy and won't let go. Then his voice cuts in again.

"You know, Rod, you may find you have a lot more in common with her if you'd let her get to know the real you."

"What are you talking about? This is the real me."

"Ask Juliana and Isabelle if this man is the Rod they know. They wouldn't recognize who you are away from them. I know Juliana wants you to be happy. She's told me before how much she worries about you and your commitment to remaining a career bachelor. She doesn't want you to end up alone and miserable."

"It's past time to drop this, Kevin. I have my reasons for wanting to stay single. I'm not the least bit worried about my future. I'm perfectly happy with the way my life is going."

"Whatever you say, man."

I won't say this out loud. Just two nights ago, Daisy was in the arms of a masked man, not knowing it was me. Tonight, she kissed me with a need and urgency that matched my own. Is she truly interested in me or ready to fall for the first guy who gives her attention?

Time will tell.

CHAPTER ELEVEN

Daisy

Rod and I take a taxi from the hotel to the national park so we can explore the area on our own. Rod's backpack is loaded with bottled water, snacks, and everything we could need for getting lost in a jungle ten times the size of the island we're on. I mean, if we walk straight in any direction, we'll find our way back to the shore. It's not as if there's enough land mass here for us to get lost for too long. But I appreciate the effort he went through to make sure we have extra rations, so I don't point out any of the obvious.

Plus, there's no telling how much he spent in the resort's stores to accumulate all these supplies, complete with an emergency blanket in case we get cold in the sweltering heat of the Caribbean. The driver pulls into the park and drops us off at the visitor center. Rod pays the driver and arranges a time for the same guy to pick us up later.

We stroll through the park toward the mountainous area hand in hand, taking in the beauty of the land, sea, and sky along our way. When we reach the edge of the forest, we stop at the trailhead entrance and examine the park map. I take a picture with my phone, just in case the trails aren't well-marked in the deeper parts of the woods.

"This one leads to a huge waterfall. Let's do that one first." I point to the trail and follow the lines to the water.

"Sounds good to me. My lady wants a waterfall, I'll give her a waterfall. It'll be the best damn waterfall on the island, too." He cuts his eyes over to me and winks. That sexy smile of his gets me every time.

We begin our trek down a well-worn path. The lush green foliage of the forest surrounding us makes it hard to look away. The trees, ferns, and moss-covered rocks are each slightly different hues, but when the streams of light filter through the canopy above, they're almost iridescent. I can't take enough pictures to capture the beauty of the real McCoy. They each turn out flat and lifeless compared to the genuine thing. This place is teeming with thriving life and vibrant colors.

"This was a brilliant idea, Rod. I'm officially in love with an island and I never want to leave."

After a short trek up the side of the first mountain, we come to an opening before the trail winds around to the right. The cliff on our left is nearly straight down, disappearing into the aqua blue water below. The white-capped waves lap at the protected cove beneath us, instantly making me wish I had wings so I could soar off this mountainside and enjoy all the views from above.

"You look more relaxed here, even after climbing that hill,

than you have any other time I've seen you. You really have fallen in love with this place."

"I feel at peace here. The trees, the breeze, the sound of the ocean, and the songs from the birds in the trees are all so soothing. It's heaven on earth."

After snapping a million and one pictures of the amazing vistas, we continue our hike under the shade of the tree limbs hanging over the trail. After a few minutes of walking, Rod stops and tilts his head, listening to the sounds coming from the thick trees on the mountainside.

"Do you hear that? It sounds like running water. A small stream, maybe? Let's hike down the side of the mountain off the trail and see if we can find it."

The thought of leaving the trail makes me apprehensive, even if we are on a small island. I'm not concerned about getting lost, but there could be deep holes or other hazards that would make it hard or impossible to get back out. But I'm determined to be more adventurous and less scared of my shadow.

"Okay, let's go." Maybe I'll just hang back a couple of steps behind him. No sense in both of us disappearing into a hidden cave, never to be seen again. At least this way I will still be able to go get help.

We hike down the hill, talking and laughing as we wind around large rocks and wide trees. The scenery is beautiful, and the undergrowth is rich. We haven't found any hidden crevices or dangerous precipices, so I dial my anxiety back a couple hundred levels. After about an hour, I notice there are no trails. Anywhere. We've alternated walking up, down, and sideways so much that we couldn't find our path back to the trail if we tried.

I'm not convinced we haven't doubled back over our own tracks once or twice by now.

"Rod, we've been walking for a while and haven't come across any water yet. Are you sure we're going in the right direction?"

"Nope."

"That's reassuring." My deadpan response makes him laugh out loud.

"I'm not worried about it and you shouldn't be either. We're having fun, aren't we? Exploring uncharted forests. Making our own path through the jungle. Getting to know each other without any prying eyes. Where in the world are we? We don't know. But I do know I get you all to myself, so there's no way our little adventure can be wrong."

"Let me get this straight. You're Waldo and I'm Dora? What if we don't make it back to the taxi in time and he leaves without us?"

"What if he does? What's the worst that can happen? I'll call another one. I have my phone." He shrugs, not concerned at all. "You love this island, so take all the time you want to explore. If we get back at three in the morning, we'll miss out on eating in the formal dining room tonight. We'll just create our own dining experience right here in the jungle. The more I talk, the more determined I am to miss our ride and just stay here."

"Are you holding me hostage now?" I smile, knowing he wouldn't do anything to hurt me.

"Hostage is such a hostile term. I prefer to call it hosting an unsuspecting guest for an extended period of time."

"Yes, obviously that description is much more accurate. My bad."

"You're forgiven. No need to grovel at my feet and beg for my forgiveness."

"Hilarious. Let's stop in that clearing over there and lighten the weight of your backpack a little. Maybe we can get our bearings while we're sitting still."

We settle on the large rocks to rest and rehydrate, and I pull out my phone to look at the picture I took of the trail map. At this point, I'm hoping to find anything that directs us to our current location and the best way to get back on track. First of all, I was honestly looking forward to seeing the waterfall and taking a swim in the crystal clear water. And second, as tempting as Rod's idea of being stranded in the jungle is, the anxiety of the entire situation may just send me to a premature death. Best not to chance it.

"Hey, let me see that picture. I think I recognize that landmark." Rod takes my phone from my hand, locks the screen, and slips it into his pocket.

I awkwardly stare at him for a few moments, waiting for his signature smile to light up his face as he hands my phone back. But neither happens. He unwraps a protein bar and sticks one end into my open mouth.

Now he smiles. Even though it's overtly playful and definitely sarcastic, it's still sexy as hell. This man will be the end of me.

I take a bite of the snack and glare at him while I chew. "Care to tell me why you stole my phone?"

"Again with the overly aggressive language, Daisy. Clearly, I didn't steal your phone. It's safe and sound in my pocket, out of your reach and away from your purview. We're on an adventure and you're cheating with a map." He *tsks* at me and shakes his head in mock disappointment.

"You're intentionally trying to get us lost so we'll miss the taxi. Are you insane and just forgot to mention that little detail before now?"

"My psychiatrist says only one of my personalities is insane. The rest of us are mentally stable."

I cross my arms and arch one eyebrow at him.

"Fine. No, I'm not crazy, I'm simply enjoying this too much to rejoin civilization just yet. We're not lost. Even if we get back and we've missed our ride, we'll be fine. Just trust me, okay? It seems you and I both had to grow up faster than most others, so we missed out on the luxury of being irresponsible. Maybe I'm using this excursion to pretend I'm footloose and obligation free for a while."

The heartfelt explanation makes me pause and take stock of my own life. He's not wrong by any stretch of the imagination. "All right, Rod. Maybe I'm the crazy one because I never thought I'd say this, but I trust you. From what you just said, you need a break from real life before life breaks you."

"You have no idea. Regardless of what happens, we have today to do whatever the fuck we want to do. Right now, I want to take you to the waterfall and swim. Eat your gooey cardboard bar so we can go."

"Do you know how to get to the waterfall from here?"

"I know exactly how to get to the waterfall from here. Did you really think I was lost on this little island?" He bites off a piece of his snack bar and grins as he chews.

"You intentionally let me believe we were lost." I grab a piece of moss off the rock and throw it at him. Even when I try to glare at him, I can't stay mad when he smiles at me with that innocent but mischievous grin.

"Sorry if I legit scared you. That wasn't my intention. I'll take excellent care of you. It's what I do." He shrugs, leaving that statement out there as if it means nothing.

When it means everything.

With our stash of snacks and drinks diminished, we set off in search of the infamous waterfall again. Only this time, he walks by my side as we make our way down the hill. The landscape flattens and we wind along the path, passing beautiful flowers and stunning greenery.

Rod stops my progress with an arm extended in front of me. Then he pushes a palm frond out of the way and reveals a stunning cascade of water.

"Did you order the waterfall with a side of stunned silence?" He grins, so proud of his cleverness.

But he's not wrong. My mouth is still gaping open from the magnificence of the scene in front of me. The spray from the twenty-foot tall waterfall carries on the wind and dampens our skin. The low roar of the water striking the rocks below drowns out any external noises. Only Rod and I occupy this small section of paradise, and I'm instantly protective of it.

"Last one in has to walk out naked." Before my words register, I take off running toward the shimmering pool.

"You want to play dirty, huh? I can play dirty too." His laughter echoes off the rock walls surrounding the private cove, reverberating back to my ears as he gains on me.

With maybe half a step left to my advantage, I lunge for the water and make it in the small pool just before he does. We're technically close enough to call it a tie, but I'll only concede that as a last resort. Until then, I'm claiming my victory wholeheartedly. When I surface, he's so close to me I can feel his body heat in the water.

"Looks like you have a long walk back to the parking lot in your birthday suit." I move my arms as I tread water and my fingers brush across his chest.

When did he have time to remove his shirt?

Now I'm acutely aware of the immediate proximity of his manly bare chest. My naked march dare may backfire on me. What if he's already naked in the water with me? So many thoughts fly through my mind. Too many scenarios play out in my daydreams to home in on just one. Flirting and teasing is one thing, but I'm not quite ready for the actual act just yet. I've spent a lot of time with him, but I still don't know his last name or anything else about him.

"Where'd you go just now?" He's in my face with his voice low and intimate, and his eyes are too discerning. "You're heating the water with how fast your mind is racing. Slow down and enjoy the waterfall."

His wet lips press against mine momentarily before pulling back. He waggles his eyebrows and swims toward the water beating against the rocks. I watch him, mesmerized by his agility, as he climbs up on the wet, slick rocks and stands under the waterfall as if he's in an outdoor shower. He stretches his arms out to the side, leans his head back, and smiles up at the sun.

He is chiseled and muscled all over—a work of art perfectly carved.

My brain makes a mental note, along with a permanent snapshot. He's not naked—he's still wearing his shorts.

Damn it.

Life on the edge, right? I swim over and meet him at the rocks. He looks down at me with the most carefree expression I've seen him wear this entire trip. He seems as if the weight of the world has been lifted from his shoulders and he can finally breathe freely for the first time. I accept his proffered hand, and he hoists me up to stand beside him under the world's most exotic showerhead. We lean our heads back and let the water wash over us.

The sound of giggles pulls me from my deep thoughts, but when I open my eyes, I realize it's coming from me.

"This fall has magical qualities," he yells over the roar of the water beating against the rocks. But I'd know exactly what he was saying, even if he whispered. "It washes away all the worries, doubts, and fears. All that's left in this place is the happiness you bring with you."

He'll crush you, Daisy. You know it. You feel it. You even can see it happen.

And yet, I wouldn't exit this wild ride, even if I could. He's all I want, wrapped up in one man. I think.

CHAPTER TWELVE

Daisy

"This was the best day I've ever had. Oh my gosh, I can't get over how perfect everything was. I loved everything about it—the views, the waterfall and the pool, the flowers, the entire island. I'm so glad we took that trip." I can't stop gushing about the off-trail excursion Rod and I took today as we step into the hotel elevator.

Tracy and Kevin made plans of their own, and she said I probably wouldn't see her until late tonight. In fact, I think her exact words were that I shouldn't wait up for her.

"It was an outstanding day, wasn't it?" Rod looks down at me with a smile, our height difference magnified while I'm wearing my flip-flops. "I'm glad we went too."

This boundless energy inside me won't be contained much longer. I'll start bouncing off the walls any second now. I feel like a completely different person. As if I've walked around in a fog for the last twenty-seven years and I'm finally awake for the first time. The colors are more vibrant, the scents more aromatic, and the sounds are clear as a bell.

Of course, it could also have everything to do with all the nerve endings in my body firing simultaneously when Hot Rod and I took an impromptu dip in the water under the cascading falls. The way his hands slid across my wet skin. His lips on mine. How he stared at me when he didn't know I'd seen him from the corner of my eye.

How we were on the verge of tearing off our clothes and going at it right there on the slick rocks, but a tour group interrupted us a split second before the full moon came out. I'm glad they showed up when they did and brought me out of my Rod-induced haze. I never allow passion to carry me too far away from logic, but in that moment, I was a goner. Tracy would've been happy, had I gone through with it, but I know myself better than that—I would've walked away with an enormous amount of guilt.

Staying true to myself is painful sometimes.

"Are you going to the costume party tonight?" I can't help but bounce on the balls of my feet to expend the bundle of energy in my chest.

"Um, yeah, sure. I'll be there. Are you going?" His expression immediately changes from playful and happy to doubtful.

"Yes, I wouldn't miss it. The last one was a lot of fun. I can't wait to see all the costumes at the party tonight. The club is so much fun. You already know I love to dance, and that DJ plays the best music. It'll be a long night, but it'll be worth it."

"Maybe I'll see you up there then. Just so you know, I'm not going to the formal dining room, but I'll find you in the club later. What are you wearing?" He folds his arms across his body and doesn't smile.

Complete change in his demeanor. He went from red hot to ice cold in less than a second.

"I'm pretty sure I'll be a genie tonight." I turn and watch him step out of the elevator, waiting for him to confirm his costume.

"Okay, I'll see you later then." The doors close and he's gone. He's not even walking me to my room this time. He always makes sure I get there safely and no one is hiding inside.

At first, I'm hurt and insulted by his sudden personality change, but then it dawns on me. I lean back against the wall and smile to myself. He doesn't realize I know, and have known the entire time, that he is Captain America. He was fine until I mentioned the costumes, then he became sullen. He thinks I'm going up there to meet some other guy, and he doesn't like it.

I can't simply sit on this information.

This is too good not to use against him in every way imaginable.

He hasn't been Mr. Forthcoming himself, hiding behind his mask and pretending to be someone else while he danced with me and kissed my cheek. Tonight, I'll push that fact as far as I can before he snaps and rips that helmet off his head. Then I'll smile to let him know I have played the player. I'm amused that he thought I wouldn't recognize him by sight or sensation. There's no way I could mistake him. My heart does that little pitter-patter only when he's around.

He asked for a first impression do over, but I refused to allow it. His overt attempts to talk to me as someone else were endearing. For whatever reason, he cared enough to want to change my perception of his character, and I couldn't resist his earnest attempt. I questioned if he was channeling the persona for the first few minutes, but I quickly realized his true mask was the one he wore every day. The helmet that covered part of his face allowed him to be his genuine self, without fear of judgment or rejection.

I played along, giving him the space he clearly needed. But tonight, we're not playing games in the dark. We'll see where we stand in the light when I call him out on the truth.

The elevator door opens on my floor and I stroll to my room, taking my time and letting daydreams about night things flow through my mind. When I open the door, the phone in my room is ringing. I snatch the handset off the cradle just in time before it rolls over to voicemail.

"Hello?"

"I'm so sorry, Daisy. I wasn't thinking straight. Now that you've made it into your room, can you check all the hiding places while I'm on the line so I know you're safe?" He sounds tortured. He's beating himself up over nothing.

I suppress a pleased chuckle because this is important to him. "Yes, I can do that. Hold on a minute."

With the handset lying on the table, I move around the room, call out where I am at each stop, and relay there's no one there except me. "Everything's okay. I'm here all alone. No monsters hiding in the closets or behind the doors."

"That's a relief. I was about to call the hotel's security officers to meet you at your door."

"I think that would've scared me more than helped me, Rod. I'm perfectly safe. No need to worry. I'm already aware of my surroundings at all times, even without you here as my private security detail."

"It just helps me to know for sure. I'm jumping in the shower now, but I'll see you soon."

We disconnect, and I nab the shower for myself while Tracy is still out with Kevin. The water raining down on my head reminds me of our time on the island. Then his words replay in my mind. I wonder what happened in the past that won't let him rest without confirming my safety today. I can't imagine I'm the only person he does this with, and that has me thinking up ways I can get Kevin alone to grill him.

"Chill, Daisy, don't get ahead of yourself. After a few more days, you'll probably never see Rod again. Don't try to fix him."

Tracy still isn't back when I've finished dressing, so I take a stroll around the grounds, lose a little money in the casino slot machines, and have dinner on my own before changing for the late-night party. Time alone enjoying drinks in the open air of the patio bar helps clear the cobwebs from my mind.

Tracy was right in saying I needed to loosen up and have fun. Flirting with Rod and nearly losing any semblance of my self-control with him has been invigorating. Feeling desired and desiring him in return has been life altering for me and my frame of mind. Maybe he's not Mr. Forever, but he's a good Mr. Right Now, and maybe that's all I need.

I don't have to be afraid anymore.

~

WALKING INTO THE NIGHTCLUB ALONE DRESSED AS A SEXY, barely dressed genie is more intimidating that I thought it would be. Saying it's a genie costume may be a little generous. It's actually more of a sexy Egyptian outfit with a faux leather bikini top, a decorative waistband, and strips of flowing see-through chiffon on the front, back, and each hip that touch the ground. Though I try to convince myself I'm overreacting, being stared at by all the men unnerves me to the point I have to fight against the urge to fly out of here.

I continue walking toward the bar with my spine straight, unwilling to allow their ogling and leering deprive me of meeting my date. My senses tingle, warning me someone unwanted has stepped too close to me. Before I turn to face him, a firm hand wraps around my elbow and halts my forward movement. The sudden jolt causes me to stumble, and he uses my imbalance to his advantage, pulling my body backward against his.

"Look, guys, I caught a genie. Isn't it against the law for her to leave without granting all my wishes?" An overpowering odor of whiskey assaults me when he laughs.

"No, it's not. But it is against the law for you to touch me without my permission. Let go of me right now."

"I like my women fiery and feisty. Must be my lucky night because you're both."

He's drunk and pawing me, despite my obvious attempts to get away from him. His friends are laughing and encouraging it. Not one member of his circle jerk speaks up in my defense.

When he slants his head and leans toward my face to plant his mouth on mine, he closes his eyes for a second. He's sloppy drunk and his movements are uncoordinated, so I wrench my knee up while he's not looking and nail him directly between the legs. The sudden impact against his balls makes him involuntarily bend at the waist and release his hold on me. The instant I'm free, I move as quickly as I can through the crowd to get away from him and his friends, but the angry shouts grow closer behind me.

I push through the crowd immediately inside the entryway and stop short when I run into Captain America himself. One look at my face and he knows something is terribly wrong. Then the irate rant from the drunk man storming up behind me, calling me names, and telling me he's not finished with me yet, catches Cap's attention.

The drunk guy with swollen balls steps behind me and glares at Rod. "Step back, fella. I've already captured this genie. She's fulfilling all my wishes tonight."

Rod drops his gaze to mine and rage fills his eyes. "This guy a friend of yours?"

"You heard me, buddy. Fuck off."

Rod keeps his gaze trained on mine.

"No, he's not a friend of mine at all." Then I recount the story for him, right up until I ran into him during my escape.

Rod nods, then turns his attention to the drunk man and his friends. Without saying a word, he gently pushes me behind him and uses his body to shield me. "She's already told you no several times, in obvious ways. You don't seem to take a hint, so I'll be blunt. You're not fucking touching her. Walk the fuck away before the EMTs have to carry your sorry ass out of here on a stretcher."

"Who the fuck are you? Do you actually believe you're the super soldier himself?"

"Nope. But I am the man who will beat you within a

fucking inch of your life if you so much as look at her wrong again. I dare you to try to touch her. You'll be missing all your fucking teeth in about two seconds."

The other guy stands stock-still for a few seconds. With a quick move, he accepts Rod's dare and tries to reach around him to grab me. Rod wastes no time grabbing his shirt with one hand and repeatedly punching him square in the mouth with the other. Blood instantly spurts from his busted lips, a tooth falls to the floor, and the other guy still hasn't figured out where the hit-and-run sledgehammer slamming into his face came from. His knees buckle and he goes to the floor, so Rod releases his shirt and lets him fall the rest of the way down.

The guy's friends surround him, looking down at the floor then back up at Rod in disbelief. Rod pushes his chest out, curls his hands into fists, and steps toward them. Two of them quickly grab their friend off the floor and stand him up.

"We don't want any more trouble, man."

"Then I suggest you stop your friend next time he lays his hands on a woman without her permission. Fucker's lucky he's still breathing."

Security personnel descend on us from all directions, and I realize the entire nightclub has stopped what they were doing to watch us. I bury my face against Rod's back and hold on to him tightly. After Rod explains what happened, and several other guests corroborate the events, the security guards let us go as they walk away with the other guy under their watchful eyes. I don't know what'll happen to him, taken to the local jail, escorted off the property, or released with a stern warning.

He glares in my direction as they walk past me. "Fucking cunt tease. Sensitive bitch."

Rod lunges at him again, but several of us keep them separated. "Let him go. He'll get what he deserves. Besides, you already knocked out one of his teeth."

"I had thirty-one more to go. I planned on claiming every fucking one of them." The way he assesses my thoughts and feelings with a glance is uncanny. "You're not okay. Come on, I'll get you out of here."

He extends his arm to the side and I duck underneath it without question, sticking to his side like a tattoo. When we reach the fresh air outside, he finds a private cove where we can be alone. He stretches out on the lounge chair and motions for me to sit between his legs. Then he wraps his arms around me and holds me while my entire body shivers uncontrollably.

"Do you want to talk about it?" His voice is soft and reassuring in my ear.

"Not right now. Do you mind just holding me until this mental breakdown passes?"

"Not at all. I'm not going anywhere."

"Thank you, Rod." I turn to my side and curl up against his chest. His arms and legs shield me. His lips press against the top of my head, and I feel safer than I have in a very long time.

When my mini meltdown is finally over, I push up from my curled fetal position in his lap and give him a sheepish grin.

"Someone hurt you."

I nod. "Someone hurt me."

He inhales a deep calming breath. "For what it's worth, you're safe now."

"I know. You don't make me nervous the way some other men do. I've learned how to listen to my intuition better. I'm not perfect with it, but better than I used to be."

"Ah, yes, that brings up one other thing. You called me Rod a few minutes ago. So you knew?"

"Did I know it was you behind the mask the entire time at the last costume party? Yes, I certainly did. You thought you had me fooled?"

"Yeah, I guess I did. Then I realized that by fooling you, I'd screwed myself, because you liked Captain America better than you liked Rod Stone."

"Stone, huh?"

"Yeah, I guess it's okay for us to exchange last names now. I mean, you seem like a cool lady and all. You're not secretly a crazy stalker or anything, are you?"

"Never convicted." I feel a little like smiling again at last.

His chuckle is low and rumbles across his chest. "What's yours?"

"Nash. It's nice to meet you, Rod Stone." I lift my hand to shake his and he takes it.

"It's very nice to meet you, Daisy Nash." He turns my wrist and places a kiss on the back of my hand.

He gently tugs on my hand, pulling me back to my spot against his chest, and simply holds me in his embrace. We talk, point out constellations in the sky, and open up more about our personal lives. I think we're moving into another unfamiliar territory here, and I'm not sure what to do with it. This feels all too real, and it feels so good.

All signs I should be running.

"Tell me about your life, Mr. Stone. Distract me." I absently trace lines on his hand, skating over his knuckles and tracking along his fingers.

"I'm afraid my life story won't distract you. It'll only depress you more and encourage you to fling yourself off your balcony later."

"Misery loves company. Don't you know that?"

"Maybe we should stick to one tragedy at a time and see how it goes. I don't want to break your streak of not leaving a friend behind."

"I can promise you this one thing, Rod. I'll stand beside you regardless of what terrible memory you share with me. I'd never judge you or leave you to deal with it alone. That's the worst feeling in the world, thinking you're on your own when you're desperate for someone to understand. A single event can shape and define so much of our lives."

CHAPTER THIRTEEN

Rod

There's so much misery in my history, I'm not sure where to start, or if I even want to share this part of my life with her. She knows I have a sister, but no details about my life or my past other than that tidbit. I'm inclined to keep it that way for two reasons. First, that shit is too sad to dump on her at a time like this. She needs to be distracted from her own demons, not tricked into carrying mine along with her own. Second, I find I have to keep reminding myself this is only a short-term fling and will be over when we check out of the hotel.

"You're not alone either, Daisy. If we allow the hard times to define us, we're no better than the people who put us in that position. The memories never really go away, but I push them away because I'd rather focus on the here and now. The way I see it, I can either let those ghosts haunt me for life, making me afraid of everything, or I can get out there and live my life despite them. The events from our past may shape us in the short run, but how we continue to react to them is what separates us in the end."

"I admire your bravery. I'm not sure I'm strong enough or bold enough to rush at my fears headfirst like that."

"What doesn't kill us makes us stronger, right?"

"Maybe. It certainly brings on panic attacks and late-night anxiety. I admire you for not allowing yours to rule your present. I'm not prying, just making an observation when I say this." She pauses for a moment. "Your story must be a hard one if it made you as strong as I think you are."

"Yeah, well, we all have our crosses to bear, right? Mine is no better and no worse than anyone else's story. The details may differ, but the tale is still the same. We live, we die, and we repeatedly mutter 'what the fuck is this shit' in between."

She lightly chuckles, but my feeble attempt to bring a little humor into the discussion is clumsy and obvious. "Your story is what makes you different from everyone else, Rod. The details of the past, how you view the tale, and the way you respond to adversity shape your personality. Under that detached playboy exterior beats the heart of a caring man."

"Playboy? Who said I'm a playboy?" I pretend to be offended, but I can't keep the smile off my face or out of my voice.

"You did the first day we met. No one else had to say a word."

"That was someone else, not me. Someone who looked exactly like me."

"You have an evil twin running around the island? That's a scary thought."

"Isn't it? What if you'd mistaken him for me? I'd have to kick his ass. You wouldn't know which one of us to root for, causing even more chaos. That would *not* end well at all. Knowing there's someone out there pretending to be me, I think it's best you just stay with me all the time. You know, just to be on the safe side so he doesn't trick you again."

"Hmm, I suppose that applies to sleeping in your bed all night too, huh?"

"We wouldn't want to risk him showing up at your door and confusing you. I should probably keep an eye on you all night."

"Maybe you're right. It would be a shame if he stole me away from you after all the time we've spent together this week. By the way, that was a very subtle way to change the subject. If you don't want to talk about your personal life, I'm not one to force you into it. But thank you for changing my focus, anyway. It's too easy to get drawn into the awful memories and let them overshadow the amazing ones."

"Like I said, I'm more concerned you'll leap over your balcony railing to get away from me. It's not that I'm trying to hide any of it from you. But I don't enjoy remembering the past, much less talking about it. The bright spots of my life are my sister and my niece. What about your family? Tell me about them." I hope I didn't just open an old wound in my attempt to distract her from my own.

"My parents are still happily married, sickeningly in love, and live in Florida. Daddy is in real estate and Mom is a pediatrician. I have one sister, Marlee, and she's three years older than me. And you already know Tracy. She isn't my sister by blood, but she might as well be considering how close we are."

"Are you close to Marlee too?"

"Yes, she and I are very close. We don't spend as much time together as I'd like, but that's for no other reason than life gets hectic and she lives in a different city. We keep in touch and see each other when we can."

"No brothers?" Focusing on her family keeps mine off the topic menu.

"No, but I always wanted a little brother. My mom said having two girls was more than enough for any mother to handle." She chuckles, but the affection in her voice is plain. "I suppose she was right. Marlee and I kept her busy enough."

"I'll bet you were both Daddy's girls too, weren't you?"

She nods. "Most little girls are, aren't they? We definitely were—still are, actually. Daddy has the best heart of any man I know, and my mom is the love of his life. He doesn't hide how much he loves her from anyone anywhere. They have the perfect relationship. If I ever get married, that's exactly what I'd want. They're best friends first, and they do everything together."

"Then you're looking for marriage, kids, the whole little neat package?" Insert cold feet here. That's just not in my cards.

"Not necessarily. If it happens, it happens. If not, I don't need a man for my life to be happy and complete. I came on this trip with Tracy as a favor, not to find my future husband. You can stop sweating bullets now. I promise not to hunt you down after our brief vacation is over."

"That's exactly what a stalker would say."

"You caught me. I only said that to hide my real plans. Thwarted again, damn it."

"Don't even try to pull the wool over these eyes." Not that I'd admit this to her, but I enjoy how easily our conversations flow and the way we banter and laugh with each other. Maybe a little too much. "Any other family to speak of?"

"We actually have an extensive family. My grandparents are still going strong. They had nine kids, so I have plenty of aunts, uncles, and cousins to go around. Do you need to borrow some? I'll send a few your way and let them pry into your business for a change."

"That's a hard pass from me, beautiful. Few people are privy to my personal business and I don't see that changing anytime soon. I'm afraid you're stuck with the nosy interlopers."

"Who said chivalry is dead? They clearly have no idea what they're talking about."

"Right? I don't know why anyone would think something like that. It's obvious you have found the ultimate prize of a man right here. You'll be the envy of the entire resort by morning. Guaranteed."

"After that display in the club tonight, I'd say I already am the envy of the resort. You were my real superhero, and every other woman who saw you fight for me wished you'd do the same for her."

"So that's all it takes? Knock a few teeth out, bust a few noses, make a fool out of a few deserving shitheads? I can do that."

"You *did* do that. I can't thank you enough for stopping them, and for sitting out here with me until I calmed down."

"Daisy, I assure you, no thanks are necessary for any of that. My sister says I'm an overprotective big brother, but she hasn't seen my protective side until some guy tries that shit with her. If I can't sit back and allow that to happen to her, then I can't allow it to happen to any other woman either. No man has that right, and no man will get away with that shit if I'm around."

"I haven't met anyone like you before, Rod. I know we joked about it before, but you really are one of a kind."

"Don't make me out to be more than I am, Daisy. Maybe I have stricter codes in some areas than other men do, but that doesn't make me a saint. If you had to spend more than ten days with me in the real world, you'd be ready to kick me to the curb."

"You think you're so slick, hiding behind that mask. I never said you were perfect, and no woman would expect you to be. But there are attributes that set you apart from other men, and that's nothing to be ashamed of, Rod. In fact, you should be proud of it."

Regardless of how much I'd like to believe her, I just can't. "You're seeing me through sea-colored glasses, beautiful. When I take this Captain America mask off, I'll be the same *Hot Rod* once again. But if that's how you want to see me for tonight, I can't stop you."

She turns in my arms toward me, chest-to-chest and face-to-face. Nowhere to hide. Her bright smile is back, and I realize I enjoy seeing it a little too much. She gently shakes her head. "I wasn't talking about your Captain America mask, Rod. I mean the other mask you hide behind every day. But now I know you're secretly one of the good guys."

Am I?

No, I'm not, and despite how much I'd like to believe her perception of me is on target, I know she couldn't be further from the mark.

"That line of thinking will only get you hurt, sweetheart. You have a pure heart, I can tell. You want to believe the best in people. I hate to burst your bubble, but people suck and will always let you down. Believe the worst, don't hope for the best, and be pleasantly surprised once in a while."

"Actually, I don't believe the best in people at all. My past won't allow me to give anyone the benefit of the doubt. When I trust someone, it's because they have earned it and proven their loyalty. You've earned it, Rod. Over the past few days, with all the small and large acts of kindness, you've earned my trust and respect."

All I can do is consciously breathe at this point. Part of me wants to grasp on to her words and never let them go, to believe them as she does. But I know I can't, not for any longer than the time she's nestled in my arms. We lock our eyes in a heated stare, each waiting for the other to make a move. I won't be the one to initiate a kiss, not after she was just assaulted in the club, and whatever memory ghosts haunting her are still stirring in her mind. It's not fair to either of us. I don't want any of those memories connected to her time with me.

Then she closes the gap between us, and her soft lips are on mine. When her tongue sweeps across the part of my lips, reason flies away in the breeze and I'm instantly aware of my fingers curling in her hair, scraping against her scalp. Controlling the tilt of her head, I deepen the kiss. I'm devouring everything about her as slowly as our overheated bodies will allow me to go. My heart is racing, my breath has seized in my lungs, and my thoughts have slowed to a singular purpose.

Worshipping her body all fucking night long.

Daisy

Why do women feel the need to rationalize and justify every decision and every move they make? That little voice in the back of my head warns me that others may think badly of me if I follow through with my plans to spend the night with Rod. It asks how I'll deal with the fallout if I have to explain my actions to anyone.

What will they say?

What will they think?

Who else will they tell?

All right, little voice. I have a question for you in return. If you can give me a valid answer, maybe I'll listen to you this time. If not, I'm moving full steam ahead.

I'm listening.

What if the worst thing that happens to me turns out to be the best thing I've ever had?

Give me a second.

Time's up, little voice.

Rod just bared part of his soul to me, showing me his sensitive and loving side, even if he didn't realize it. It's definitely there buried under a world of hurt from his past. He didn't share much about his family except how much his sister and his niece mean to him. What he didn't say tells me just as much as what he shared. But I can't judge him for hiding his heart away when I've done the same for years. I've allowed previous injuries and insults to color my current view of the world. Though I meant every word when I said I don't believe in love anymore, I believe the decisions I make affect my happiness.

The moment our eyes locked in a heated battle of desires, I knew exactly what I wanted to do. The bliss of the present is the only thing that can erase the pain of the past. Even though I partially feel as though I'm using Rod to forget my pain, maybe we can be each other's saving grace. Since we've spent time together, we've danced around moving our highly emotional connection to an intensely carnal one. But neither of us has wanted to be the one to make the proposition, until this moment. It's clear we're only making each other crazy and spending nights alone needlessly.

His eyes searched mine, and he waited on bated breath for me to make the first move. The signals I've sent until this point must have been well received because he allowed me to take the wheel and set the pace. Knowing he cares that much about my welfare only endears him to me that much more. Recognition lit in his eyes the moment I made my decision.

Was that a glimmer of hope I saw in those gorgeous blue eyes?

My lips touched his, and it felt as if I'd touched a live electric wire. The current flowed through my veins and ignited all my nerve endings at once. The kiss started off slow and tender, testing the waters and giving the opportunity for either to pump the brakes. When it was clear that wouldn't happen, sparks flew behind my eyes and any self-control I possessed disappeared when he threaded his fingers through my hair.

For the last several years, my decisions haven't made me happier in far too many ways. The reins have been in my hands all along, and it's my fault for not using them. That changes tonight.

That changes right now.

In our current position, I'm essentially lying on top of him with our bodies perfectly aligned. Every inch of me is on fire from the heat of his body underneath mine, making even this skimpy genie outfit feel too heavy and confining.

He gradually ends our kiss and pulls his face back while sliding his hands down to cup my face. "Daisy, you don't have to do this. Short term isn't your style, and this vacation will be over in a few days. I don't want you to remember me as your worst mistake."

I gently shake my head at his words. Rod could never be my worst mistake. "You still have three wishes to make, Master. Would you care to rub your genie's bottle and tell her all about your first wish?"

His eyes darken with pure lust and desire. Even in the dim lighting out here, I can feel the heat emanating from them. "Daisy, I'm warning you—"

With my arms supporting my weight, I push until I'm straddling his hips. Then I lean over to whisper in his ear.

"Last chance before I give your three wishes to someone who will use them."

"Let some other fucker even try to take them. He'll be fish food before anyone even knows he's missing. I can't be held responsible for what I do to any other man who touches you." One of his hands slides to the back of my head, threading my hair between his fingers again until he has enough to grip tightly in his fist.

It's funny, but when Rod takes control of my body, I don't feel as he's trying to dominate or confine me. His touch, even when it's firm and powerful, promises nothing but pleasure and thrills. That same move from any other man would send me scrambling away from him.

Rod pulls my head backward to expose my neck, and hungrily licks, bites, and kisses the sensitive skin until goosebumps break free over my entire body. "All my wishes involve your naked body, my name screamed from the top of your lungs, and complete privacy from prying eyes. Although, if you're feeling extra adventurous, I'm game for making good use of this lounge chair. I can't guarantee we won't be escorted off the grounds as soon as we're done, though."

"Maybe we should finish this conversation in my room … where I can be as loud as I want." The bulge in his pants is growing, pushing against the barely there fabric of my genie costume and making it impossible to think straight.

"I don't know. It would do a lot for my ego to hear all the chants and cheers from the other guests when the manager makes us do the walk of shame out of here." He waggles his eyebrows and winks seductively.

"All right. You stay out here and do your thing while I go to my room and do mine. We'll see how the crowd cheers for

Hot Rod then." I stand from my straddled position on his lap and sashay away from him.

My squeals of laughter erupt before I even realize what's happening. He rushes up behind me, grabs me around the waist, and hoists me with a twist over his shoulder with virtually no effort at all.

"As I recall, you invited me to your room, you very attractive temptress. Now you think you can just walk away and leave me out in the cold alone? I don't think so."

"We're in the Caribbean. It's not cold out here. And you were the one who wanted to stay outside. How many times do I have to say you have three wishes? Use them wisely."

He playfully pops me on the ass while carrying me through the busy hallway. Other guests stop and stare before laughing out loud at my predicament. "Don't talk back to your master, little genie. Every time you get sassy with me, I get another wish added to my account. I'm already up to five."

"Five? How do you figure?"

"Now it's six. You want to go for seven?"

I pause for a moment to think about it.

"No, not until I have all the details."

He barks out a laugh, then picks up his pace. "Where is your fucking room and why is it taking so long to find it?"

"You can put me down and I'll lead the way."

"Nope, not a chance." He stops abruptly but his hand on my ass keeps me secure against his shoulder. "This is your hall. You need to move your room closer to mine, Daisy. This distance is unacceptable."

"Is that your first wish?"

"No, it definitely is not. Stop trying to trick me into wasting my wishes. Where's your key card?"

When I hand it to him, he turns his face toward me with a bewildered expression before looking at the key card again. "Where the fuck did you have this hidden in that outfit?"

"If you'd hurry and open the door, I'll let you search me and see if you can find the hiding place yourself."

"I'm taking you up on that offer, but it still doesn't count as one of my freebies." He unlocks the door and rushes inside.

He abruptly stops again.

The overtly sexual moans and groans and other noises are instantly replaced with shouts and curse words hurled in our direction.

"Oh, shit. Sorry. Sorry. We're leaving—right now. Don't mind us. We didn't see a thing." He tries to turn around, but with me still on his shoulder in the narrow entryway of our hotel room, he can't without walking all the way into the room.

Laughter rolls through his entire body as he rushes into the open space. The way his shoulders shake from his uncontrolled amusement mimics how an earthquake must feel.

"Rod, just put me down, you lunatic." Now I'm laughing too.

"Nope. We're leaving right now. Right this instant." He whirls around and rushes back to the door. "Kevin, just plan on sleeping in here tonight. Daisy's staying with me."

"Good. Now get the fuck out." Kevin's response only makes us laugh harder.

"We're batting a thousand tonight, aren't we? Good thing we know for certain my room is empty now." Rod takes off in a jog toward his room, jostling me the entire way and garnering more attention from the innocent bystanders we encounter.

"God, let's hope no one is crashing in your room for some reason after all this." Since he refuses to put me down, I have no other recourse than to stare at his fine ass and how muscular it looks under his tight costume. Curiosity gets the best of me, so I poke it with my finger.

"What are you doing back there?" He jerks forward and jumps a foot off the ground at the same time.

"I wanted to see if your outfit is padded or if that's your actual ass."

"Satisfied now?"

"I'm satisfied with the answer to that question, yes. I'm happy to report your ass is not artificially enhanced." Our snickers and cackles echo down the hall. Anyone who was already asleep is wide awake now.

"Fuck, we're finally here. We need a fucking GPS to get from your room to mine." When Rod opens the door, the unmistakable sound of snoring rattles the windows and reverberates throughout the suite. "You've got to be shitting me. Jace, wake up!" Rod yells before we even reach the bedroom. "I know you're in here. Get the fuck out of my room right now."

"Dude, quit fucking with me. This is my room and I need some rest. I've only had a few hours of sleep the entire time we've been here, not including when you left me passed out at the fucking dock." Jace is on his stomach and doesn't bother to open his eyes when he speaks. Then he slides deeper into the bed, gathering the pillow in his arms as he prepares to go back to sleep.

Rod grips me tighter with one hand while jerking the covers off Jace with the other. Then he grabs Jace's foot and drags him off the bed until his ass hits the floor, leaving him shocked and bewildered.

"Go back to your own room, fucker. I'm locking the adjoining door so you can't come back in here."

Jace grumbles and the stench of alcohol emanating from him fills the room. He's had way too much to drink, but he finally staggers to his suite next door.

Rod locks the main door and the connecting one before he deposits me onto the bed. The question in his eyes only confirms I've made the right choice. To reassure him I haven't changed my mind, I sit up and move to the edge of the bed. He's standing between my legs, so I run my fingers up his legs and palm his erection. The spandex material of his costume leaves little to my imagination.

When I glance up at him, he pulls the helmet off his head and tosses it across the room. "I'm the only man you'll think about tonight. No masks, no costumes, no characters. Just me —your Hot Rod."

"Hot Rod with the hot bod, you're definitely the only man on my mind. No question about that."

I peel his pants down and his erection springs free. When I slide my tongue across my lips to wet them, he groans out loud. In a split second, he flings his shirt to the floor. Before I lose my nerve, I take him into my mouth as far as I can, and he thrusts his hands into my hair. He's not controlling, but he's guiding with expert skill. There's no hint of demanding in his touch, only urging and encouragement. He's not dominating, but he's empowering me by giving me silent control of the situation.

He draws in a sharp breath between his teeth before bringing my ministrations to an abrupt end. "That's definitely wish number one. You feel so fucking good. You have no idea how much it hurts me to stop you. But I have too many other plans for your body tonight to let it to end this way."

"I like the sound of that. What's wish number two?"

His cocky, sexy grin sends shivers down my spine. "For my second wish, I wish you would take off those clothes. All of them."

"Yes, Master." I playfully bat my eyes and stand, my body skimming his as I rise. Then I take my time unbuttoning and unzipping until my complete belly dancer costume is in a pile on the floor. "Wish number two granted."

His eyes roam across my skin, taking in every inch of my naked body without a shred of shame or embarrassment. "I just realized something... I don't have nearly enough wishes to last the rest of the night."

"We'll just take it one at a time then and see where the night leads us."

I lift on my bare toes and stretch to reach his lips. He bends to meet me and slides his hands under my bottom. When he straightens his back, he lifts me until my legs wrap around his waist. Then he carries me toward the door leading to the balcony. He stops to grab protection from the bedside drawer then walks outside, still holding me up with one arm.

"Don't worry. It's dark, and it's late. No one will see us."

Their balcony is much larger and more private than ours. The table and four chairs sit in one corner while two lounge chairs are in the other. The teak flooring meets full walls on either side, completely blocking the view from other rooms. He walks over to a lounger, straddles it, and places me on the thick pad. Then he moves backward, grabs my legs behind my knees, and lowers his chest. The first touch of his mouth on me draws a loud, involuntary moan from my throat. My fingers grip his hair in a tight fist, tugging as I ride the wave of pleasure.

When his hands slide under my ass and lift me off the seat, I'm not sure what to think or what his plan is, but he wastes no time in showing me.

"Just like eating watermelon." He lifts his brows then dives back in, voraciously licking, sucking, and biting every bit of me.

Then he makes this weird flipping and rolling movement with his tongue, and suddenly I don't care who hears me or sees us. The climax tears through my body with the force of a thousand flippy-rolly tongues. The inky night sky above us parts, rays of sunshine beam down on us, and a chorus of angels sing glorious notes of harmony in celebration.

Then his name falls from my lips like a breathy prayer.

"That was wish number three, to hear you calling my name in ecstasy. Now I know what it sounds like and I want to hear you scream it over and over."

He continues his sensual onslaught. The sensation of his fingers filling me doesn't quench the fire in me. It becomes a raging inferno of need. "Rod, now."

Those two words are all I can manage to speak, but that's enough. He makes quick work of the wrapper and condom, but still pauses, waiting for permission before proceeding. My response is to dig my heels into his ass and pull him toward me. His blue eyes darken to a deep blue-gray while they're locked on to mine when he thrusts his hips and fills me to the hilt.

His mouth and tongue move along my neck as he stretches my delicate skin with every move. He wraps his lips around my nipple, grazing the tip with his teeth, and making my back arch off the chair while driving into me harder and harder. The humid air only adds to the perspiration already covering our bodies, making our skin slicker and harder to grab on to. My nails scrape across his chest and his back in my desperate attempts to delay the total body explosion that's imminent. Time passes in the blink of an eye as he repeatedly reduces my body to a shuddering, shaking mess. At the end, we find the edge of the cliff together, neither able to hold out any longer.

We lie in each other's arms under the stars to let our racing hearts return to normal. We're out of breath and our chests heave with exhaustion, but soon the cocoon of warmth mixed with the gentle breeze from the ocean lulls me to sleep in Rod's arms.

When I stir again, the sun is rising, people begin to stir, and Rod and I are still naked outside.

CHAPTER FIFTEEN

Rod

The morning sun rouses me from the deepest sleep I've had in years. The warm body lying beside me all night certainly didn't hurt.

Then my eyes fly open. *We fell asleep outside last night.*

Voices carry from all around us as the other guests enjoy breakfast and mimosas on their balconies. Daisy is stirring beside me, probably trying to figure out how to run inside the room without flashing half the hotel in the process.

"Good morning, gorgeous." I pull her tighter against me and throw my leg over her, covering her backside from any prying eyes. "Sleep well?"

"Yes, apparently a little too well." She chuckles over our predicament as she lifts her head and looks around. "Should we make a run for it now?"

"Now's as good a time as any. We're in a high-rise hotel,

145

sweetheart. It's not as if the people down there will get a good look at anything."

"What about the people leaning against the railing behind you? The ones staring at your fine bare ass and snapping pictures with their phones? Will they get a good look at anything?" She tosses my words back at me with an arched brow.

"No more than the people behind you gawking at your luscious bare ass will."

Her lips part and a surprised gasp immediately follows. I can't help but smile, despite my best efforts to keep a straight face. "Are you serious, Rod? Are they really looking at me?"

For a moment, I consider teasing her more, but the horrified expression in her eyes won't let me. "No, there's no one there. Even if there were, they wouldn't see anything except my leg. Even if someone saw that fine ass you have, it wouldn't be the end of the world. Not yours anyway. I'd have to kill them for looking, so it would be the end of theirs."

She laughs and rolls her eyes at me. "Okay, smart ass. Let's make a dash for the door and hope it didn't lock behind us last night."

"Now *that* would be a worthy challenge. I'm kind of hoping it is locked now."

"Don't even joke about that!" She darts toward the door and sighs heavily in relief when it opens.

I follow her into the suite and stop in my tracks when I realize what she's doing. That I'm standing here buck naked has no effect on me. I fold my arms across my chest and stare her down. "Daisy, what the fuck do you think you're doing?"

Her head jerks in my direction then she quickly averts her eyes, her face flushing bright red. "What does it look like? I'm putting my clothes on before heading back to my room. You don't expect me to roam the halls naked, do you?"

"No, of course not. I think I made it clear I'd have to kill any man who tries to take you away from me, and you walking to your room naked would definitely send the wrong message. That's not what I meant, though."

She straightens and turns to face me. "What do you mean then?"

"Why are you leaving? Why would you go back to your room?" Her eyes keep dropping to my cock, then back up to my face. The more she does that, the harder it gets and the more it stands at attention. I intentionally wiggle it, making her stare at it for more than a heartbeat before she jerks her gaze away.

She glances around the room, unsure of what she should say. The answer is there, but she's unsure of saying the words. "Well, all my things are in my room. I need to shower and get ready for our outing today. I mean, I'm not wearing this genie getup all day, so I'm not sure what you expect me to say right now."

"Are you trying to ditch me right now? Are you running out of here and avoiding me the rest of the day?" I tilt my head to the side and raise my eyebrows.

The irony of the situation is not lost on me. I'm choosing not to acknowledge this is the one time I don't want my overnight guest to walk out on me.

"No." Her statement sounds more like a question. "I don't believe in overstaying my welcome and I need different clothes. And a shower. And my flat iron. Hairbrushes. Sunglasses."

"You know, I have a very nice shower right here. It doesn't

require clothing to enjoy it. And maybe you've forgotten, but Tracy and Kevin claimed your room last night. They may not be ready for you to barge in on them again so early in the morning."

"Maybe you're right. Are you trying to ask me to stay here with you, Rod?" There's a hint of doubt in her eyes, but the smile attempting to break free is genuine.

"Stay, Daisy. Don't leave me yet. We'll order room service, enjoy the walk-in shower while we wait for breakfast, and avoid the crowded shore excursions. I'm sure you and I can find plenty to do today, without including everyone else."

"All right, then. I'll stay."

"Good. We'll call the room phone to warn them before we show up to get your things. You can wear one of my T-shirts as a dress. No one will think twice about it. You could be wearing your bathing suit cover for all they know."

"Sounds like a plan."

"That's what I wanted to hear. I'll call in our breakfast order right now." To save time, I order one of everything available on the breakfast menu then turn my attention back to Daisy.

"Now, you mentioned a walk-in shower?" She licks her lips and I briefly consider holding her hostage in my bed all day.

"I did. Let me walk you into it right now. Drop your drawers and come with me." I waggle my eyebrows.

She giggles and does as I ask. "Wow. This bathroom is enormous. It's almost the size of our entire room. We can't even wash our hair in our shower stall without bumping our elbows on the sides. The next time Tracy and I go on vacation together, we're upgrading to a suite."

"The suites do have their perks." I adjust the temperature then pull her underneath the water raining down from above our heads. "Last night was only a taste. What do you say to a four-course meal now?"

Her reply is to run her hands down my chest and grip my already hard cock in her delicate little fingers. "I say I'm starving."

When she drops to her knees and nearly swallows me whole, my eyes roll back into my head and I'm amazed my legs can still hold me up. She works her mouth and her hand in tandem, bringing me to the point of no return. I try to warn her, though my entire being would revolt against me if I stopped her. But she keeps going of her own will, determined to see me crumble to my knees with her.

When I open my eyes, she's looking up at me. This time when our eyes lock, it's not from an overabundance of raging hormones. Something deeper calls to me, regardless of how hard I try to turn a deaf ear and a blind eye. With no effort at all, I lift her into the air and push her back against the cool tile wall. We both feel it, this invisible link connecting us, drawing us in closer with each passing moment.

I cover her mouth with mine, savoring every inherent sensation. Her sweet lips. Her soft tongue. Her unique taste. Her exclusive scent. The hot water continues to pour over us, making our bodies slick as her breasts slide against my chest. Her arms tighten around my neck, her legs tighten around my waist, and her hips move in tight circles over my cock, searching for release. I grasp her ass and surge upward, burying myself as deep inside her as I can go.

Her nails claw into my back and she releases a loud cry before digging her heels into my ass and urging me on. The water sloshes, her moans increase, and her inner muscles tighten around me, milking me for everything I have to offer her. Our foreheads are still pressed together as we try to regain control of our senses. When we finally come up for air, and our eyes meet once again, I realize the dire mistake I just made.

Before I can apologize profusely for my lapse in judgment, she shakes her head. "It wasn't all your responsibility, Rod, so stop feeling so guilty. I'm just as much to blame for not keeping my head on straight. We both got carried away. Just so you know, I haven't been with a man in, let's just say it's been a very long time. You have nothing to worry about with me. I'm clean and I'm covered."

"To be perfectly honest with you, I'm ashamed of myself, Daisy. I've taken a lot of pride in never having had sex without protection, even when I was a teenager. I'm clean, regardless, so you can rest easy about that. But I won't be the least bit offended if you want to be tested for everything. I'll even pay for it. This isn't exactly the sweet pillow talk I had in mind for you today."

"It's real life talk, Rod. I'd rather have that than unobtainable fairy tales any day."

"I'm willing to let you thoroughly inspect me, make sure there's nothing suspicious on any inch of my member. You can get as close and personal as you'd like."

"And he's back, folks. There's the Hot Rod I know."

"I don't know what you're talking about. I've been trying to introduce you to *Hot Rod* this whole time."

Now that we've dispelled the tension and restored our easygoing banter, we can move on to more important things. I turn off the water, grab a towel, and rub it over her skin, everywhere, without missing a single spot. When I finish, that heated expression is back in her gaze and her skin is flush. I fucking love how my simplest touch affects her, something I rarely pay much attention to with other women.

Maybe Daisy is the missing link in my life. No one else has ever made me want to pay close attention before her.

"If you keep looking at me like that, you'll have me for breakfast instead of the bacon and eggs we ordered." I arch one eyebrow at her in a direct threat.

"I'm not hearing a downside to this ultimatum. Is there supposed to be one?" She has the nerve to smile at me.

"I've created a monster. You will be the death of me. You know that, right? No food. No drinks. No sunlight. Locked inside a suite, pleasuring my woman day and night."

"Again, exactly what are you trying to persuade me to do? I'm not clear."

"Get out of this shower before I tan your backside." I wrap the towel around her to hide her gorgeous body from my overactive libido.

"Really, Rod. It's as if you're intentionally trying to provoke me."

She steps out of the shower and purposely drops her towel on the floor. She swings her hips from side to side, knowing damn well I'm watching her like a stag in rut, my tongue hanging out of my mouth, and my eyes unblinking.

"I'm changing your name, Daisy Nash." I announce as I follow her into the living area. "Daisies are sweet little dainty flowers. They're delicate and elegant. They don't try to kill people."

She's visibly amused at my sudden outburst. "Is that so? What is my new name then?"

"I have to do some research on that subject before I announce it."

"Because you have no clue what the other flowers are, do you? Besides a rose. Everyone knows that one."

"You're not a rose either." I pitch a T-shirt to her, mere seconds before there's a knock at the door. "Room service is here. We're not finished with this conversation."

Her smile nearly splits her face in two. "No, we're certainly not. Now peel my grapes and feed me, man slave. I'm hungry."

I'm enjoying this time with her way too much.

CHAPTER SIXTEEN

Daisy

"Aha! I've got it!" Rod exclaims, rather loudly, as we pick up more bottles of spiced rum and Tortuga Rum Cakes from a small store in town.

"You've got what?" I glance around the small store, noting all the eyes intently fixed on the two of us.

"Your new name. It just came to me."

"Oh, God. Let's hear it then."

"You're no longer Daisy. You're Mahoe." He grins broadly, proud of himself.

I'm stunned speechless. The snickers from around the store are quickly covered by fake coughs and hands firmly placed over mouths. This isn't embarrassing at all.

"Rod. Did you seriously just call me your *ho*? And you think I'll be all right with that?"

"No, I didn't call you my ho. I said Mahoe."

"You're not making this any better."

"It's also called a sea hibiscus. A Mahoe." He spells out the name, but my deadpanned expression doesn't change.

"Again, you're not making this any better for yourself. Do you honestly think I'll answer to 'ma-ho' when you call me that in public?"

"Hmm. I see what you mean. That could pose a slight problem. How about I only call you my ho in private then?" He waggles his eyebrows and I can't help but smile in return.

With a roll of my eyes, I shake my head. "No, not even in private. Find another nickname."

"That's the state tree of Jamaica, if that makes you feel any better."

"It doesn't." I walk off to grab a bottle of banana-flavored rum, leaving him alone with his Mahoe thoughts.

"Your husband is hilarious." The lovely woman behind the counter smiles at me, then cuts her eyes toward Rod. Our banter over the nickname he tried to give me amuses her. "Are you two lovebirds here on your honeymoon?"

Before I can correct her, Rod is at my side with his arm draped over my shoulders. "As a matter of fact, we are. How could you tell?"

"I've been married for a very long time. My husband and I have three boys. If there's one thing I know, it's that a man only teases and laughs with a woman the way you are if he's head over heels for her. You, my friend, are crazy about this one." She nods her head toward me, her sweet smile still securely in place. Rod freezes in place. I'm not sure he's even breathing anymore.

"Now you've embarrassed him. He hates showing his feelings. He'd prefer for everyone to believe he doesn't actually have any. It's okay, honey. Your secret is safe with us. It won't go any further than the bottom of this bottle of banana rum." I playfully jab him in the ribs with my elbow, partially to get him to breathe again before he passes out—and also to play along with the big fat fib he just told.

"Whew. That was a close one. You're not recording this, are you?" I glance over at him in time to see him smile and wink at the store owner.

"No, of course not." She swats her hand in his direction. "No need to do that. Everyone can see it anyway. You're not fooling anyone but yourself, mister."

Before this conversation turns more uncomfortable, and we dig ourselves deeper into a lie, I place the goods to the counter in a not-so-subtle move. "Looks like we have enough alcohol to hold us over until morning now."

Rod insists on paying for our booty, so I back off and let him. I was fully prepared to pick up the tab for the entire bill. After all, Rod has done more than enough for me on this trip. But it seemed to be important to him, bordering on a matter of pride and dignity, even, so I let him have his way.

We say our goodbyes to the store workers and walk outside to our waiting taxi. The ride back to the hotel is quieter than usual.

I thought we already passed the awkward stage of our vacationship.

I'll be damned if I let one offhanded comment ruin the four days we have left together. This is the most fun I've had in years and I'm not ready to let it end just yet. Check-out day will be here soon enough, and I've mentally prepared myself to say goodbye to him then.

But not one minute sooner.

"Rod? Is something wrong?" I finally just blurt out the question that's on my mind. At least if he runs away from me now, it won't be because of a simple misunderstanding.

"No. Why would you think something's wrong?"

"You're just too quiet. It's not like you, so I thought maybe what that woman said spooked you beyond repair."

"Why would she spook me?" He arches one eyebrow, trying to look cute. He succeeds.

"Because you're in love with me, Rod. She knows it. I know it. Even you know it deep down. It's embarrassing for me too, but I know you can't help it. Can we just go back to pretending you're not already fully attached to me, that you won't be emotionally devastated when you have to let me go?"

A slow smile crawls across his face. "For you, my ho, I will do my best to act natural again."

"Thank you. But we're changing my name to something else. Anything else. Because I'm ninety-nine percent sure you said 'my ho'—two separate words—on purpose just now."

He exaggeratedly feigns his shock and bewilderment. "I can't believe you'd accuse me of something so heinous. You'll pay for that later."

"Is that right?"

"Yes. My hos don't disrespect me like that and get away with it."

The taxi driver sniggers from the front seat, causing Rod and me to burst out laughing. Any unease between us disappears, but it makes me wonder why Rod's so averse to love. What happened in his past to make him run from his feelings? I wasn't kidding when I said he hides any trace of emotion from others. I may be damaged, but I can spot a kindred soul.

"So, tell me about Daisy Nash. What do you like to do when you're not working? What lights your fire?"

"You really want to know about me? Like, personal information?"

"Yes, I do." His sincere expression nearly melts me on the spot. I wish he'd show this side of his personality more.

"Tracy and I have been best friends pretty much all our lives. We grew up on the wrong side of the tracks, so we had that in common from the start. Even still, our families were polar opposites. Hers was very cold and unloving while mine has always been the epitome of love. We were so poor back then. When I say we had nothing when I was growing up, I mean that literally.

"My parents are great, don't get me wrong, but they did everything backward. Got married way too young, had kids right away, *then* Mom went to college. Attending undergraduate then medical school and residency with small kids at home was harder than it sounds. Dad worked all the time, but money was always tight, and it seemed we could never catch a break.

"The other kids relentlessly teased and bullied Tracy and me in school. For me, it was because of the holes in my clothes, my run-down home, or my parents' old broken-down vehicle because we couldn't afford a better one at that time. That takes a toll on kids in ways many people don't understand. So, a few years ago, I started a summer camp for underprivileged kids. I love teaching, but extending the camp has become my mission in life."

"That's fascinating, Daisy. What kind of activities do you do at the camp?"

"We have a lot of fun things built in the program. But the

primary focus is to teach them the life skills they don't learn in school so they can be more successful adults. We have experts from various fields come in and give us a glimpse into their lives. We recognize everyone isn't cut out for college, so we have focused time on technical vocations. We arrange internships for the older teens to work with mentors and give them on-the-job experience to put on their résumés. Plus, we cover room and board for the kids to ensure they have a full stomach and a safe place to sleep."

"Not to pry, but how is this program funded? Do you get government grants for it?" He turns in his seat and faces me, fully engaged in the conversation.

"I've tried, but there never seems to be enough money left over to help those who are trying to help themselves. Our funds come from local corporate sponsors who want to invest in the community. They get tax credits for their donations, and we get to stay open for another summer. But our model is too dependent on corporate donations. Changes in the stock market could wipe out all our hard work, so I'm looking into different funding options for future camps. I won't give up."

"You are amazing. Instead of letting your past make you cold and unfeeling, you used your experiences to make you more compassionate and giving. Not many people are like you, Daisy. You're absolutely one of a kind." He rubs the pad of his thumb along my jawline, slowly and seductively. A shiver runs up my spine from the contact and intimate expression in his eyes.

"The kids are the amazing and resilient ones. They keep me going the days I feel defeated. I know I can't wallow in my pity party because they're counting on me."

"That's a lot of responsibility to put on your shoulders." He searches my eyes. What is he looking for?

"Who else will step up and help them if I don't? I can't wait and hope someone else feels compelled to undertake the project. I'd never be able to sleep at night."

He's not sure how to respond, so he simply shakes his head in disbelief instead.

"What are you thinking, Rod? Do I not qualify for ho status anymore?"

"You never did. I hope you know I was only kidding about all of that. I'd never disrespect you like that."

"If I thought you were serious, I wouldn't be here right now. I'm a big girl, I know how to call my own cab and everything. You've mentioned your sister a couple of times and how close you two are. I don't think any man who cares about his sister the way you do would purposely hurt another woman." I link my fingers between his, reinforcing my message.

"You're incredibly perceptive. My sister and I have been close all our lives, not in a creepy way or anything. We also had a rough childhood and learned to lean on each other to get through life in general. Even though we're both grown, I'm still overprotective of her. She's used to it by now, though."

"I get the sense she doesn't have much of a choice in the matter." I chuckle, picturing Rod as a big brother.

After we reach the hotel, I'm unsure of where I should go, back to my room or to Rod's room with him. Maybe he wants some time alone before dinner? Maybe he's had enough of me for the day? My insecurities rear their ugly heads again.

Before I have a chance to say anything to embarrass myself, Rod grabs my hand and silently answers all my questions.

When we walk into his suite, my packed suitcase is there waiting for me. We quickly check the closet and drawers and find Kevin's belongings are missing. Apparently, our friends decided a swap in roommates was in order without consulting the other two people in this scenario. Rod and I stare at my bag for a moment before turning our gaze to each other. He shrugs one shoulder.

"Works for me. Now I have full access to gawk at your body at any time of the day or night."

"Funny, I was just thinking the exact same thing."

"I fucking love that smart, sassy mouth. Come here." He places the shopping bag on the desk and scoops me up, tossing me over his shoulder with ease.

The mattress hits my back and a sexy muscular body covers my front. When his lips touch mine, my entire body lights up like a Christmas tree. He takes his time moving his mouth over every inch of me. His fingers tease and explore. His tongue licks and flicks. He accepts my every moan as a challenge to elicit another. Every cry becomes a scream. When my entire body is spent and shuddering uncontrollably under his touch, he falls over the edge with me.

When he collapses on top of me, our bodies meld into one. He slides his arms underneath my back and squeezes me closer to him. I'm lying here cradled in his arms, and I know one thing without a doubt.

I'm in way over my head now.

CHAPTER SEVENTEEN

Rod

"When are you and Tracy getting married?" I intentionally throw that unexpected bomb at Kevin during our early morning run to see how he'll respond.

"Married? What are you talking about?" He stops jogging and his eyebrows lift well over his sunglasses. "When are you and Daisy getting married?"

"We're not, and you damn well know it. This is a vacation fling—nothing more. I've made that clear from day one."

"So you've said. But you've been with the same woman for a week now, not even looking at all the other hotties running around here in their thong bikinis. You don't want to admit it, even to yourself, but you've got it bad for little Miss Daisy."

"Wrong."

"I'm not wrong. The day Daisy and Tracy went off

together and left us out, you were in a foul mood the entire time because you couldn't get your Daisy fix."

"Lies and slander."

He laughs, but it's the sardonic, I know you better than that kind. "You're right. There are lies, the ones you're telling yourself. You've been in two fights over her, in the club and at the pool. The only other woman you've fought for is Juliana, but she's your sister, so that doesn't count."

"She's the only woman I love, so she does count."

"That was true before. But do you know what I think?"

"No, and I don't want to know."

"I think you've already fallen in love with Daisy, to the point you can see yourself settling down with her for a nice, long life. That scares the ever-loving shit out of you, and you know it."

I turn to resume our jog on the beach, refusing to dignify that ridiculous notion with a response. He's quick on my heels, though.

"Typical Rod. Shut down when anything resembling emotions toward another human surfaces. You're not your father, man. You've already proven that. Look at Juliana and Isabelle."

"What's it to you? Why do you care so much?" I roar at him, directing my anger and frustration at the closest outlet.

"Because you're my best friend, Rod. If you don't acknowledge what's going on with Daisy, you'll regret it for the rest of your life. Losing her will haunt you day and night. The girl is crazy about you, and anyone willing to put up with your bullshit deserves a fucking gold medal."

"All the more reason for her to get away from me after the next three days end. Actually, it won't even be that long because you and I have an early flight out on our last day. So, we have a couple of days and some change."

"What a superb role model you are for Isabelle. You should remember this moment the first time some jerk breaks her heart. When you want to kick his ass, just remember you're not one bit better than he is."

"What's your fucking deal, Kevin? Did Tracy cut you off unless you can convince me to pop the question to Daisy before the trip is over?"

"Don't bring Tracy into this and try to lay any blame on her. You're way out of fucking line right now."

"You're in love with her, aren't you? How the hell can you be in love with someone after a week?"

"Yes, I love her, and I tell her frequently. Don't worry about my relationship with her. At least I have one—a real one. You've trapped yourself in the past for so long, you're emotionally stunted now. The sad part is, you have no reason to be, but you won't face your own demons. You are not to blame for what happened a lifetime ago. It's time for you to move on because your sad song is old."

He doesn't give me a chance to respond before he turns on his heel and jogs off in the opposite direction. His words sting more than anyone else's would because he's been my best friend since middle school. He knew me way before my company's success launched me into the stratosphere of multi-million dollar business contracts, writing software programs for some of the top Fortune 50 companies, and expanding to a full staff of five hundred employees just to keep up with the demand.

He was my biggest supporter when I taught myself the various programming languages as a teenager because that was the only way I knew how to support my family. Today, I'm the president and CEO of my own company. He's my vice president, a position he earned on his own because of his work ethic, brilliant mind, and innovative ideas.

He's the only person I would trust to run the billion-dollar enterprise in my stead.

Despite all that, for some reason, I can't bring myself to take his word about my current predicament.

For the next thirty minutes, I sprint as hard as I can in the sand, weaving around people enjoying the bright sunshine, warm water, and white sand. I've seen more fucking couples in love in the last half hour than the rest of my days here combined. Everywhere I look, they're smiling, touching, kissing, or taking a stroll with their fingers laced together as a public declaration of their love. I never wanted this bullshit. All I wanted was a fun vacation on a tropical island with a beautiful and sexy lady warming my bed at night.

When I stop, I yank my phone out of my pocket and drop on my ass in the sand. Before I lose my nerve and change my mind, I call Juliana.

"Rod? What's wrong? Are you hurt? Sick? Should I have the National Guard deployed to come get you?"

"Hi, Juliana. I'm fine. Not sick or hurt. And the National Guard wouldn't come to a foreign country to get me. I need an honest opinion and realized no one knows me as well as you do."

"All right." She draws out the syllables as confusion kicks in. "Tell me what's going on, Rod. What happened?"

She listens silently while I fill her in on all things regarding Daisy. From the first day we met, her spunky attitude, my reaction to the dudes who try to flirt with her, how I completely ignore every other woman on the island. The only sound she made was a sharp gasp when I admitted Daisy has been sleeping in my room every night ... and we spoon. I finish with the argument Kevin and I had a few minutes ago.

"That's it. That's the complete story. What do you think?"

"Rod, you know how much I love you and appreciate everything you've done for Isabelle and me. There's no man in the world I trust the way I do you. So, when I say this, know that I mean it with all the love I have in my heart."

"Okay."

"You're a complete and total dick to women. You have a full jar of hearts you've broken over the years. I've had to ask a dozen or so women to leave your house because you didn't want to face them the morning after. Unfortunately, I think I'm the only one who knows what a great catch you are. The ugly truth is, I'm afraid you'll end up alone and miserable because you've pushed every woman who has cared about you out of your life. From what you just told me, I'd say you're doing it again."

"This time with Daisy wasn't supposed to be anything more than a short vacation fling, Juliana. Nothing more. Why am I the terrible guy suddenly? She came to a singles resort in the Caribbean. Did she really expect to meet the man of her dreams *here* and live happily ever after? That's like going to a club every weekend thinking the men are just waiting for their true love to walk through the door. It's ridiculous."

"Ridiculous or not, you've never spent more than a night or two with the same woman. You've never asked about her life, what she's passionate about, or anything else remotely resembling a genuine interest in her as a person. Even if it wasn't supposed to be more, it *is* more. What's so different about Daisy?"

With a heavy sigh, I reply with the first thing that pops into my head. "Everything."

She covers a giggle with a fake cough. "Can you be a little more specific?"

"All the usual characteristics you'd imagine. She's beautiful, smoking body, sassy mouth. She's also funny and thoughtful and genuine. She helps underprivileged kids every summer. She spends her time gathering corporate sponsors to give these kids a fighting chance, even though she doesn't have much herself. She has enough backbone to call me on my shit and she makes me want to protect her at the same time. Something about her is so familiar, I feel as if I've known her forever. But she does not know who I am or how much my company is worth. It's refreshing."

"Big brother, I don't know how you could ask for a better sign from the universe that you two belong together. Everyone isn't after your money, Rod. If she was a heartless gold digger, you would've figured that out already. You haven't told me anything that would make her seem like that type, though."

"I don't think she is. We had a run-in with one woman who recognized me and wanted to sink her claws in for the kill. If Daisy's lying, she deserves an Oscar for her performance."

"How about you try the opposite of your usual approach this time? Try trusting her until she gives you a reason not to, but not a second before then."

"It's not a matter of trust—"

"The hell it's not. You don't trust anyone enough to keep

them around. You have Kevin, Isabelle, and me. I'm not counting Hunter and Jace. They're hopeless cases. There's no one else in your life. Take it from me, finding someone you love and who loves you back is a veritable miracle. Don't make the mistake of thinking she'll always be there, waiting for you to decide."

"I hate it when you're right."

She laughs out loud. "Yeah, I know you do, but get used to it. I know what I'm talking about. Worrying about you being sad and alone keeps me up at night, Rod. You deserve to be happy. You won't make the same mistakes he made."

She doesn't have to define who "he" is. We both know all too well.

"You shouldn't lose a wink of sleep over me, baby girl. I'll be fine. Besides, maybe I'm making a mountain out of a mole-hill. We have a couple of days left here, but she hasn't mentioned continuing anything once we leave. She may not have any desire to see me again."

"Don't start making up excuses to hit the self-destruct button, Rod. Please. For me. Just this once—let it ride and see where the chips fall on their own."

"Damn, you know me far too well. I need to change up my tactics to keep you on your toes."

"Go get the girl, big brother. Don't come home without her."

"Yes, ma'am."

"Hey, before I forget, Isabelle and I are staying at your house for a few nights while you're gone. Your house is closer to her school than mine. I can forward my work phone line to your house since I'm eyeball deep on a big project. It'll be the munchkin and me when you get texts from your alarm company, so don't worry."

"That's fine with me, you know that. Make yourselves at home."

We chat for a few more minutes about what she and Isabelle have been doing since I've been away before we disconnect. Then I stay planted on the beach, watching couples frolic in the water or families build sandcastles. Regret fills me, flooding my senses, when I think about the hundreds of millions I've made, the days, nights, and weekends I've spent working, and the time I've lost with my family along the way.

In the years since my business took off, we could've had annual family vacations and seen the world. Instead, I dedicated my life to the almighty dollar, even after I'd made more than enough to sustain us. Dissecting my reasons will take more time and effort than I'm willing to waste this morning, but I have a sneaking suspicion this won't be the last time it comes up.

My jog back to the resort is slower than the race I ran getting away from it, but I have more time to think about what both Kevin and Juliana said. Their depiction of me is eerily similar, too much to consider it a coincidence. In the late hours of the night while Daisy was in my arms, we talked about so many things and I've gotten to know her much better than I ever planned. When she asked questions about my life, I found ways to steer the question back around to her instead.

If she has noticed my tight-lipped nature, she hasn't mentioned it, and I have to wonder why. The thing is, I know how clever and inquisitive she is, so the most likely explanation is she's giving me the space and privacy I've insisted on since we met. While she bares her soul to me. Without fail, the topic returns to the summer camp she coordinates and the kids who have touched her heart. Her passion is contagious and makes me want to sign up as a camp counselor.

But what endears her to me more than anything is how unpretentious she is about the selfless work she's doing. She runs it as a true nonprofit, only taking enough money in donations to keep the doors open and the lights on. Every penny she takes in goes to the kids in some form or fashion. During one conversation, she let it slip that she'd bought clothes and shoes for one girl using her own money because the camp didn't have the extra money to spare. The others had made fun of the little girl for wearing the same clothes a few days in a row when she didn't have a choice.

I'd never been so glad to have the lights off. I clamped my eyes shut, rested my forehead against the back of her head, and fought back the demons trying to take me back to my childhood. It didn't work.

One day when I picked Juliana up from elementary school, I heard a couple of little snot-nosed girls making fun of her off-label clothes. They laughed and pointed at her tattered jeans and out-of-style shirt. Her bottom lip quivered, and she was so ashamed she wouldn't even make eye contact with me. Maybe it was wrong of me, since I was sixteen at the time and they were much younger, but I shut them up when no one was looking. A little rough talk and a threat of public humiliation resulted in two scared former mean girls.

Looking back on it now, I wonder if I only made the conditions at school worse for Juliana, only she never told me out of fear of what else I'd do. The truth today is the same as it was back then, there's not much I wouldn't do to protect my little sister. But I wonder what Daisy would think of me if I shared the deep secrets of my heart the way she has. Would she find the honorable man she thinks I am?

Or would she see the real me?

The man who pursued success more out of vengeance than passion. The selfish side of me that simply wants to live my life with no one expecting anything, without additional obligations or responsibilities on my shoulders. The guy inside who screams to have the young and carefree life I was robbed of when I was only fourteen. I had no choice but to grow up, literally overnight, and I've resented that for as long as I can remember, despite how much I love Juliana.

Do I expose Daisy to the real Rod Stone, or let her live with a lie of a man?

For the next couple of days, I'll keep those thoughts to myself and maintain the happy go lucky fantasy world version of my personality. If she mentions seeing me again after this trip is over and we've returned to the real world, I'll slowly introduce her to the parts of me that aren't so attractive or appealing.

Then I'll watch her run away as fast as she can, because no one wants to be around *that* guy.

CHAPTER EIGHTEEN

Daisy

The sun soaks my skin in its warmth as I relax on beach chairs closest to the water at our luxe resort. We have front row seats to the most beautiful scenery on the island, oceanfront with a light breeze. Tracy lies beside me, snoring after complaining she didn't get enough sleep last night. Rod and Kevin got up early for a run on the beach, which woke Tracy and me earlier than we'd prefer while on vacation. Rather than waste the sunlight, I dragged her lazy ass out of bed to spend time with me.

I got about five minutes of girl time out of her before she dozed off.

More beachgoers emerge from the resort, claiming the surrounding chairs and chatting about the various water sports they've reserved for the day. Since my partner in crime wimped out on me, I lean back and close my eyes, enjoying the quiet time. My black shades provide just enough cover to shield my eyes from the rising ball of fire in the sky. Sleep tugs at my senses, pulling me under its warm blanket with help from the sound of waves lapping at the shore.

"Holy shit, man. Would you look at these ladies? Where have they been all our lives?"

"I don't know, but we have to convince them to change this egregious oversight. It would be a shame to let this chance for true love pass us by."

When I open my eyes, two familiar guys wearing swim shorts, designer sunglasses, and broad smiles stand at the end of our lounge chairs. The one with blond hair smiles, then blows a kiss at me. The dark-haired guy wears a sexy smirk and waggles his eyebrows.

"Sorry, guys, we're not interested. We're both already taken."

"You have to give me a chance to change your mind. I've never seen a more beautiful woman in my life. From the first second I laid eyes on you, I knew I had to meet you. Fate has spoken, and she wants you and me to be together forever. Not with some loser you've wasted your time around." The blond lays the charm on thick, but I see right through his bullshit.

"Hunter, get the fuck out of here. She said she's not interested in you or your shitty lines." Rod approaches from my left, fresh from his beach run.

He wordlessly motions with his head, but I know exactly what he wants. I sit up, slide forward, and he sits behind me. With his legs on either side of mine, I lean back against his chest in what I now consider "our thing," how we stake our claim on each other.

"Now my chair is complete. What took you so long?"

"Sorry to keep you waiting, my blue-eyed beauty. I had to get my exercise in so I can maintain my stamina for you." He leans around and kisses my cheek. "Daisy, this persistent guy is my friend, Hunter. The one beside him is Jace. These are the guys I've warned you about."

"The guys in the adjoining suite? The ones who passed out waiting for the boat to the cabana? The one who was drunk and sound asleep in your bed?"

"The same."

"So that's why you locked and barred the door. He obviously doesn't remember seeing me in the room with you."

Rod throws his head back in laughter. "You are a smart, delicious cookie. Two minutes after meeting them and you already get it."

"Very funny, fucker. What gives, Rod? When did you start letting a woman stay in your room overnight?"

"Since I met Daisy. She and I have spent several days together now, and I have no intentions of letting her go. Move on down the line, boys. She's one of a kind, and she's all mine."

Hunter and Jace openly gawk at Rod, but he doesn't flinch a muscle behind me. In fact, his words make me question if he wants our vacationship to last past our getaway. I'm trying not to get my hopes up, but my feelings for him deepen every day. As hard as I've tried to keep them contained and maintain my "love isn't real" mantra, he makes it almost impossible to resist falling when he shows his thoughtful side.

Tracy wakes from her nap and looks between our visitors and Rod and me. "All four of you are very noisy early in the morning. You need to keep it down and let a girl get her beauty sleep. My man will be back from the gym soon."

"Sounds like you're shit out of luck with her too. By the

way, she's been with Kevin the entire time, and you know how he is about other men hitting on his girlfriend. You can pull up a seat and join us if you promise to behave." Rod motions to two vacated chairs beside us.

"We'll catch you later. This party is a little too tame for our taste." Jace grins and walks away, Hunter falling in line beside him.

Rod leans down to my ear and whispers, "I hope I didn't spook you with what I said."

"Did you mean it?" I hold my breath and wait for him to say he only meant to get rid of Hunter and Jace.

"Every word." His lips brush against my ear as he speaks. I'm almost stunned speechless. Can this be real?

"You didn't spook me. But if we're being completely honest, I'm scaring myself."

"Let's take a walk and find somewhere we can talk in private."

After I wake Tracy to tell her we're leaving, Rod takes my hand in his and we walk off together.

"I have an idea. Let's rent a Jet Ski and have a little fun. We'll be far enough away from everyone out there, and we can float on the waves while we talk."

"Perfect. I've always wanted to ride one."

"Your wish is my command." He kisses the back of my hand and my heart flutters. It really is the little things.

With the half-day rental secured, we climb aboard our water motorcycle and head offshore, away from the crowds. When we're far enough out to float on the deep, clear water without being in the way of the other riders, he kills the engine and maneuvers his body until he's facing me.

"This may seem like it's coming out of left field after the

other talks we've had, but it's something that's been building since the day I met you. Kevin called me out on my bullshit attitude this morning, and that made me take a long, hard look at my life. I even called my sister and asked her opinion, asked her if Kevin was right about how people perceive me. When the two people who know you best have nearly identical views, it makes you stop and think."

"What did they say?" I'm not holding my breath. But I'm fairly certain I'm hyperventilating instead.

"In a nutshell, that I'll end up miserable and alone because I won't let anyone get close to me. But I'm different with you, and I shouldn't limit what we have to just a vacation fling. In fact, my sister doesn't want me to come back to the Atlanta area if I don't leave my old personality here." He chuckles, but the humor doesn't reach his eyes. He looks off toward the horizon. "Since the day we met, I've felt a strange connection to you. One I've never experienced with another human being before now, so I'm not even sure how to handle it. I quit believing in love a long time ago. For years, I've said it was nothing more than a fairy tale that'll inevitably end in disaster.

"But you make me want the fairy tale, Daisy. So much so I can't imagine going back to how my life was before I met you. I need you to be honest with me about how you feel."

A small gust of wind could blow me over right now. My mouth is dry, my heart is pounding, and my entire body is trembling. Vulnerability isn't in my repertoire of emotions under normal conditions, but the time I've spent with Rod has been anything but ordinary. Contrary to my preferred response of deflecting, I decide to go with complete honesty... after I confirm one thing.

"What if your feelings are because of the setting? Vacation brain is an actual thing, and you may make wrong decisions based on the euphoric feeling it gives you. But those feelings aren't real, and you'll realize that after you return home and put distance between you and paradise."

"I've given it a lot of thought, even before today, and my feelings have nothing to do with where we are or our escape from the problems of everyday life. This is all about you, who are you, and how I feel when I'm with you. I couldn't walk away from you now if I tried. What I want to know is if you feel the same about me."

"I do. I absolutely feel the same way about you. I've tried so hard to fight against falling so hard for you, to hold on to my convictions against remotely related to love. But I can't control these feelings any more than I can control the tide. When we're together, I can barely hold back from showing and telling you how much I adore you already. I don't want to hide it anymore, but I don't want *you* to freak out and run from me. Whether you believe it, you deserve to feel loved, appreciated, and needed. If you'll give me a chance, you'll finally believe you're worthy of being loved."

Now I feel especially vulnerable after dumping all my feelings onto his lap. In my mind, I calculate roughly how far we are from shore and whether I can make it back if I jump in the water right now. I asked him not to run, but I'm the one about to have a panic attack because I've allowed this to happen in the first place. I swore off men more than seven years ago, only venturing out when Tracy convinced me with strong coercion to go on a blind date.

"You'll be the one who runs, Daisy. But I'm not going anywhere. Whatever we have to do to make this last when we get home, I'm game." He takes my hands in his, staring at them in silence for what feels like forever. When he speaks again, his voice is so low I can barely hear it over the waves gently breaking. "How could you possibly know I don't feel worthy of being loved?"

"Because I don't feel like I am either and my spirit felt it in yours. Maybe two damaged people can find a way to heal each other. If they can find a way to trust each other."

"You don't know how fucked up I really am. What if you decide you can't deal with my bullshit and you want to take off, get as far away from me as possible?"

"Your bullshit can't be any worse than mine, Rod. What if we both tried a novel approach and trusted each other?"

"I'm willing to try it." He doesn't verbalize the question, but I see it in his eyes.

"Me, too."

With a reassuring squeeze to his hands, I lean over to kiss his cheek. He turns his face at the last second, pressing his lips against mine. He moves his hands to my face, cupping my cheeks with tenderness and affection. His caress isn't as demanding or heated as usual. It's full of love, warmth, and openness. It's his way of showing his vulnerable side, using a method that makes him feel safe. I return the sentiment in every way—my hands covering his face, letting him take control, and knowing he wouldn't take advantage of his power over me.

We seal our agreement with a kiss that's filled with much more than pleasure and desire. It's a guarantee we're both committed to seeing this through, past the end of our vacation and back into the world awaiting us. It's an assurance we recognize our collective painful past so we can move forward with a promising future. It's a verbal contract assuring the other understanding and patience when working through the ghosts that are sure to reappear from time to time.

In perfect sync, we stop, but hold the connection for a minute longer. Our foreheads remain pressed together, and his eyes are closed, but the bliss on his face fills my heart with so much hope and longing for a genuine relationship. For the first time since that awful night in my past I've worked so hard to forget, I'm ready to move forward. I want to give this man my full trust, my heart, and my soul.

"I don't know how you did it, but you broke through the wall of ice I've built around my heart. You saw through the disguise I wear every day and gave me your love despite it. You should've run away as fast and as far as you could, Daisy. But it's too late now, because I'll be damned if I let you go … and I mean that literally. I'll be damned to a life of eternal hell if I lose you now."

He inhales a ragged breath, possibly regretting his last admission.

"No pressure, though." His smile breaks free, and it's the most carefree one I've seen on his face yet.

"There's my Hot Rod, back again." We chuckle together, dispelling the tension before I respond with all the sincerity I possess. "Hearing you say that doesn't make me feel pressured, Rod. It makes me feel even more connected to you than I already did. I've felt bound to you in a way that's hard to explain since the moment I first saw you. Now, I'm not fighting that bond anymore."

"You're all I want, Daisy."

My heart is bursting with overwhelming feelings, but

focusing on the handsome face of the man I love brings everything into perspective.

"Then you have all you want, for as long as you want it."

"How do you know exactly what I need to hear without me telling you?"

He wraps his arms around me, pulling me onto his lap and holding me as close to him as our lifejackets will allow. To others, we probably look silly. But this is as real as it gets, and I wouldn't change a single thing. His question was rhetorical, uttered in the moment, but it reveals more about his psyche than he realizes. I should know. I've had enough therapy sessions of my own to be recognized as an honorary therapist.

"We still have a few hours left on the Jet Ski rental. Are you up for going full throttle with a powerful engine between your legs and squealing loud enough for the entire island to hear you?"

"Sure, but we did all that in your room last night. How is this any different?" I lean back and give him my best seductive grin.

"Fuck, I love that sassy mouth of yours. We'll put it to better use later. For now, I want to hear you scream in public."

After we're back in our original positions, Rod hits the throttle and we skim across the top of the water at what feels like blinding speeds. Instead of squeezing my eyes shut and holding on for dear life, I release my anxiety and allow myself to feel everything. I feel the wind in my hair, the sun on the face, the spray of water on my body, and the freedom of giving up my tight control on life so I can live again.

CHAPTER NINETEEN

Rod

Today marks one week since I met Daisy—the day she first arrived. One week I've spent every day and well into the night with her. Seven days and nights that she's been on my mind, in my arms, or in my bed, often a combination of all three.

I'm not an idiot. There's no such thing as instant love. It's not a feeling that just needs a dash of salt, sand, and surf to create. All the free flowing liquor in the world can't create feelings that aren't there. But I do believe two people can have instant chemistry and a strong physical attraction to each other and build on that foundation. There's so much more I have to learn about her and details about her life I want to know, need to understand.

Somewhere between day one and day seven, we've started a new chapter in the book of Rod and Daisy, and now all I want is to find out where this plot twist will take us.

If that means we end up back in Atlanta together, so be it. Worse things could happen. I've lived through enough of them to know. We've shared vague references of where we live in our time together, mostly in the getting-to-know-you stage, so I'm sure there's a way we can work it out to see each other after we leave here.

That makes our new relationship all very real.

"You're drinking bourbon?" Kevin steps out onto the balcony where I'm sitting alone with my thoughts.

"Yep."

He sits across the table from me and leans back in his chair, his eyes narrowed while carefully scrutinizing my face. He props his elbow on the armrest and covers his mouth with an open fist. That's his signature move when he's concerned, but knows he should approach cautiously.

"This is the first time I've seen you drink bourbon in a long time, a very long time. Want to tell me what's going on?"

"I told Daisy I love her."

He's silent for a couple of minutes, shocked beyond words. "You actually said those three words?"

"Well, no, not verbatim, but in a roundabout way."

"I'm confused. How did you say, 'I love you,' without saying the actual words?"

"I told her I want the fairy-tale life, and I want it with her. I said I don't want to be without her." I shrug, trying to appear aloof and nonchalant about the entire conversation. The truth is I'm still freaked out about it on so many levels, even though I meant every word.

"Well, that's a start, I guess. What was her response?"

"Long story short, she returned the sentiment, so we're on the relationship track now." I empty the tumbler of bourbon and pour another shot from the decanter.

"Don't bolt on her, Rod. She deserves to be treated better than your usual dates."

"Did you hear what I just said, what I told her?"

"Yeah, I heard the words, but I also see the actions. The only time you drink bourbon is when you're dealing with the devil, and he makes you do stupid things. You don't listen to the expert advice your best friend gives you. But you need to hear what I'm saying, Rod, because I mean every word. If you turn your back and hurt her, don't expect me to help you put the pieces back together."

"Wow. I can't believe the best friend I've ever had just said that to me."

"It's called tough love, brother. You've sabotaged yourself for as long as I can remember, and I've helped you back on your feet every time. I've enabled you in your dysfunction and made it too easy for you to make excuses for your behavior. Because I have mad love for you, I can't do that anymore.

"Put the bourbon away and deal with the demons causing your confusion. You took the first step and admitted she means a lot to you. Now prove you're a man of your word and not a lame loser who can't live up to his promises."

"Don't you need to go make sure Tracy hasn't lost your balls in her purse?" Even though I hate that he's right, I put the stopper back in the decanter and push it out of my reach.

"She and her purse are off shopping with your girlfriend. Daisy was excited about some secret date you've arranged for this evening. They're buying new jewelry and whatever else they find to dress her up."

"She told me." He waits for me to elaborate on my plans with an arched eyebrow and a disgusted expression. "Fine. It's a romantic dinner on a catamaran, just the two of us, besides the crew."

"You're going all out for her. I like it. Let's up the stakes. You ready?"

"Hit me."

"Tonight, give her your cell number and your address, and take hers, to show you really do want to continue this relationship after this vacation is over. Nothing says commitment like sharing street addresses."

Have I mentioned how much I hate my best friend?

"That's kid stuff. I don't even have to wait until we leave for dinner to do that. I'll give her all my information when she gets back from her shopping spree, and I'll get hers. Happy now?"

"Ecstatic. I'll put the bourbon away on my way out. It's time to get dressed for my date with Tracy tonight. By the way, we've already shared all our contact information, even our email addresses. We're way ahead of you."

He swipes the glass from my hand when he stands and takes the bottle from the table, leaving me alone with my thoughts once again. He's right about one thing, I'm in an ominous place when I turn to bourbon, and it takes me to even deeper levels of moodiness. Time to shake that shit off and make sure Daisy has a good time tonight.

After raiding the in-room snack bar to help counteract the alcohol, I take a quick shower to wash off the day's worth of salt and sand I accumulated on the Jet Ski and beach. Standing in front of the mirror after, I take a long, hard look at myself. I can't deny what Juliana or Kevin said about me. When it comes to my sister and my niece, I'll fight to the death to meet their every need. My automatic response with matters of the heart with anyone else is to flee, far and fast.

That's why I'm taking this new status with Daisy one minute at a time.

Reaching in to grab my hairbrush, I realize the bathroom vanity drawer is mostly empty. The thing is, it was full of Daisy's makeup and hair accessories this morning. Rifling through the other drawers and cabinets reveals the same—her belongings are gone. Did she pack everything before she left to go shopping with Tracy? Was their outing a lie so she could get away from me?

I stomp over to the closet and jerk the door open, preparing myself to see more missing items. But her suitcase and clothes are still there, in the same place she left them when she first unpacked. For a minute there, I honestly believed she'd taken all her things and ghosted me.

The thought of her leaving me bothered me more than I thought it would and opened old wounds I'd rather not contend with right now. Or ever, truth be told.

Just to be sure, I want to call her and ask what time she'll be back. But as Kevin so eloquently pointed out, I don't have her number. I could go through the hassle of having Kevin get it from Tracy, but that makes me look desperate.

Knowing she'll be back calms my churning stomach enough to finish dressing for our evening out on the water. It's still hot as hell outside, so I dress in a collared pullover and khaki shorts for dinner. I can't wait to surprise her with our reservations tonight. The cruise is usually for multiple couples, but I rented the entire boat for the night so we can enjoy the views with a modicum of privacy.

Before long, I hear the click of the doorknob turning and she walks in, dressed to the nines and all made up for our date. She stops in her tracks when her eyes meet mine, the hunger in them radiating in heated waves. I take in her appearance slowly and fully, from head to toe. When I make my way back up, her flushed cheeks and rapidly rising and falling chest leave no doubt she feels it too. The intense attraction, the powerful spell we're under, the passion threatening to boil over at any second.

Now I realize why I've never grown attached to anyone else. These feelings make me feel alive and buzzing with energy, and only she invokes them in me.

"Damn, you look amazing, Daisy. Excuse me while I pick my tongue up off the floor."

The way she fills out a little black dress should be criminal. Her matching jewelry only accentuates some of her best assets. The silver chain hangs low, drawing my eye to her cleavage. She pulled her hair up off her shoulders, leaving soft curled tendrils hanging loose around her face. Long, shiny earrings dangle from her ears and match the bracelets on her wrist and the ankle bracelet that sits above her heel.

She walks toward me, keeping her chin up, and her eyes locked on mine. Now I know why her makeup bag was missing from the bathroom. Her smoky eyeshadow adds an extra layer of sex appeal to her already sensual look. No more doubting her on my part. She's outdone herself today, and she did it all for me.

I meet her halfway and slide my hands along her waist until they meet behind her back. Before she has the opportunity to say anything, I lean down and steal a long, lingering kiss.

"Wow. What did I do to deserve that?"

"I missed you." That's the truth. Despite everything that happened in this room while she was away, it all boils down to that simple answer.

"Should I go out and come back in again?"

"Are you coming back in naked, wearing nothing but those heels? If not, then forget it. I'm not letting you out of my sight again for anything less."

"We can save that for dessert later tonight."

"Don't tease, woman. You're killing me as it is. We should probably get going now before I change my mind and keep you to myself all night."

"Lead the way, handsome. You haven't told me what we're doing, but I'm game for whatever you have in mind."

We walk hand in hand to the docks with her admiring the large yachts along the way. When we reach the catamaran, I extend my arm toward the gangway, signaling for her to board first.

"We're doing a sunset cruise?"

"We are, with dinner, music, and dancing too. Just you and me for as long as you want to stay out on the water."

She's beyond excited as she hurries on to the boat. The staff greets us with a glass of champagne and offers various types of hors d'oeuvres while we wait to cast off. We explore the ship together until we feel the movement as we pull out of the slip. We're escorted to the sole table at the front of the wide deck, giving us the best view of the sky and water in every direction.

"Rod, this is incredible. I can't believe you arranged this, but thank you so much for this experience. I love everything about it."

"It's my pleasure, Daisy. I'm happy you're enjoying it."

The small band plays softly in the background as we enjoy the multi-course meal. We've already had an emotion filled day, but this romantic atmosphere seems to amplify it. After the waitstaff clears the table, we move our chairs to sit side by side and enjoy the view together. With my arm draped around her and her head against the crook of my shoulder, we watch the sun disappear into the water on the horizon. Dusk turns to dark, and stars sparkle in the nighttime sky.

Daisy lifts her head and looks up at me, an innate innocence shines in her eyes. "I've loved every second of today, Rod. And..." She swallows hard but doesn't avert her gaze from mine. "I'm falling in love with you."

I dip my head to capture her lips in response, but I can't bring myself to say those words yet.

CHAPTER TWENTY

Daisy

When the bright sun streaks through the curtains, the warmth of a hard body behind me brings an instant smile to my face. His arm is slung over my side, holding me close in his sleep. It's early still, and his rhythmic breathing confirms he's still in a deep sleep. My mind drifts back to the events of yesterday and last night. The feelings he shared were so unexpected, I was in complete shock at first. But then I let go of the fear and embraced the truth.

The time we spent together last night on the boat was nothing short of pure magic. Sunset in the arms of the man I'm crazy about, a romantic cruise under the stars twinkling in the black sky, and a full night of him ravaging my body until all my energy was completely spent. He ordered midnight room service as an extra dessert, an ice cream sundae will all the toppings. But he was the sweet one, being so attentive, affectionate, and adorable.

For the first time in years, I'm happy and have hope for a genuine relationship, one where we can grow and flourish together. Even though I wouldn't have believed it from my first impression, I think Rod feels the same. But I also think he's much more afraid of admitting his feelings than I am. Seems we both have our own hang-ups and ghosts from the past still haunting our present. Mine has kept me from pursuing love ... and accepting it. That's how I knew Rod didn't feel worthy to be loved. It's easier to see the signs in someone else than to see them in myself. It's also easier to tell him he deserves it than to convince myself of the same sentiment.

From the cadence of his gentle snores, I don't think he'll wake anytime soon. Instead of waking him, I close my eyes and allow sleep to pull me back under its alluring spell. I'm safe and secure in Rod's embrace, and no dream is better than the real thing.

When I feel him stirring later, I wake again with a smile that seems to be permanently affixed to my face. He's no longer pressed against my back, so I carefully turn to see him, so I won't disturb him if he's still asleep. The tortured expression on his face steals my breath. He's so deeply lost in another world he doesn't even realize I've moved beside him. He fixes his eyes on the ceiling, draws his eyebrows down, and a painful grimace mars his handsome features.

Then he drags his hand down his face and exhales a forceful breath. He squeezes his eyes shut and covers them with his forearm. Without knowing which demon he's wrestling with this morning, I'm hesitant to strike up a conversation out of the blue. But I can't lie here and pretend everything is all right either.

"After seeing that gorgeous sunset last night, I almost woke you up a couple of hours ago to watch the sunrise. But you were sleeping so good I didn't want to interrupt your slumber."

He lowers his arm and turns his gaze toward me, but his eyes are distant and cold. "You probably should have woken me after all."

"Maybe tomorrow morning I will. Want to tell me what's going on in that handsome head of yours?"

"It's nothing. I'm going to shower, then we can head down to the restaurant for breakfast."

"Okay." Normally at this point, I say I'll join him in the shower, but the detached tone in his voice keeps me at bay.

We walk down to breakfast in awkward silence. He holds my hand, but the intimacy I felt last night is gone, replaced by an enormous gulf separating us. When we reach the table, he pulls my chair out for me before taking his seat, then he disappears behind the menu.

"Rod?" I love rollercoasters, but not this one.

"Hmm?"

"Can you look at me for a minute?"

He slowly lowers the menu, and his gaze follows it to the table. But I'm determined to wait him out. He's an intelligent man. He'll pick up on the social cue, eventually. When he finally gives me his undivided attention, I reach across the table and take his hand in mine.

"Talk to me. Tell me what's wrong, what's on your mind. You're not acting like yourself this morning."

"You know the old cliché *it's not you, it's me*? In this case, it's entirely true. Memories I'd rather forget reared their ugly heads in my dreams last night. Sometimes it takes me a while to shake off the bullshit and get back to my normal, charming self."

"Maybe I can help move that along. You don't seem to be in the mood for crowds or company today. How would you like to rent a couple of kayaks and do our own river tour? Later this afternoon, we can have a couple's sunset massage on the beach. What do you say?"

"That's a great idea. Let's get away from everyone and escape from reality for a while. In fact, I'll have the concierge arrange it right now. If you'll order our breakfast, I'll go take care of the reservations before they're all booked."

Though he still doesn't seem overjoyed, at least he is livelier than he was a few minutes ago. I'm counting on the rest of the day and evening alone to help pull him out of this depressive funk. I can sympathize with bad dreams dredging up memories that are better forgotten. There was a time mine would throw me into a near catatonic state for a day or two while I dealt with the aftermath.

After a lot of therapy sessions and a lot of introspection, I realized I wasn't handling my problems constructively. That's when I changed my mindset and started the summer camp project, putting my focus on helping others rather than wallowing in my self-pity. It wasn't easy, by any stretch of the imagination, but my behavior had negative effects on more than just me.

Some people are worth the extra effort, regardless of how hard it is or how much effort it takes to change.

The waitress stops by our table, and I give her both orders while waiting for Rod to return. Tracy, Kevin, Hunter, and

Jace walk in and spot me sitting alone, so they fill the empty chairs.

"Hey, guys. What are you up to today?" I greet them with a smile.

"Since Hunter and Jace have alienated every single woman left at this resort, Kevin and I get the absolute pleasure of spending the day with them. If they're left to their own devices, they'll end up either in jail or killing each other." Tracy rolls her eyes exaggeratedly, clearly irritated with her situation.

While I feel bad for her, there's no way I'll volunteer to babysit those overgrown boys for her.

"Where's Rod?" Kevin looks around the restaurant.

"He went to make arrangements for our trip today. He should be back any minute now."

"What are you two doing today?" Tracy cuts her brown eyes at me and flashes a sly grin.

"Kayaking today and a couple's massage later this evening."

"The whole paddling the boat thing is too much work. I think we'll take the brats to a water park and let them play." She laughs at the shocked expressions on Hunter's and Jace's faces.

Rod rounds the corner just as Tracy finishes. "You know, I like that idea better. Let's go with them today, Daisy. We can cancel the kayaking trip and still spend the day playing in the water."

He slides into his seat beside me and starts chatting with the guys. Tracy shoots me a look that says she's sorry, but she's also confused. To say the least, I'm puzzled too. Not only because of his sudden shift in behavior, but I thought he wanted to be alone with me. But then again, he came here with his friends, not me. If he wants to spend the day having fun as a group, I can't begrudge him that time. The expression on Tracy's face, however, says differently.

After breakfast, Rod and I quickly change then meet the others to ride to the water park together. The crowds have already descended, looking for another fun day in the sun. Kids run past us, elbowing their way through the masses to reach the next ride, while we wait in line for a locker to store our belongings. A group of young women wearing little more than dental floss strut by us, and one purposely slows her gait, wordlessly offering an open invitation for Rod to join her.

When I glance up at him to see his reaction, my heart plummets to my feet. One brow is arched, a sexy smirk covers his face, and his eyes wander up and down the length of her body. I stare at him in disbelief for several seconds, unable to verbalize my feelings. I'm not the type of person who thinks a man can never look at another woman, that's just not feasible.

But he is doing more than looking, more than admiring a pretty face and nice body. He's bordering on accepting that invitation with me standing right beside him. That's one of the cruelest ways to disrespect someone he supposedly cares about. When he finally turns his attention to me, his face drops and his lips part as if he's about to say something, but he quickly closes them again.

Tracy and Kevin openly gawk at Rod—one with pure contempt and the other with utter shock. Rod's eyes dart between the three of us before he draws his bottom lip between his teeth. He knows he crossed a line that he never should've gotten close to, much less stepped over.

He clears his throat nervously, then drops his eyes to the ground.

I'm teetering on the edge of leaving the park altogether, or sending Rod with his fuck-buddy wannabe, while I spend the day with the rest of the group. At the moment, I feel like the dumbest woman on the planet. Staying with him today will make me appear weak, and I've worked too hard not to feel that way ever again. Walking away will make me question if I'm overreacting and being too emotional.

"That was a real dick move, Rod." Tracy can't hold her tongue any longer. "If I were Daisy, I'd knee you in the balls until you puked then walk away laughing. Have you ever tried not being a piece of shit?" She throws her bag in the locker along with Kevin's stuff and slams the door.

Our four companions take a few steps away to give us room to access our locker. While Rod unlocks it and empties his pockets, I make my decision. Without saying goodbye, I turn and quietly walk away. The farther I get away from him, the quicker my pace becomes. When I reach the front entrance, I grab the taxi another group is vacating before someone else does.

As the car pulls away from the curb, I glance over and see Rod standing at the chain-link fence, his fingers gripping the metal as he watches me leave.

Back at the hotel, I approach the front desk and request a room for myself. While Rod is gone, I'll move all my shit out of his room. Rather than upsetting Tracy and Kevin's plans for the last couple of days on the island, I'll get a separate room and enjoy my time alone to decompress before we go back to Atlanta.

"How many room keys do you need?" The clerk is only doing her job, but that question hurts more than it should.

"One."

With my new room key in hand, I rush to Rod's suite and throw all my things in my suitcase as fast as I can. After checking the bathroom, closet, and drawers one last time, I'm sure I have everything. I leave the extra key card on the night-stand and walk out the door, the loud click of it locking behind me somewhat befitting of the moment. That door is closed and locked behind me.

A tiger can't change its stripes.

A leopard can't change its spots.

A Hot Rod can't change first impressions, no matter how good of an actor he is. His true colors will always bleed through.

"Daisy, where are you?" Tracy called my cell phone from hers, so I know they're back from the water park.

"I'm in my room. Why?" I know why, but that's a required question so I can appear nonchalant.

"Rod just came from your room and said all your clothes are gone. He's sitting here in my room, bleeding."

"Why is he bleeding?" It's more curiosity at this point than concern.

"Because I beat the hell out of him with your Harley Quinn baseball bat when he showed up at my door without you."

"It's a plastic bat, Tracy."

"Well, it's warped to shit now and has Rod's blood on it. I busted his lip." She's obviously proud of her actions. I can't say I blame her.

"Hot Rod got his ass beat up by a girl, huh? That amuses me, probably a lot more than it should. But, to answer your original question, I'm in my own room, not his suite. I moved out of there as soon as I got back from the park."

She relays our conversation to Rod with an emphasis on her convictions in her tone. I can't help but giggle at my best friend.

"Rod wants your room number. He said he's coming over to talk to you."

"I don't think so. I'll give it to you, but there's no reason he needs it. You know I don't demand much of anyone in my life, but disrespect is one thing I will not tolerate from anyone. My initial impression of him was spot-on, and I should've listened to my gut. Now that he has his suite to himself again, he's free to do whatever he wants."

"Rod, she said you can go fuck yourself with Lucille from *The Walking Dead*. I'm paraphrasing."

I hear Rod's response in the background. "Who the fuck is Lucille?"

"She's a baseball bat covered with barbed wire. She's very effective." Tracy fake coughs to cover her laugh. I can only imagine the horrified expression on Rod's face. "Daisy, what room are you in? I'm coming to see you in a few minutes. *Alone*."

We disconnect after I give her my new room number and strict instructions not to share it with Rod. I feel like a big enough fool as it is. From the moment I first met him, I knew I shouldn't trust him, shouldn't fall for him, shouldn't get involved with him, but I didn't listen to my instincts. I thought I had gotten better about that, but I obviously have a long way to go.

A few minutes later, there's a soft knock on my door. After checking the peephole to confirm it's Tracy, and only her, I open the door and let her in. She wraps her arms around me in an uncharacteristic display of affection and kicks the door shut with her foot.

"Daisy, I'm so sorry. There's something I need to confess, and I'm afraid you'll be mad and never speak to me again."

"What could you have done to make me never speak to you again?" I step back to gauge the seriousness of this conversation by her expression.

Shit. This doesn't look good.

"We'd better have a seat." She moves to the sitting area and pats the cushion next to her on the couch.

When I sit, she grabs my hand and gives it a light squeeze. "Okay, here's the whole truth and nothing but the truth, so help me God."

I arch an eyebrow, waiting for her confession with anxious reservations.

"Kevin and I have been seeing each other for the last several months. When we met, we immediately clicked, and everything has felt so right from day one. He talked a lot about Rod because they've been best friends since middle school. Kevin is the vice president of Rod's company.

"One night, Kevin and I were talking about how happy we are together, and we both wished our best friends could find someone, too. You've been closed off from feeling anything for years, with reason, but I wanted someone other than me to know how amazing you are. Kevin told me about how Rod dotes on his sister and niece every day, but that he had commitment issues, too.

"Kevin and I hoped you and Rod would find each other the same way we did. So, we arranged this trip as a way you two could meet, but without the usual awkwardness of a blind date. You've found something wrong with every guy I've tried to set you up with anyway, so I hoped a more casual setting would make it easier for you to relax and have fun. I'm sorry I kept everything a secret from you. This fiasco is all my fault. Are you mad at me? Can you forgive me?"

At first, I'm more than mad. I'm livid. When I read about others "seeing red," I always thought it was a metaphor. Now I know it's not. It's an actual response when someone, such as myself, is so furious she could spit nails. Before I answer her, I take a minute to think about what she said … and about my inability to move past my traumatic experience. She arranged this entire trip to help me break free from the bonds of my past. Regardless of the outcome, I know she had the best intentions in her heart and she only arranged this trip because she's worried about me.

"I am mad at you, Tracy, but I also understand why you went to such great lengths to lie to me and hide shit from me. For future reference, I'd prefer an honest conversation instead of an elaborate scheme to hook me up with some guy. That said, you did tell me not to fall for Rod. You warned me not to like him, to get that shit out of my head. I think that was the phrase you used. But I fell for him anyway, and that isn't your fault. It's mine. Even though I knew better, I jumped in with both feet. That's not a mistake I'll make again."

"He wants to talk to you, almost to the point of desperation. He tried to follow me here, but Kevin stopped him from leaving our room. The entire time we were at the park today, he moped around with a miserable attitude, downturned lips, and vacant eyes. I don't think he even recognized any other women were there after you left.

"I was so proud of you for that move, by the way. You just

turned on your heel and left him standing there at the lockers without so much as a 'kiss my ass' on your way out. It was brilliant. I don't know for sure, but I had this sense he pulled that stunt on purpose, just to test how you'd react."

"Talking to him now won't change anything. He probably assumes I walked away because I'm jealous over him looking at someone else. Nothing could be further from the truth. He acted as if we weren't together when he was making 'fuck me' eyes at someone else, while I stood beside him, after saying he wanted us to be a real couple. If he changed his mind, I'd rather he man-up and tell me straight. Unfortunately, his true colors aren't attractive to me. I'm glad I saw them sooner rather than later.

"Of course I still love you—you're my best friend. But, Tracy, listen to me very carefully right now. Don't ever do anything remotely like this to me again. When I'm ready to subject myself to the humiliation and pain of dating again, I'll tell you."

"That'll be the day after never."

"Most likely."

CHAPTER TWENTY-ONE

Rod

hen I woke this morning, I knew I was in for a horrendous day, but I had no idea it would become the complete shitshow it turned into. Before I even opened my eyes, I had a sinking feeling in the pit of my stomach. A recurring dream about my parents returned last night, one I can't escape from because it's too close to real life. My mind warps my memories, exaggerating some of the worst points of my life the way dreams do—with moments of clarity mixed with others that make no sense. But the end result is always the same. I open my eyes and accept the painful scenes are part of me and have been since my early teens.

I needed some time and space to get out of my head, so I took a long shower alone, hoping the fog would clear out of my mind. Daisy felt the distance I put between us, I knew that, but I needed it to ground myself again. The truth is, I wasn't intentionally pushing her away, but I couldn't stop myself either. When I'm transported back to that time in my life, every nerve in my body feels raw and exposed and everything irritates me. It's not pretty and that's no excuse for my terrible behavior, but it is what it is.

By the time we left for the water park with the rest of the Scooby Gang, I was looking for anything that could distract me and remove the black cloud from over my head. To distract myself, I chose thrill rides over quiet tranquility, and constant stimulation rather than down time to reflect and turn the events of the past over in my mind. I needed laughs with friends over solitude from the world and one-on-one bonding time with Daisy. For my sanity, I took the opportunity to put a little separation between me and what prompted the dream in the first place.

I never want to turn into my dad.

However, the colossal mistake I made when we arrived at the park was all on me. It was entirely my fault and nothing I can blame on anyone or anything else. Sadly, my deed confirmed my belief I should remain a bachelor for the rest of time. As long as I do, I will never turn into him. The pain I saw on Daisy's face as the taxi drove away was far too similar to the sorrow my mom wore when she didn't know I was watching her.

The stabbing in my chest as I watched her leave me there, clinging to the fence that separated us, acted as another time machine, dredging up feelings I haven't felt in decades. My focus changed from the trauma of my past to the distress of the present. She stayed on my mind the entire time, regardless of how hard I tried to have fun with my friends and put everything else behind me. I can't count the number of times I considered going to her, throwing her over my shoulder, and rowing our kayak miles from shore. When the group had enough of water slides, I couldn't wait until we reached the hotel again.

But I walked into the suite, ready to apologize and grovel at her feet after a miserable day at the park without her, and found she wasn't there.

Her suitcase had been packed, and she had moved out of my room without leaving a goodbye note, or a conversation, or a knock-down drag-out fight until all our cards were face up on the table and we had emptied our combined emotional baggage.

I felt abandoned, even though I deserved it.

Before giving up and writing this entire trip off as a loss, I made an honest effort to find her by going to the room she shared with Tracy. I was met with a plastic baseball bat to the face and body at Tracy's hand. When she'd bent the bat so badly she could no longer use it, Kevin calmly took it from her hands and told me to have a seat.

"Where is Daisy?" I crossed my arm over my chest.

"How the hell should I know? You're the one sharing a room with her now." Tracy stood over me, her eyes firing daggers at me.

"Apparently not. All her things, including her suitcase, are gone. I thought maybe she came back to your room."

Tracy froze, her eyes grew wide as her jaw dropped open. She grabbed her cell phone to call Daisy, keeping her glare trained on me while she spoke. At least then I knew Daisy was safe and in her own room, but knowing she'd rather be alone than spend one more minute with me was a jagged pill to swallow. Tracy made sure I didn't follow her to

Daisy's new room, so I devised a plan to find her on my own.

After a quick search on my phone, I located a florist nearby that offered same-day delivery. When I called and explained I'd severely screwed up and needed to make amends immediately, the friendly lady on the other end understood my plight and took mercy on me. Two dozen red roses and $500 later, the flowers arrived at the front desk. I watched the box like a hawk until the concierge picked it up to deliver it to her room.

Now I'm following him.

Like a crazy stalker.

But I have no intentions of hurting her. Not that my exploits are completely benign since she said she didn't want to talk to me and didn't want me to know which room she's in. I'm not respecting her wishes, but my desperation to fix the situation is driving me to extreme measures. I'm risking everything only to talk to her through the door, to make one last-ditch attempt to show her I'm not the completely self-absorbed asshole she believes me to be.

That I've shown her I am.

When she opens the door, the concierge offers the box with the long stem roses in it and she hesitantly accepts it. He carries on his way, leaving the hallway empty except for the lurker waiting in the wings. My feet carry me to the door before I realize I decided to move.

I knock softly and sit with my back against the door before beginning my monologue. She needs to know it's me before she reaches the door, so she's not startled by my presence. The last thing I want is for her to be afraid of me, to think I'm here for anything other than to apologize profusely.

"Daisy, it's me. You don't have to say a word or even crack the door open. I'm not here to harass you or debate anything I've said or done. My only objective is to tell you how very sorry I am for today, everything about it. You have been nothing short of amazing. I've had more fun with you in the last week than I can ever remember, no matter what we were doing. You have an incredible heart, an infectious laugh, and a beautiful soul. It's a cliché, and it sounds like a really cheesy line, but what I'm about to say is the honest to God truth. Every minute I've spent with you has made me want to be a better man, because that's exactly what you deserve, nothing less. You bring out the best in me.

"When I woke this morning, I was nowhere near being the man you should want. Old memories resurfaced and brought me back down to the tenth level of hell, my own private floor. My thoughts tormented me, and I did what I always do when I can't deal with the past. I pushed you away, even though that isn't what I want. But you didn't give up on me, you walked beside me, quietly and patiently giving me space to deal with myself.

"Deep inside my soul, I know I deserve nothing you have to give me, and that fact made me even madder, at myself, so I pushed harder. The girl at the water park couldn't hold a candle to you. No one can, to be honest. I'm so sorry that my inadequacies and insecurities hurt you, and I'm so sorry *I* hurt you."

Now that I've put my heart and my pride on the line, all I can do is wait to see how she'll respond. Will she open the door and let me back in her life? Will she pretend she didn't hear any of my confession and apology? Will she simply thank me and go on without me?

I close my eyes and lean my head against the door, not caring that I'm sitting on the floor, in the hallway, of an upscale luxury resort. I'll wait here all night for her answer if that's what it takes.

Then I hear the sound of metal sliding against metal and the distinct click of her deadbolt locking in place.

That wasn't the answer I hoped for, or even expected, but she made her position crystal clear.

I push myself up to stand, take one last look at the door separating us, and walk away without a fight. The suite's minibar doesn't hold enough booze to take the edge off what I'm feeling, so I take a detour toward the main bar in the hotel lobby.

Vacationers party all around me as I take a seat at the bar, but their smiles only piss me off. When the bartender approaches me, I order bourbon and tell him to keep them coming. My plan is to numb every inch of myself, including my mind, rather than going to the black places it usually takes me. If the hotel staff has to pour me into my bed when they shut down the bar before dawn, so be it.

My cell phone vibrates in my pocket, and my first thought is Kevin is looking for me. I'm sure Daisy has already called Tracy to replay my every word for her best friend. Since I haven't checked on my business since the day I arrived on the island, I decide it's probably best to check the alert before I'm too hammered to understand the words. But when I glance at the screen, I realize it's not a text message at all.

It's an alert about an unheard voicemail from my home line. Before I left for vacation, I forwarded voicemails from my office phone and my home landline to my cell, knowing my executive assistant wouldn't contact me, even for urgent issues, while I was out of the country. She was too adamant I enjoy my first vacation in forever without the hassles of working *that* remotely. If someone got past her to my voicemail, the issue must be escalated and need my attention.

As I dial into the digital voicemail system, my mind is on all the possible problems that could've erupted since I've been away. A breach of contract? A client who missed their payment? A specialized software program malfunctioning? I'm so lost in thought I almost miss the computerized voice saying I have no new messages on my work number. Finding that odd, I disconnect and check my home voicemail instead. A couple of my largest clients have my home number, so it's feasible they would've contacted me there if my assistant thwarted their attempts to reach me at the office.

The voicemail on my home phone is for my sister, Juliana … and the message makes my blood turn to ice in my veins. My free hand grips the edge of the bar to keep me steady on the stool. The room spins around me as if it's a merry-go-round competing on the NASCAR circuit. I drop my cell on the counter and stare at my glass, trying to focus on a single object until I can calm my racing heart.

The words replay on a continuous loop in my mind.

"Hi, Juliana. This is Claire, reminding you of your appointment tomorrow at one o'clock with Dr. Tomey. If you have any questions, give me a call back."

I know who Dr. Tomey is. He's a medical oncologist. There's only one reason she'd have an appointment with him.

Her cancer has returned.

CHAPTER TWENTY-TWO

Rod

It took an inordinate amount of finagling, but I eventually got on an evening flight back to Atlanta. Even though I won't make it home until the early morning hours, at least I feel as though I'm doing something rather than just sitting in my room, waiting with my bags packed. I didn't call Juliana before I left. The conversation about her diagnosis and prognosis requires a face-to-face, sit down, come to Rod meeting.

Somehow, I did remember to send Kevin a quick text to let him know I was leaving early, so he doesn't waste his time looking for me. But I didn't say anything about why in the message. For one, Juliana's medical status isn't mine to tell. But even if she's okay with sharing the details, I don't have any to give and Kevin would have questions. He's known Juliana almost as long as he's known me, and he's always considered her as his little sister too. I'll fill him in when he returns from the Caribbean and his life returns to normal.

The flights and layovers felt as if they took forever, but I finally pull into my tree-lined drive just as the sun peeks over the horizon. I don't bother with any luggage when I jump out of the car and rush inside. Juliana will be up soon, and I want to be parked at the kitchen table with a tall mug of piping hot coffee in my hand when she comes downstairs.

Once the coffee is ready, I don't have to wait long for her to come flying around the corner, expecting to see Louise, my house staff manager, in the kitchen. She screams when she sees me instead.

"Rod! What the hell are you doing home so early? You scared the shit out of me." She puts her hand over her heart and huffs loudly.

"You know, I had the same reaction when my phone alerted me to a voicemail … and I heard the oncology center confirming your appointment for today. Is there something you forgot to tell me? Because I'm fairly certain I would've remembered that minor detail."

She at least has the decency to appear uncomfortable about withholding vital information from me. "I may have neglected to mention a detail or two. Yes, it's back, but I don't have time to go into all the details right now. Isabelle will be down in a minute for breakfast. Can we talk about this later?"

"If you promise we'll have a very long talk and you'll tell me every single detail."

"I promise. Actually, I'm glad you're here now. Can Isabelle stay with you after school today? They only have a half day of class today."

"Of course. You know I never turn down time with my

best girl."

"Thank you. I'll drop her off on my way to the doctor."

Juliana kisses me on the cheek just as Louise walks in the back door. She's shocked to see me at first, but the way her eyes dart between Juliana and me confirms she already knows the score.

"I'll make breakfast. You can help Isabelle get dressed for school." Louise pats Juliana on the shoulder and starts pulling food out of the refrigerator.

Once Juliana is upstairs, Louise turns her attention to me. "She's been trying to find a way to break it to you. She's been worried more about how you'll react than about herself."

"She should already know we'll get through it together, whatever it takes."

Louise nods and turns back to the stove. "Isabelle will be happy to see you. She has missed you."

"I've missed her too." But at the moment, I can't stop thinking about my little sister.

Isabelle walks into the kitchen, sees me, and flies into my arms, squealing, "Uncle Rod!"

"Good morning, munchkin. Guess what? You and I have a date after school."

"Yay!" She sits in my lap while she eats then Juliana shoos her toward the door for school.

After my girls leave, I retreat to my home office to work and try to focus on something other than the fiasco my life has become, seemingly overnight. When it's time for Isabelle to get home from kindergarten, I've accomplished nothing more than taking a shower and a nap.

Spending the evening with Isabelle isn't work for me. She and I are thick as thieves. We have a standing date, one we both look forward to when she comes to stay with me. We can be whoever or whatever we want to be. She's in this phase where teatime from *Alice in Wonderland* is the best pretend game ever. We even use horrible English accents.

Okay, so I'm wrapped around her little finger and never want to be cut loose.

Sue me.

"I've made tea, finger sandwiches, scones, and petit fours. If you don't need me anymore for now, I have a few errands to run." Louise gathers her personal effects and starts for the door.

"Thank you for getting all this food ready. You're a life-saver, Louise." I kiss her on the cheek as she walks by me.

"What you do for those two little ladies, it means more to them than you'll ever know, Rod. You're a generous man with an incredible heart. You need to let it show more."

"Those two ladies are the loves of my life. You know what Juliana went through as a child. Then what happened with Isabelle. There's nothing I wouldn't do to take care of them."

"It's more than just taking care of them, Rod. You're their rock, their stability. They look up to you. They need you." She pats me on the shoulder as she leaves. "It's past time for you to meet someone, settle down, and have a family of your own, though."

"Now why would you wish something like that on me after all those kind words?" I openly gawk at her as if she's lost her mind.

She laughs while looking me square in the eye. "Rod Stone, if you think today is the first time that I've said that prayer over you, then you don't know me at all. Your time is coming when you least expect it."

"I'm crushed you would say such a cruel thing. I thought you loved me, Louise. But the truth eventually comes out. What's sad is it's always those closest to you who betray you the worst."

"Yes, I'm such a terrible person for wanting you to have the best life possible. How will I be able to sleep at night?"

That's a rhetorical question, apparently, because she walks out of my home without the common courtesy of giving me a chance to answer her.

"Uncle Rod!" I hear my little munchkin yell as she steps through the doorway. "Do you know what time it is?"

"Time for high tea, my little love. Everything's ready. Get a move on before it gets cold."

"You know I have to change clothes first. I can't have tea dressed in these old rags." She rolls her eyes at me and I burst out laughing.

"Don't even look at me like any of this is my fault. This is all on you, big brother." Juliana shrugs and drops Isabelle's book bag beside the table. "You're the one who takes her shopping and spoils her with everything you find."

Yeah, that may be true. No sense in confirming her accusation, though.

"I wonder if she'll let me in the palace with my T-shirt and shorts on."

"I'm sure she will. You can do no wrong in her eyes, Rod. That little girl is crazy about you."

"The feeling is mutual. What time do you think you'll be back?"

"My treatment may run a little long today. They're fully booked. There's no need to call the police to track me down, again, if you don't hear from me for a little while."

"Define 'a little while.' Because if I don't hear from you for several hours, the police will raid every doctor's office in the Atlanta metro area until they find you."

"Or, you could do what normal people do and use the app on your phone to find me. What do you do for a living again? Software developer and professional hacker, isn't it? Surely you know how to use the GPS in my phone to figure out exactly where I am."

"Of course I do. I can even tap into your phone and use your camera to check your surroundings if I wanted to, but it's much more fun to use the police force to prove the lengths I will go to just to keep you safe and sound." I waggle my brows at her, knowing this is a complete double standard, but not caring.

She didn't raise me. I raised her.

Enormous difference. Huge.

"I love you, Rod. I don't tell you enough how much I appreciate everything you've done for me, and for Isabelle, our entire lives. Have fun with Isabelle and try not to spoil her more than you already have."

"I can't make that promise, little bird. One can never have too many crowns." I pull her into my arms. "Please be careful. Come back home in one piece. I love you." I kiss the top of her head as her arms squeeze me tighter.

"Stop worrying about me. We only live once."

I watch her leave and a twinge of pain shoots through my chest. She's all I have. If anything happens to her, it'll be the end of me. Since I know how much I love Juliana, I can only imagine how much Mom's diagnosis broke her heart, for us more than for herself.

"Uncle Rod, I'm waiting." The little girl's singsong voice

pulls me from the dark thoughts in my mind before they take over completely.

"I'm coming, Princess Isabelle, with hot tea in hand. I hope you're hungry because we have a lot of sandwiches and scones to eat today."

~

JULIANA CAME BACK IN THE LATE AFTERNOON, LOOKING exhausted and pale with a hint of green tinge. The lethal cocktail of medications is already working on the cancerous cells in her body, but since they can't tell the difference between good and bad, they wipe out everything.

Knowing she didn't feel well enough to eat a big dinner, I made soup and grilled cheese sandwiches for us. She ate, slowly and meticulously, but the food at least gave her a little more energy than she had when she got home.

"You relax. I'll throw the munchkin in the bathtub and read her a story before bed. Then when I come back down, you can give me the condensed version of everything you've been hiding from me."

"Thank you. I appreciate the help."

Her not arguing with me confirms she feels much worse than she's saying. Every horrible thought about her illness and her future fly through my mind as I carry Isabelle up the stairs, thrown over my shoulder, with her laughing and squealing like any other five-year-old.

Exactly the way I want her to stay as long as possible. She deserves the best carefree childhood we can give her. The one Juliana and I never had.

After a bath complete with bubbles, toys, and drenching

Uncle Rod, Isabelle kisses her mom goodnight before bedtime. She convinces me to read her two stories, but she's sound asleep before we're halfway through the second one. I place a gentle kiss on her forehead and leave her door slightly ajar on my way out.

Juliana is lying on the couch with her arms held tightly against her body when I walk in the den, so I grab a blanket and cover her.

"Let's hear it." I purposely keep my voice low and neutral. No sense in shaming or guilting her.

"It's acute lymphoblastic leukemia. I found out about three weeks ago. I just started the chemotherapy protocol. This round lasts four weeks."

"And then?"

"And then, they'll tell me if I'm in remission or not. But for the next four weeks, I'll need your help with Isabelle. These drugs will kick my ass, and I may be in the hospital for part of that time because it'll kill my immune system."

"You know I'll do whatever you need me to do. There's no question about that. Why didn't you tell me you suspected the cancer had returned?"

"Because I had no idea it had. I had heavy periods and terrible headaches, and I just felt tired a lot. I thought the doctor would change my birth control pills or put me on iron supplements. This diagnosis caught me completely off guard. Really, I haven't stopped long enough to deal with it yet. I'm only doing what I have to do to stay alive, one day at a time."

"You and Isabelle can move in with me until you're completely well. I'll take care of both of you. If the doctor needs to admit you, all of Isabelle's things will be here for her. Maybe that'll make the changes a little less of a shock to her system. If you're not inpatient, I'll get to spend more time with you. Plus, I can work from home whenever you need me here."

"Okay, Rod, you've convinced me. You don't have to keep going with your arguments. You win, I lose." A small smile plays on her lips, but she doesn't seem to have the energy for a full one.

"You probably should go to bed now, too. I'll take care of all the logistics in the morning—packing clothes, forwarding mail, whatever else you need me to do."

She pushes up from the couch and heads for the stairs. When she reaches for the rail, she looks at me. "You are the best big brother in the world, Rod. You've taken care of me my entire life, even though it cost your childhood. I don't know what I'd do without you. I love you."

Her declaration takes me aback and makes me feel guilty for all the times I resented not being footloose and carefree during my teenage years. Not that I ever let her know I had those thoughts of betrayal and resentment because of our situation. It wasn't as if she asked for the perfect storm of a fucked-up life.

"I wouldn't have it any other way. I love you too, little bird."

She climbs the steps, each one taking more of a toll on what's left of her energy than the last. I watch with my heart in my mouth as she reaches her bedroom door, holding on to the doorframe to steady herself.

"I don't know what I'd without you, Juliana. You can't ever leave me." My whispered words are out in the universe.

I hope someone is listening.

CHAPTER TWENTY-THREE

Daisy
Two weeks later

The first day in my new teaching position has been nerve-racking. Not because of the students, since I haven't even made it to my classroom yet. I've been in the office all morning trying to sort out my employment paperwork. Somewhere between leaving my previous school, moving from a small town outside of Atlanta to the Buckhead area, and taking a Caribbean vacation, I somehow failed to ensure the superintendent's office had received all of my documents.

A few calls and a lot of pleading with others to email additional copies eventually works in my favor. My class lines up in the in the hallway, waiting for their turn to enter the cafeteria when I finally join them. I walk down the line and introduce myself to each student personally. As expected, there are a few who are not shy at all and others who aren't so sure about me yet.

Five-year-old kids are my favorite age group to teach. Kindergarten can be so much fun and a time of tremendous discovery, given the right encouragement, or they can be tiny terrors.

There's no way to tell which way the wind will blow from one day to the next.

At the end of the line, watching all the students march toward the cafeteria, a young lady greets me with a smile as I approach. "You must be Daisy. Welcome to Peachtree Elementary. I'm Glenna Porter, the paraprofessional assigned to your class. I'm looking forward to working with you."

"Nice to meet you, Glenna. I'm not late for work, I promise. We ran into a paperwork snag that took all morning to correct. I hope you haven't had too hard of a time keeping them occupied alone."

"Not at all. Don't worry about it. Ours is the best of the four kindergarten classes." She smiles as she opens the door and reminds the kids to keep their voices down as they go through the line.

As we walk in with them, Glenna gives me the rundown on the school lunch policies and expectations. I'm relieved to find there's nothing out of the ordinary from the last school where I taught. This one is much more upscale, being a private school. Everything is still bright and shiny. The walls are freshly painted, the tables are new, and the floor is squeaky clean.

Nothing but the best here.

After we ensure all the children have their lunches and find their seats, Glenna and I take ours.

"How long have you worked here, Glenna?"

"Three years, and I still love it. The staff here is great. Everyone is so easy to work with and gets along like family. I've never seen a school like it before. Usually the politics and mean girl cliques make life miserable. Maybe it's different here because the teachers aren't friends with any of the parents. We're on opposite ends of the tax bracket range from the parents of our students." She laughs good-naturedly, but I know exactly what she means. The teachers and parents don't run in the same circles, so the chances of nepotism are low.

We chat over our meals until it's time to line up the students again. When we reach the classroom, everyone automatically goes to their assigned station for free art time. I walk around and ask each child about their painting. I'm not a psychiatrist, but I've learned a lot about what's going on inside their little heads just by talking about their art. Most of the boys draw their favorite superhero, giving me a glimpse of how they'd like to see themselves one day. Most girls draw something pretty, sunshine and flowers, friends and family, or princesses and castles.

"What a pretty picture. Who is this?" I kneel beside one beautiful little girl with thick black hair and big, beautiful blue eyes.

"This is my mommy in my room with me. We play dress up and I get to wear a crown, like a princess." She smiles brightly as she tells me about her home, animatedly explaining every detail. She's a bright little girl, seemingly already ahead of some of her classmates.

"That sounds like so much fun."

"It is. But we haven't played this in a long time." Her face drops and her demeanor changes noticeably.

"Oh, I bet she's just busy with work and stuff. She'll play with you again soon."

"Yeah, she will when she comes back home."

Not knowing the family situation in the home, I decide against pressing for more information today. Her sunny disposition has already dimmed somewhat. "Well, you've drawn a beautiful picture."

Her bright smile is back, making her eyes sparkle and her face light up. "Thank you, Miss Daisy."

One subject bleeds into another as we move through the day. Keeping the class of twenty busy and entertained is both exhausting and rewarding. At last, their time for free play arrives. The leaders from two of the four classrooms alternate supervising playtime activities for the entire grade, giving us a much needed break. While the kids are outside enjoying their recess time, Glenna and I take some time to talk openly and get to know each other better.

"Is there a Mr. Daisy around?" Glenna props her feet up on her desk.

"No, definitely not. What about a Mr. Glenna?"

"Unfortunately, not yet. My charm and wit seem to be lost on the average male around here. Maybe I need to move." She purses her lips to the side, half kidding and half serious.

"Don't waste your time. No matter how far from home you go, men are still the same. You'd be better off sticking around here, finding someone who sucks the least." I should know. I flew over fourteen hundred miles only for some jerk to dump me the day before our vacation ended.

He didn't even say goodbye. That's how much I meant to him.

"You're probably right. Plus, searching for some fictional

man isn't worth leaving my friends and my incredible job. Not that I'll ever become a millionaire doing this, but my peace of mind is worth much more to me." She speaks as though she has a story to tell behind that statement. When she's ready, she'll tell me.

"Have you not met any single fathers here, bringing their kids to school? Surely there are a few available dudes in the Buckhead area you'd be interested in dating."

"You'd think so, right? The only problem is the single men who come here are part of the multi-millionaire club in this area, if not the billionaire club. The rich keep getting richer, so it's hard to keep up with the minimum allowable net worth. In case I haven't made it crystal clear, I'm looking for the rare species of man who doesn't care so much about the almighty dollar."

"You know, I sensed you had a message in there, but I was having a hard time figuring it out." I wink, letting her know I'm teasing, and we chuckle together.

"As I was walking around, talking to the kids and getting to know each one, I realized you were right about our class. It is the best, even though I have no firsthand knowledge of the other classes. We have some incredibly bright children in here."

"I agree. They make every day a new adventure for me." She pops a goldfish cracker in her mouth.

"Do you know anything about what's going on in Isabelle's home? She seemed so sad when I asked about her picture."

"Her mother has cancer and has been in and out of the hospital. She's fighting it but I don't think she's holding up too well." Her face falls, emphasizing the severity and sadness of the situation.

"That breaks my heart. Even if kids don't understand all the details, they feel how these events affect the family. I'll keep an eye on her, in case it gets worse before it gets better." I drop my eyes to my desk, already contemplating the ways I can help Isabelle through this dark time.

"Juliana, her mom, is the sweetest person too. You'd love her—she's not the pretentious kind. Earlier in the school year, she was so involved in Isa's school events, and she'd interact with all the other kids like they were her own. It's a hard adjustment for that little girl, not having her mom around all the time, so I'm sure it's equally hard on Juliana."

"I can't imagine all the conflicting feelings they both have right now. Is there anything we can do to help her?" I can't imagine being in her shoes.

"Not that I know of, but from what I've heard, she has a strong support system in her family. When you get to know Isa better, you'll see that little girl is so adored at home. She's not spoiled, but she hung the moon and stars in someone's eyes."

We get busy setting up the room for the next activity before the end of the school day, but what I just learned about Isa's mom is stuck in my mind. The empath in me can't stand the thought of that sweet little girl potentially losing her mom to such a terrible disease. Even if I can't do anything to change her health condition, maybe I can find small ways to help lift her spirits.

The children return to the classroom and we eventually get everyone settled in their seats. We're so busy working with each child to complete their sight words, I don't realize how fast time has passed. When I glance at the clock, I realize the dismissal bell will ring soon, so we quickly gather their book bags and help them put their work away until tomorrow.

I can't help but smile when I watch all the littles file out of the room when the bell rings, knowing exactly where they're going and what they need to do. I'm lost in my own musings until the voice of the only male I trust with my heart calls my name.

"Mommy! I had the best day. This school is awesome." Landen, the seven-year-old love of my life, rushes into my classroom and straight into my arms.

"I'm so glad you had a great first day. Just remember this next time you don't trust your mom." I feel him smile with his cheek pressed against mine.

"Don't get carried away now, Momma."

This is our personal comic routine, a private joke between mother and son. He's all boy, rough and tumble, and into everything he's not supposed to be. But he also has the best heart and sense of humor, even if I'm biased in my beliefs. He and I tease each other regularly as a reminder not to take life too seriously. We started this schtick when he was old enough to understand humor.

I secretly hope it helps us both survive his teenage years.

"You think you're smart, don't you, little boy?" I playfully honk his nose before packing my bag to leave for the day. "You can tell me all about your new class on the way home. I'm almost ready to go."

"Can I go get a drink of water in the hall?"

"Sure, but no running off anywhere else."

He likes to visit other classrooms and meet my peers. Not that I mind, usually, but since we recently moved, we're still decorating the house I recently bought. I'd planned to drag him along with me on a shopping spree before going home.

Before putting my planner away, I glance at the lesson plan for tomorrow and mentally check off everything I'll need to work on it at home tonight.

"No, I can't leave it here. I need it. My teacher said it's a beautiful picture and I want to give it to Mommy." A little girl's voice echoes down the hall, the urgent pleading in her tone is unmistakable.

She sounds like Isabelle, but I'm not certain. So I turn my gaze toward the door, waiting to see if she appears.

"Is it in here?" He's looking down at his miniature doppelgänger when he steps through the doorway into my classroom.

My heart stops. I can't breathe, move, or speak. I'm completely and utterly dumbstruck. How did I look at her all day and not see the resemblance?

Rod is standing in my classroom beside Isabelle, silently staring back at me.

She looks so much like him. Same color hair, same color and shape of eyes, same dazzling smile. Is Isabelle his daughter?

"Mommy, can I play baseball next season? My new friend, Jason, said he's playing. We can request to be on the same team." Landen scurries around Rod and joins me behind my desk, chattering as usual and completely oblivious to the tense stare down I'm in.

"Sure, baby. We'll find out when signups are, okay?" Now that I've found my voice, I turn my attention back to Rod and Isabelle. "What can I do for you two?"

"Miss Daisy, I left my picture here. Can I take it home to

show my mommy?"

"Yes, you sure can, sweetheart. I'll get it for you." I robotically move to the back to the room where I put her painting away for safekeeping, feeling Rod's eyes burning holes in the back of my head the entire way.

"Color me surprised and speechless. *You're* my niece's new teacher?" His eyes narrow, his lips are parted, and he tilts his head to the side as I hand the drawing to Isa.

A fleeting memory of a Caribbean conversation about family comes back to me. He mentioned his affection for his sister and niece. Now he's here with her.

"Apparently so."

His eyes cut over to Landen, then back to me. I know what he's thinking without him saying a single word. Today holds more than one unexpected surprise for him.

I may have neglected to mention I have a son, who was staying with my parents while I ran off to a tropical island with my best friend.

My bad.

"Come on, Uncle Rod. Let's go see Mommy now." Isa tugs on his hand, but his eyes never leave mine.

"To be continued."

That felt like an ominous warning. He was the one who deserted me on a tropical island, not the other way around. If he thinks I owe him any kind of explanation, he can think again, but on his own time and far away from me.

There's nothing between us that needs to be continued. My only connection to him now is I'm Isabelle's teacher, nothing more, nothing less.

"Sure. We can talk during the next parent-teacher meeting."

CHAPTER TWENTY-FOUR

Rod

When I left Daisy in Punta Cana two weeks ago, I accepted the notion I'd never see her again, that what we had was only a vacation fling, and my mind would return to normal once I was home. Over the last couple of weeks since returning home, I'd convinced myself those lies were true. That when I hurt her, it was for her own good, so she'd see the real Rod Stone before it was too late to save her from me. So she could turn her back on me and walk away now rather than later.

Then I walked in Isa's classroom, and there she was, long blonde hair, big blue eyes, smoking hot body, prompting every possible meaning of _hot for teacher_ to float through my mind. The odds of the sexy siren I met in the Caribbean being my niece's teacher are astronomical. There's no way this was all because of chance. But, in that first second when I laid eyes on her, it didn't matter who, how, or what was behind our reunion.

She was there, and the living, breathing connection between us was still thriving.

"I can't wait to show Mommy my drawing. Miss Daisy said it was beautiful. Do you think it is, Uncle Rod?" Isa looks up at me, hope blooming in her eyes.

"Miss Daisy was right. You drew a beautiful picture for your mom. She will love it."

Speaking of *mommy,* it would seem there's something rather significant Daisy failed to mention when we were getting to know each other better. Even after we bared our souls and decided to try a genuine relationship, before I fucked it up at the water park. She has a child with someone else. He's older than Isa, but not by much.

Was she married before? Is her ex still in her life? Does she have any other children? So many questions present, one after the other, until I question everything I thought I knew about her. Having a son is a more than a minor detail from her past that she may or may not have wanted to share. A ready-made family is an enormous responsibility for a career bachelor like me to consider.

Even though I can't deny how my blood pressure spiked when I saw her, my focus is on getting Juliana well and ensuring Isabelle feels safe and secure while her world is upside down. Now that I've put some distance between us and can think straight again, I remind myself of one thing, *wrong time, wrong place, wrong man.* There's no chance of picking back up where we left off before she abruptly moved out of my suite, regardless of how often she's on my mind.

Or how many times per week I'll have to see Daisy now

that I'm helping Juliana by taking Isa to school or picking her up.

Isa and I walk into the hospital to see Juliana. The treatments—chemotherapy medications and radiation therapy—have taken a toll on her body, and her immune system can't fight off even the most basic infections. For her safety, the doctor put her in isolation. Since children are walking petri dishes of germs, Isabella can only talk to her mom on the phone and see her through the window. It's hell on both of them to be apart, but we'll get through it for the short term. This pain will be worth it in the end.

The nurses have been extra accommodating to Isa, including her in everything except going into Juliana's room with them. When we arrive on the floor, Isa takes off running to the nurse on duty. We've gotten to know everyone who works in this area over the last week.

"Lexi, look what I brought Mommy!" Isa holds up her artwork and beams with pride.

"You did so good, sweetheart. Let me grab the tape and you can hang it up for her, okay?"

"Yes!" Isa nods enthusiastically, still wearing the innocent smile of a loved child. I'll do whatever it takes to keep that smile intact.

Juliana sees them approach the window, so she gingerly climbs out of bed and shuffles to the window. She looks paler and thinner than she did yesterday. Her hair began coming out in large chunks, so she had the hospital staff shave her head and save her from the daily reminders. Now she wears colorful bandanas Isa and I picked out to help keep her head warm.

"Look what I made you in school today, Mommy." The

nurse holds Isa on her hip and the phone against her ear so Isa can put her masterpiece on display.

I can't hear Juliana's reply, but I have a good guess, anyway. Her energy is zapped, but she gives her little girl every ounce she has in reserve. Juliana slides her fingers along the inside of the glass, touching the drawing with her heart and committing it to her memory. These are the times she uses to keep going in the middle of the night, when it's pitch-black and eternal sleep would be so much easier than fighting the heavyweight in the ring with her.

The lump in my throat is the size of a watermelon, but I force it down and bottle my emotions with it. My girls need me, and I can't be the one who breaks under the pressure. I watched my father do that to his family, decimating all of us in the process. That spineless sack of shit didn't deserve to be in our lives.

I'll never be that man.

"Mommy wants to talk to you now, Uncle Rod." Isa hands the phone to me then Lexi takes her behind the nursing station desk to give Juliana and me privacy.

"Hey, little bird. How do you feel today?"

"This little bird is ready to fly the coop, Rod. I'm going stir-crazy in here. There's only so much public television I can watch before my brain rots." She leans her weight against the wall separating us, already tired from the few minutes she's been out of bed.

"Do you want me to have a recliner or something brought in there so you can sit by the window?" I'm afraid she'll fall down right in front of me.

"No, I'm okay. The bed is usually here, but I asked them to

move it to the opposite side of the room so I can get my daily exercise."

"That's not funny, Jules. You're here to rest, get the best medical care, and stay away from all germs. Walking back and forth across the room uses energy you don't have to spare."

"So does arguing with you. Now listen. You need to talk to Isa's teacher and tell her everything that's going on with me. Right now, she's still having fun with Uncle Rod. But the time will come when she feels like I've abandoned her. She may not come out and say it, but she'll show it in different ways at school. They need to tell you right away if she does or says anything out of the ordinary. I shared some information with Glenna when I picked Isa up last, but they need to know everything."

"Consider it done. Don't worry about anything except getting well."

"Thank you for always being the best big brother anyone could ask for, Rod. All my life."

"Don't do that. Don't start saying your goodbyes. I'm being straight with you. I can't handle that."

She nods, compassion shining in her eyes. "I know there's nothing you won't do for Isabelle. Just like there's nothing you haven't done for me. And I was thinking, maybe you should get in touch with Dad."

"No."

"You can't stay mad at him forever."

"Yes, I can."

She shakes her head but doesn't push the issue any further. "There's something you have to do for me, and you can't say no. I *need* this, Rod."

"Name it."

"My lawyer sent papers over for you to sign. The nurse can call the hospital social worker up here to notarize them." She inhales a ragged breath, fighting back the tears. "I'm signing over temporary power of attorney over Isabelle to you. If she needs medical care or anything from a parent at school, you wouldn't be able to stand in for me without it. While I'm in treatment, you'll have to be her father. Will you do that for me?"

"I would never say no to that request, little bird. You know I'll take care of whatever she needs while I'm also taking care of you."

"I do know, and you're the only person in the world I'd trust with her. Thank you, Rod. I'm sorry you were never given the chance to live your own life. You've always had to take care of me, then Isabelle and me. You could never be selfish and only think of yourself at any point."

"No, Juliana, don't think like that. Mom offered me a choice of whether I'd raise you or Dad's parents would take you. But there was never a choice in my mind, and I've never regretted it for one second."

She wipes a stray tear away with a shaky hand. "I need to get back in the bed now. I love you. Tell Isa I love her too."

"We love you, too. Call or text me if you need anything."

I place the receiver back in the cradle and watch her move across the room toward the bed, slower than usual, even slower than when she got up a few minutes ago. After she's safely lying down, Lexi calls the social worker to bring the legal papers for me to sign and her to notarize. Even though I expected this would be the case when I learned of Juliana's diagnosis, actually signing the papers and taking guardianship of my sister's daughter feels far too final.

It's what's best for Isabelle at this point of Juliana's treatment, I know that.

But it also makes me think we're preparing to say goodbye … and I'm not strong enough to do that.

As I walk into the school's front office the next morning to deliver the temporary guardianship papers, part of me hopes to run into Daisy and another part of me hopes to avoid her all together. My motto is playing on repeat in my head the entire time I look for her, *wrong time, wrong place, wrong man.*

After filling out additional paperwork with my contact information, the secretary files the temporary guardianship papers with Isabelle's records and assures me everything is in order. But I still need to have that conversation with her teacher, the one about any changes in Isa's personality. That means I have to find Daisy and talk to her, for my family's sake, not for my own.

When I step into her classroom, another woman is in there instead. I glance around the room, expecting to find Daisy working with one of the kids, but she's not there.

"Can I help you?" The non-Daisy woman glances around the room, then turns her attention back to me with a cautious eye.

"Yes, I'm looking for Daisy Nash. I'm Isabelle's uncle, and I need to give her some vital information."

"Miss Daisy is in a staff meeting with the principal and the other teachers. I'm Glenna, the paraprofessional assigned to this room to help her with the workload. If you'd like, you can give me the information, and I'll make sure she gets the message."

Damn.

I can't withhold the information now that I've stated it's vital. This means I'll get to keep my oath of steering clear of Daisy at all costs. I relay the message from Juliana and explain the temporary guardianship arrangement, so they're not surprised when they see me standing in for my sister. She takes all the information down and slides the note into a file inside Daisy's desk with a promise to share it verbally too.

As fun as it could be to fill my days with kindergarten activities, I've been away from work long enough as it is, so I turn and walk out to my car. Nowhere along the path between Isabelle's classroom and the front door do I run into Daisy.

Not even a single glimpse of her.

When I walk into the office, everyone is busy working, but Kevin isn't in his office. I glance at my watch and realize I'm twenty-five minutes late for an important meeting. With everything in my personal life blowing up in my face, I completely forgot about it. After I rush to my office and grab my laptop, I quietly enter the large boardroom and take a seat in the back.

Kevin, ever the consummate professional, doesn't miss a beat when he catches me sneaking in and taking a seat along the back wall so I won't disturb the clients around the table. He continues the presentation we were scheduled to give together, covering my ass as the second-in-command of the company. He doesn't mind since he didn't rise to the level of vice president based on his good looks, but missing anything work-related isn't in my DNA. My business has been my life since I was a teenager, studying computer language late into the night after Juliana and Mom had fallen asleep hours before.

When the lights brighten at the end of the demonstration, Kevin recaps the important details of the meeting and provides a reminder of the next steps. After a quick introduction and vague explanation of my tardiness, I thank them for considering our company before they leave. When they're out of earshot, Kevin turns his attention to me.

"How are you holding up, brother?"

"I'm taking all of this one step at a time. Juliana. Isabella. Daisy."

"Daisy?" His bewildered expression would make me laugh if I didn't have this elephant sitting on my chest, making it impossible to breathe.

"Yes, Daisy. She's Isabelle's new teacher."

"Oh, shit."

"That about sums it up."

CHAPTER TWENTY-FIVE

Daisy

"How do you like it here so far?" Cam Brooks, the fifth-grade science teacher, strolls up beside me as Landen and I walk into the school early one morning.

Cam is the schoolgirl crush of every young girl in this elementary school. With soulful brown eyes, dark brown hair, classic good looks, and a genuinely friendly smile, it's easy to see why he also turns the heads of the single teachers. Since the day of our teacher staff meeting last week when we first met, he's gone out of his way to help me learn the ropes and be a friendly face.

"I love working here. Maybe I shouldn't say this, but I'm glad the previous teacher made her maternity leave permanent. Everyone has been so helpful, and I haven't found the mean girls club among the teachers like I have in other schools. I'm convinced the smaller classrooms keep us sane here." We laugh together while he holds the door open for me.

"I'm glad to hear that. The staff here is more like a family than anywhere I've taught. We've all experienced the politics you're talking about, and we've agreed to keep that mentality out of our school. Since we spend more time with each other than at home during the school year, we all have to get along."

"That's exactly the same argument I made at my last school, but it fell on deaf ears. You and I seem to think a lot alike."

"Yes, we sure do. I'd be willing to bet we have a lot more in common too." He smiles down at me with a mixture of teasing and appreciation in his expression.

"Possibly." I'm not trying to flirt with him, but I can't seem to stop batting my eyelashes and smiling like a dork at him.

When we reach the corner that separates the upper grades from the lower, he stops walking and turns his full attention to me.

"There's something I want to ask you about, but I don't want you to think I'm overstepping my bounds or anything,"

"You can ask me anything." *Seriously, stop it, Daisy.*

"I've been thinking about the summer camp you organize every year, and I'd like to help if you'll have me. I have a few ideas of how to raise the capital you need to fund the program, and even some ideas on subjects to add to the teaching lineup. Would you like to go to dinner tonight and brainstorm? Landen is welcome to join us, of course."

My standard answer is always "no."

No, I'm way too busy this week.

No, I don't have a babysitter.

No, I have other plans. Maybe some other time.

"Yes, that would be great. I can't wait to hear your ideas." How easily I accepted his invitation is foreign to me, but somehow it feels right, too. Maybe I'm finally moving on, not simply turning the page but starting a brand-new book.

We settle on a time and place to meet for dinner before going to our classrooms. We plan to drive separately, and I'm relieved to avoid the awkward goodbye scene at the front door. Kiss or no kiss? Handshake or hug? Friendly smile or awkward wave? All these unknowns and ambiguities make dating not worth the effort.

But meeting a friend for dinner then driving myself home? I can do that.

After I walk Landen to his room, I head into mine and start setting up for the day. I can't stop thinking about the note Glenna took from Rod regarding Isabelle and their home situation. When I talked to the school counselor about it, she filled me in on the rest of the story of why Rod had to take temporary guardianship of his niece.

Despite how many times I've tried to put the thought out of my mind, I can't help but wonder if his sister's diagnosis is why he left the island early and without saying anything to anyone about it. If so, he's trying much harder than I origi-nally thought to hide his soft heart under a false shell of apathy. He briefly mentioned them while we were together, and I could tell they were important to him from the slight change in his tone.

But then I remind myself how and why we parted, and I have to accept I'm not the woman he cares about. He proved that to me beyond a shadow of doubt with his actions, both then and now. If he had any regrets about shredding my heart and my pride, he would've tried to make amends by now. He's had plenty of opportunities to talk to me, and waiting for him to man up only reveals how foolish I am.

No more promises in the dark. He was so convincing that morning after his run on the beach. I fell for his lies and lines and kept falling until the truth slapped me in the face. I wanted him to be real so badly I convinced myself to ignore all the warning signs. That's something I swore I'd never do again before I met him. Now I'm considering having it tattooed on my ass as a permanent reminder.

Cam, on the other hand, is handsome, kind, and thoughtful. He doesn't set my nerves on edge or send the fluttering in my chest into overdrive, but he could be good for Landen and me. Damn Rod for obliterating my belief that I could be happy alone. After spending nearly all my time on the island with Rod, I'm craving companionship and someone to share my life with, and to find someone who wants to be with me too.

Could Cam be that someone?

Glenna has noticed the sly way we flirt with each other over the last few days, consciously avoiding anything too overt. Naturally, the first couple of times he did it, I didn't read much into it. He's friendly with everyone, but doesn't give off the player vibe like Rod does. But I still chalked his covert advances up to him knowing how handsome he is and using it to his advantage. Glenna set me straight on that immediately.

"He's hot, Daisy. Like, hot hot, and several other women here have made it clear they were interested in him. He made it clear he wasn't interested in any of them, though. He likes you. Maybe you should give him a chance."

She doesn't understand why I'm so hesitant. I haven't been

able to bring myself to tell her about the fiasco with Rod yet, Or about Landen's father.

Sometimes I feel as if I'm trapped in prison, one I've built around myself one wall at a time.

"Good morning." Glenna's eyebrows are high on her forehead, she's doing a slow wave, and one side of her mouth is quirked upward. No doubt she's been in that same position for more than a few minutes now. "Where'd you go? Because you have not been in the same solar system with me since I walked into the room."

"Cam asked me to go to dinner tonight and talk about the summer camp. I said yes, and now I'm trying not to freak and back out of it." That's the partial truth. The full truth is far too complicated and not anything I'm prepared to share yet.

"That's the best news I've heard in a long time. You're definitely not backing out on him. Just think about how awkward that would be the next time you see him here."

"You know, that's a fantastic point. If we start something and it ends badly, we'll both feel awkward here. Everyone else will feel it too. It's best not to start anything at all. Thanks for helping me think this through."

"Hey, that's not what I meant, and you know it. You need to live a little, Daisy, while you're still young enough to have fun. There comes a time when all you can see are the years passing by, and all the opportunities you've missed because you let fear rule you. Don't waste your life hiding your heart away."

～

"Are you still mad at me?" Tracy is already at my house when I get home from work, which is odd since she normally works longer hours at her office downtown than I do at the school.

"Of course I'm still mad at you."

"But you said you love me." She pouts, pursing her lips and giving me her sad puppy eyes.

"I never said I'd stopped loving you, but that doesn't mean I'm not still mad at you for the elaborate blind date disaster." I unlock the door and tell Landen to start on his homework since we're going out to dinner later.

"Who are you having dinner with?" Her eyes are wide open, and her jaw goes slack, so I crook my finger under her chin and close her mouth.

"The fifth-grade science teacher." I purposely keep my voice as neutral as possible, not giving anything away. She still deserves to be punished for her deception.

"Can I dare to hope this is something akin to a date? Not just a girls' dinner date?"

"Mommy's going on a date with Mr. Brooks. I heard my teacher talking about it with the other second grade teachers. Miss Germann said she's so happy Mr. Brooks is finally dating again."

Tracy and I both stare at Landen for a full minute while he concentrates on his homework at the kitchen table. He's oblivious to our stunned silence. My peers are discussing my personal life at work, and that makes me very uncomfortable. This is even more reason I should cancel our plans and quell the rumors before they even get started.

"Don't you dare even think about it. You're going to dinner

with him if I have to drive you there myself." She crosses her arms over her chest and quirks one brow.

"Fine. But only because I don't want to hurt his feelings and I'm too tired to fight with you today." After making a quick snack for Landen, I walk toward my bedroom to rifle through my closet for something to wear tonight. Tracy follows me, leaning against the doorframe while I rant about a lack of suitable clothing.

"Wear your black leggings with the shimmery silver top. You look extra sexy in that outfit."

I cut my eyes toward her and decide she has a point. "What are you doing here, anyway? You're usually still in meetings at this time of day."

"What? I can't stop by and see my best friend in the world whenever I want?"

Now it's my turn to fold my arms across my chest and arch my brow at her.

"Okay, so there is something I need to talk to you about, but it can wait. Why don't I stay here with Landen while you go meet Mr. Chemistry?"

"Seriously. What is wrong with you? Are you dying? What's going on?"

She sighs heavily, then blurts it out all at once. "Kevin insists on meeting my family, including my parents."

"That is the worst idea I've ever heard. Have you not told him about how they are yet?"

"Well, I've told him a little about them, but not everything. He thinks he can change their minds, make them like him even though he's white. They're causing problems between us and he hasn't even met them yet. The more I resist, the more he thinks it's because I'm ashamed of him, or that I don't have enough faith in him, or that maybe I'm more like them than I'll admit." She wipes the stray tears from the corners of her eyes, holding on to the belief she has to be strong and independent at all times. "I just need some space to think, and I need you to help me talk this through. I'll stay with Landen while you go out, then we can talk when you get home."

"Okay, but only because I know you're not ready to talk right now. If I push the issue, you'll just clam up and say you'll handle it on your own. But I will make one point I want you to think about while I'm out.

"He doesn't think you're like your parents or he wouldn't be with you. The bottom line is the two of you will have to face others like them at some point. Is it possible he's pushing this meeting because he's insecure about your feelings? If you'll stand by him or walk away? Maybe facing this together is what he needs to feel confident with you."

The more I think about it, the more I'm concerned his meeting her parents will hurt Tracy as much as it will Kevin, even if the reasons differ. I'll leave her to sort out her thoughts while I have dinner with Cam, but I already know how this scene will play out. All I can do is offer to go with them, to act as the moral support they'll both need afterward.

Tracy and Kevin stay on my mind the entire way over to meet Cam. He's already waiting inside the restaurant when I arrive, patiently waiting at our table with two glasses of wine. His eyes skim over me appreciatively, but not too suggestively. He stands and pulls my chair out for me. His warm and welcoming smile instantly puts me at ease.

"You take my breath away, Daisy."

"Thank you, Cam. That's so sweet of you to say."

We order our food and chat while we wait, getting to

know each other better. He asks about the camp programs, why I started it, and where I see it going in the future. His interest in helping seems genuine, and his enthusiasm about being part of the program brings back the initial excitement I felt when I first started it.

"You know, almost all the parents are independently wealthy. They own lucrative companies, they inherited large estates, or they work for corporations who would donate. You operate as a nonprofit, so their donations are tax deductible. I think we could share the vision with them and pick up several sponsors, maybe even enough to cover the costs for several years out."

We're so engrossed in conversation about the possibilities and various approaches we could use, I don't realize we have company standing beside our table.

Then I look up into those mesmerizing blue eyes, strikingly handsome face, and chiseled body covered by a custom-tailored suit that fits his frame exquisitely.

"How are you, Daisy?" Rod is not pleased to find me here with another man.

Isn't that unfortunate?

CHAPTER TWENTY-SIX

Rod

"Oh, hello, Rod. I'm sorry I didn't see you standing there. We must've been deeper in conversation than I realized. Do you two know each other?" She gestures toward her date, who looks like a poor man's version of a short-haired Keanu Reeves, as if I have any interest in meeting him. But I can play along with the best of them.

"No, I don't think we've met. Rod Stone." I extend my hand to shake his.

"Rod is the uncle of one of my students." Daisy's color commentary feels like a bucket of ice-cold water was dumped over my head. I didn't expect her to introduce me as the love of her life, the one who got away, the one she's still pining for, but being relegated to a student's distant kin is a sucker punch to the gut.

"Cam Brooks. Nice to meet you." He takes my proffered

hand with a smile, not the least bit intimidated by my intrusion on their date.

"I don't mean to interrupt your dinner. I wanted to make sure you received the message I left with Glenna. If you have time soon, I think it'd be best if we had that parent-teacher conference you mentioned so we can discuss it."

"Yes, I'd be glad to talk with you about Isa. Whatever day and time is convenient for you is fine with me. My after-school schedule is open for the next couple of weeks."

"Would it be possible for you to come to my house tomorrow evening around six? It's unorthodox, I know, but Isabelle's mother wants to be part of the discussion. With her health concerns, she only leaves home when she goes to the doctor. You're welcome to bring your son, though. He and Isa can play together while we talk."

"That's not a problem at all. I'm happy to help, and I'm looking forward to meeting Isa's mother. Isa talks about her a lot. I'll see you tomorrow at six then."

"Thank you, I appreciate it. Enjoy your dinner." I nod at Cam and walk away, taking Daisy's polite hint.

I'll see you tomorrow at six then. That was a gracious way of dismissing me from the table so she could get back to flirting with her date.

When I walk out to my car, the cold late November rain drizzles, leaving a chill in the air that permeates my jacket with its bite. From the looks of their plates, they should finish dinner soon. Unless they linger over dessert and drinks, casting longing glances over their wine goblets until they decide to finish in a more private setting.

My imagination hits the overdrive button and goes from zero to one-sixty in three seconds.

If my car were that fast, I'd lose my license within a week, but somehow there's nothing in place to regulate my overactive mind. The stupid things I do are my fault, one hundred percent, but that doesn't stop even when I recognize I'm doing them. Like right now, while I'm sitting in my car waiting for Daisy to come out of the restaurant so I can try to talk to her alone.

Now that the idea is stuck in my head, my tenacious personality won't let me change course. I've had fight for every inch of progress I've ever made, overcoming the odds stacked against me every day of my life. Today's challenge is no different, only the stakes. When I was young, I was fighting for the food on our table and the roof over our heads. Tonight, I'm fighting for the one I'm sure I'm supposed to be with, even if I don't know how that's supposed to work.

What I do know is seeing her with someone else only confirmed I'm in way too deep with her. It's been weeks since we parted, since I sabotaged everything we'd built between us, and this feeling hasn't subsided or even diminished. Every time I see her is harder than the last, because I know what I had and what I'm missing.

My ringing cell snaps me out of my Daisy-induced obsession. When I glance at the screen, I'm relieved to see Kevin's name instead of Juliana's. Every call from her jacks my heart rate up, waiting for more unwelcome news.

"Hey, man. What's up?"

"Are you busy, Rod? I need your advice on something."

"I'm halfway between busy and not busy."

"What the fuck does that mean?"

"I'm sitting outside the restaurant waiting for Daisy's date to end so I can talk to her."

The line goes silent for several seconds. I know he's still there. He needs time to process my blunt confession.

"Leave her alone, man. She's way out of your league, and she deserves someone who will treat her like a queen. You're not the man for her and you know it."

Wrong place. Wrong time. Wrong man.

Sometimes I think he knows me better than I know myself.

"What makes you say I'm not the man for her?" He may be right, but that statement stings coming from my best friend.

"Rod, I do not understand how you develop and nurture your business relationships the way you do. You can work the room, make people trust you with tens of millions of dollars, and seal deals when other companies can't even get their foot in the door. Your clients love you.

"But you are clueless when it comes to how to treat women. What you did in Punta Cana was over the line, man. You don't deserve a second chance with her. The sad part is, I think she's kind enough to give you one. When she does, you'll only use it to hurt her when she gets too close again. You'll tuck your dick between your legs and run in the opposite direction like a scared little girl. Leave her alone and let her be happy."

Now it's my turn to sit here in stunned silence. The rain is coming down in solid sheets now with occasional gusts of wind to render umbrellas completely useless. Dark gray clouds cover the skies, threatening to release harder downpours at any time. Nothing could rival the storm swirling inside me, though.

"I want to apologize to her. She's Isa's teacher, so we're stuck with each other at least until next summer."

"You're not fooling me, man. And I must be desperate to call you for relationship advice." I can see Kevin shaking his head in disgust, with both of us.

"What's going on with you and Tracy?"

"Never mind. I've changed my mind and don't want to talk about it with you. I'm hanging up now. Drive home. Keep things professional between you and Daisy. Don't screw it up more than you already have."

He disconnects, but we both know I'm not taking his advice. I'm here, she's here, and the conversation I've imagined is rooted in my head. We need to talk it out and move away from the mistakes of the past.

My mistakes.

When they finally emerge from the restaurant, I'm relieved to see them going in different directions toward their vehicles, walking fast with their heads down to keep the driving rain out of their eyes.

Nothing says, "you're in the friend zone," like going on a date in separate cars.

Cam reaches his first and drives away as I jump out of mine with an umbrella in hand. Daisy looks shocked to see me, but steps under the offered cover, regardless. The fact that he left her to walk through the parking lot alone, in the rain no less, thoroughly pisses me off.

"What are you still doing here, Rod?"

"Where did you park, in the lot across the street?" I chuckle but keep pace with her.

"At the end of this row. All the closer ones were taken when I got here. You didn't answer me."

"I'm still here because there's something we need to talk about, and we need to be alone."

"Is it about Isabelle or your sister?" She stops walking and looks up at me, her eyes and face expressionless.

"No, it's not about either of them. It seems Kevin and Tracy are having problems. I know he's crazy about her. What can we do to help the situation?" I'm grasping at straws, but I have to keep her talking.

She narrows her eyes, rightfully suspicious, but she loves her friend too much not to take the bait.

"The only thing we *can* do—be there as their moral support and cheerleaders when it all goes down."

When what goes down? I should've made Kevin tell me what's bothering him when I had the chance.

"Obviously. But there has to be something else we can do."

She crosses her arms over her chest and glares at me. She knows. "You have no idea what the problem between them is, do you? What is this really about, Rod? I don't have time for your lies and games."

Time to man-up.

"It's about you and me."

"Let me stop you right there and save us both some time. First, there is no you and me to talk about. Second, there won't be a you and me ever again. Third, you and I only had a vacation fling, nothing more, and vacation is over now. We're back home, living our lives in the actual world. You don't do relationships and I don't do late-night booty calls. I'm Isa's teacher. That's the extent of our involvement.

"And, for the record, if Kevin is your best friend, you should already know what he's facing and be prepared to support him. If the roles were reversed, he would've already been giving you advice and asking how he could help you."

She steps out from under the umbrella and continues on her way.

"Daisy, I miss you. I'm sorry for what I did to you at the water park. I'm sorry I was such a dick and hurt you when you absolutely didn't deserve that. I'm asking for a second chance. What we felt was not just an island fling. It was real and you know it. You still feel it too. Don't walk away now. We can move past this hurdle together."

Her steps halt and she stands stock still for several heartbeats, the rain drenching her hair and clothes, but she doesn't seem to notice. She slowly turns to face me again. I'm convinced the anger in her eyes would burn holes through me if I were any closer.

"You're *what?* You're *sorry?* If you think an apology makes it go away, you're fucking crazy. I opened up to you, Rod. I trusted you in ways I've never trusted a man before, and never will again. What you did to me can't be fixed with a simple apology and thinking I should just let it go. When you say 'move past it,' it's essentially the same as telling me to get over it. You don't get to belittle how you made me feel or pretend it never happened. *You* did this, Rod. *You* move past it. *You* let it go. *You* get over it. *Without. Me.*"

She turns on her heels and jogs the rest of the way to her car, leaving me standing in the middle of the aisle. The open umbrella hangs loosely at my side while the rain soaks through my clothes until my skin is drenched too. But it's not the cold from the temperature outside that leaves me chilled to the bone.

I have to face the harsh facts, regardless of how much it hurts to admit. Not only am I a shitty boyfriend, I'm also a terrible friend to the best man I know.

The first thing I do when I'm in my car is call Kevin back.

"What?" His greeting isn't exactly inviting, but I can't blame him for not wanting to hear from me.

"Talk to me, man. Tell me what's going on so I can help. Whatever you need from me, you've got it. I'm sorry I've been MIA lately."

He sighs heavily into the phone. "It's okay, Rod. You have enough going on with Juliana and Isa as it is. Honestly, I forgot about that momentarily when I called you before because I'm so wrapped up in my own problems. The last thing I want to do is heap more onto your shoulders."

"They're wide enough to help carry your burdens, too. You'd do no less for me, no matter what else was happening in your world. We all have problems, man. Some may be lighter than others, but that doesn't make them any less important. Talk to me. Let me help."

"I'll meet you at your house so you can get home to Juliana. We'll have a beer or twelve and I'll tell you all about it."

"I'm on my way."

WHEN KEVIN FINISHES TELLING ME ABOUT THE ISSUES BETWEEN him and Tracy, all I can do is stare while trying to formulate a coherent response.

"Shit, man."

That's the best I've got.

"Right?" At least he understands me.

"We are in the twenty-first century, aren't we? I mean, I can't believe people actually still think in those bass-ackward ways. You're the best man for her, regardless of what color skin either of you has. I'll stand shoulder to shoulder beside you, defending you with my last breath. Just tell me what I can do to help. You know I've got your back, Kevin."

"For now, that's enough. When I figure out how best to approach this, I'll let you know. If you come up with any bright ideas, throw them my way, brother. I need all the help I can get."

"I'll do my best."

"You waited for Daisy, didn't you?" He needs a change of subject, I get it. That one is still sore, though.

"Yeah, I did." I recount the entire conversation, including how I realized what a terrible friend I am, and wait for his agreement.

"You've never been a terrible friend to me, Rod. We've been best friends since middle school, but you never allowed me to ride your coattails. You helped me realize the value of hard work and applying myself to learn everything I can at an early age. But you were always there to pick me up and dust me off when I fell, and there hasn't been one day I've doubted your friendship."

"Don't make me cry. You've already called me a little girl today as it is." We laugh and take another swig of beer. "You don't give yourself enough credit. You were already working hard and making your own way. We simply encouraged each other to keep doing better than we did the day before."

"You know I've got nothing but love for you, brother, so believe me when I say this. You are the wrong man for Daisy. I know the word failure isn't in your vocabulary, but you have to accept defeat in this situation. You tried to make it work, then you tried to fix your mistakes, and both attempts ended in disaster. Now stay away from her so she can be happy with someone else."

I can't make that promise, even if it would be for the best.

After we finish the twelve-pack, Kevin takes the bedroom in the area where the man cave is and where we've spent the night drinking and talking. He'd normally sleep in the guest bedroom upstairs, but he understands the need to distance himself from Juliana.

Since Juliana officially moved in with me after her hospital stint, we've taken extra precautions and kept visitors away to avoid passing germs to her. The treatments she has to kill the cancer are brutal, decimating her immune system to the point a common cold could kill her. Even Isa has become an expert on washing her hands and being careful around her mom.

Still, Juliana insists on being part of the meeting with Daisy tomorrow night. Not that I don't understand her need to be part of her daughter's life. I'm just trying to keep them both in mine.

CHAPTER TWENTY-SEVEN

Daisy

Knowing I had to go to Rod's after work made today the longest day I've experienced in years. I think I looked at the clock every minute of the day, watching the second hand tick at a relentlessly slow pace. I don't mind going to meet with him and Juliana to talk about Isa, but anything personal is off-limits. His apology was more insulting than endearing, and my anger and humiliation haven't diminished.

He's in my life by necessity, but I'm not allowing him back into my heart by choice.

Cam and I had the same free period today, so we spent it together mapping out possibilities for expanding the summer camp to help more students than ever before. He has as much enthusiasm about this project as I do, and it's so refreshing to have someone else to share the load. He asked about Rod in a roundabout way, but he was respectful to not cross the line into prying. There's no way Cam didn't feel the tension while Rod stood beside our table, so I admitted to meeting Rod before realizing his niece attended our school.

I left the conversation with a very vague reference of "meeting" him. There's no need to get into the intimate details.

The *intimate details* should be the last thought on my mind as I drive to Rod's. I jotted down his address from the updated forms he turned in to the office with the guardianship papers. Tracy and Kevin said he was well known in certain circles for his lucrative business, but I had no idea he'd amassed this level of wealth until I pull into his gated driveway.

Thick woods line each side of the drive and surround the enormous mansion, providing complete privacy. The lush lawns and shrubbery beds are professionally manicured and maintained. Directly in front of the long, palatial steps leading to the door is an ornate fountain with choreographed spurts of water, creating a circular drive in front of the house.

I've never seen such a posh home in person, so I'm not entirely sure what the proper protocol is. Erring on the side of caution, I pull around to the far side of the fountain and park out of the way before Landen and I make our way to the front door. When I press the doorbell, elegant chimes ring throughout the multi-level entryway. Within seconds, a staff member dressed in a stylish suit welcomes me inside.

The tailor-made suits, expensive watches, and overall wealthy air that Rod exudes in person never could've prepared me for the opulence I see all around me. I feel very underdressed and overwhelmed simply standing in this enormous living room while we wait for the lord of the manor to arrive.

"Hi. You must be Daisy and Landen." I turn to find a stunning young woman smiling at us from the doorway. Her head is covered with a long stylish scarf that matches her outfit. "It's so nice to meet you both at last. I'm Juliana, Isabelle's mom."

"There's no doubt about that." I laugh lightly as I extend my hand. "Isa looks exactly like you."

"She's my mini-me, that's for sure."

Isa comes bounding into the room, full of energy and smiles. She wraps her arms around her mom's leg and looks up at her with the most adoring expression for a moment. The bond between mother and daughter is made of steel, that much is clear. Then she turns her attention to Landen and me with a shy smile and red-tinged cheeks.

"Hi, Miss Daisy." She waves at me by wiggling her little fingers up and down.

"Hi, sweetheart. Do you remember Landen from the other day?"

"Uh huh." She nods enthusiastically and her cheeks turn a deeper shade of red.

"Yeah, I remember you too." Landen smiles at Isa.

"Why don't you two come in the kitchen? Louise, the house manager, made an entire buffet of delicious food for us. Then the kids can enjoy the playroom while we chat." Juliana absently strokes Isa's hair, but I see the signs of a loving family very clearly. Isa knows she's loved by both of her caretakers, but her sense of security comes from her mother.

"That sounds perfect, but I hope you didn't go to any trouble for us."

"It's my pleasure, and it's no trouble at all. I'm grateful to have an adult female to talk to for a change. My best friend, Karen, has been traveling for work a lot, so I've been stuck here with Rod. Alone. I love my brother and I don't know what I'd do without him, but there's only so much testosterone I can take."

"Oh, I already like you. You and I will become best friends, I can tell."

"I certainly hope so. I can't whip my brother into shape by myself. If twenty-five years as his sister has taught me anything, it's that he's as stubborn as he is generous. Come on, let's feed these kids so we can have some girl time."

We follow her into the enormous gourmet kitchen. My jaw drops when I see the expansive spread with too many types of food to count. An older lady is busy at the double wall oven, removing hot scones that smell so good they make my mouth water.

"This is Louise. She manages everything related to the house, the staff, and she keeps Rod in line in her spare time." All three of us laugh, knowing there's not much chance of that, and Louise and I exchange hellos.

"Make yourself at home, my dears. The house may look formal, but nothing could be further from the truth." Louise plates the desserts and urges us to eat as much as we want.

When I look to Juliana to let her go first, I realize the walk between the living room and kitchen depleted any energy she had when I first arrived. Her skin is pale, and she's gripping the back of the chair to remain standing.

Though I'm not certain of exactly what she's going through, I know Rod has temporary custody of Isa. Glenna said Juliana has cancer, but she didn't have more information than that. Nothing about the prognosis, type, or how long she'll be out of commission. The scarf tied around her head and draped over her shoulder must be to hide her hair loss, so my best guess is she's undergoing treatments now.

"Juliana, why don't you have a seat with the kids, and I'll make our plates. You've already done so much, it's the least I can do."

She manages a slight smile, but her eyes reveal the truth. "You're so polite, and I appreciate it, but it's really not necessary. We can talk openly. Isa knows everything about what's happening to me. I've taken a lot of time to explain my condition to her. I have a form of leukemia, so the high doses of chemo and radiation make it difficult to perform even the easiest tasks. But I'm not in inpatient isolation anymore, so I consider that progress."

Louise sets a plate in front of the chair where Juliana stands, then winks at me when she returns to the oversized island for more food. "It's no wonder Rod's wrapped around your little finger. You are beautiful on both the inside and outside."

"Um, I think you have me confused with someone else." I pick up two plates and pile them with food for both Landen and me, while Louise makes Isa's. "If you know about me, then you know Rod and I didn't part on the best note."

"Why don't I move the kids into the playroom and let you ladies have the kitchen to yourselves?" Louise takes Landen's food from me and calls for them to follow her.

After I take the seat opposite Juliana, she studies me closely for a moment before speaking. "Louise is right, you know. I'd never betray my brother, but he's betraying himself in this case. Did you know he called me from Punta Cana and told me all about you?"

My chest feels like it's been hit by a two-by-four at full force. My lungs seize and I can't breathe for a moment. Why would he call her to talk about me? I'm too curious about this conversation to remain cool and unaffected by her revelation. Now I need all the details, what he said, what she said, what his fucking problem was our last day together.

"No, I didn't. That's not what he told me about the call. He said he asked questions about his personality flaws. Why would he tell you about me?" The plate full of scrumptious food has lost its appeal. I'm not sure I could force the first bite past the lump in my throat now.

"Rod and I didn't have the best childhood experience. Our dad left to pick up medicine for me and never came home. Mom worked herself to death just to make ends meet, so Rod became a parent in addition to my brother. No matter what we faced, we had each other, and he has more than tried to make up for what we went through as kids. But those experiences have scarred him in ways he doesn't even recognize.

"When he called, he said he wanted me to verify if something Kevin said to him was true. But I know him better than he thinks. The underlying reason for the call was because he fell head over heels for you, and that scared the shit out of him. I had a frank conversation with him. He and I are extremely blunt with each other, and I thought I'd gotten through to him. Before we hung up, I even told him not to come home without you."

"But he did. He made sure of that before our trip was even over."

"If you don't mind my asking, what happened? He

wouldn't tell me anything, only that I didn't need to worry about him right now."

Before I can catch myself, I word-vomit the entire story, beginning to end, telling her every humiliating detail of that day and how badly it ended. When I finish, I realize how quickly I unloaded on her and immediately regret it.

"I'm sorry. That was inappropriate of me, but now I can't take it back. You probably weren't expecting all that."

"Don't be sorry. I'm glad you told me. Now I can kick his ass when he gets home." She nibbles on a finger sandwich, but her pallor still hasn't improved yet. "He knows better than to treat *anyone* like that. He has a lot of explaining to do."

"When will he be home? Should we expect him anytime soon?"

"No, I told him to stay away until I call him. He confessed to approaching you in the restaurant parking lot and para-phrased what happened, so I banned him from this meeting so you and I can talk freely."

"The last thing I want is to cause problems between you two. Even from the few times he mentioned you, it's clear he loves you very much. What happened between us was a shame, but it's hardly the worst thing I've endured. I'll find a way to move on and put this behind me too."

"Don't worry about my relationship with my brother. After everything we've had thrown at us, no problem in this world will ever separate us. But you're right, you need plau-sible deniability, so I'll drop the subject for now. How is Isa doing in your class? I was so worried about her when my doctor put me in an isolation room in the hospital."

"She has her good days and bad days, but I haven't seen anything that would be considered out of the norm for kids her age. She's very smart. I get the impression she understands more of what you're going through than she has stated outright."

"What do her bad days look like? What does she do?"

"Sometimes she's quiet and doesn't interact with the class as much. Other times she's more irritable than usual and can't seem to concentrate. Nothing has been severe enough to cause a specific concern about her, though. Should I be looking for something in particular?"

She shakes her head slowly, then stares at the food on her plate. "You'll think I'm being a helicopter mom with an overactive imagination."

"Try me. I had you two figured out in three seconds flat."

"Her father, Gabriel, skipped out on us when she was three months old. The situation with the two of us was different than what my parents faced, though. I've become the queen of the Google symptoms search, and I've diagnosed him with either bipolar disorder or clinical depression. I haven't decided which yet.

"Isa has so much on her at such a young age, moving in with Rod, the uncertainty she must feel when I'm in the hospital, knowing I'm sick. My fear is his mental health issues are hereditary, and they will surface in Isa because of all this stress."

"I'm not a doctor by any means, but I have seen a lot of behavioral problems in children. Nothing in her demeanor has suggested an underlying mental health issue to me so far, but I'll keep watching her. You'll be the first to know if there's the slightest concern."

With her concerns about Isa settled for the time being, she finishes her meal and her color improves. We move to the lanai which has large patio heaters spaced between the lounge chairs surrounding the enormous pool. Why wouldn't the outside be every bit as stylish as the inside?

Juliana and I talk for hours, sharing our life experiences and heartbreaks, until Louise interrupts to tell us the children fell asleep in the playroom floor. She and I built a genuine connection within the last few hours, and I feel as if I have a new friend for life. When I glance at my watch, I'm surprised to see it's already almost eleven o'clock.

I can't hide my smile when I realize we have banned Rod from his own home all night.

"Before you leave, can I ask for one more imposition?" Juliana bites her lower lip, obviously anxious to finish the question.

"Sure. What's on your mind?"

"With my rigorous chemo and radiation schedule, I rarely have the energy to work with Isa when she gets home from school. Are you available to come over and help, maybe tutor her, even if it's only a couple of days a week? I'll gladly pay you for your time."

"You want me to tutor your kindergartner? You don't think she gets enough learning at school all day? She's a very bright little girl."

"I'm really afraid that Gabriel is bipolar, and he passed it on to Isa. If she's under too much stress, disrupting her schedule could cause some of those behavioral issues to present. I just can't stand to think of her being alone or lonely because of me. Landen is welcome to come with you. We'd love to have a standing playdate for both of them."

"That's a very sneaky way of using the guilt trip method." I arch one brow at her, and her lips curl upward into a full smile. "This isn't a secret ploy to get me to spend time with Rod, is it?"

"No, I wouldn't do that to you. If he's being a jerk, he has to fix that on his own. My request might be as much for me as it is for Isa. I've enjoyed spending time with you tonight, and I think Isa will need more motherly love as my treatments progress."

"All right, then. For you and Isa, I will do it. We should be finished before Rod gets home from work, anyway."

"Thank you so much." She throws her arms around my neck for a hug. "You don't know how much I appreciate this."

Despite her statements to the contrary, I suspect her request is a plot to force Rod and me together. But I'm not worried about that. Avoiding him won't be a problem.

CHAPTER TWENTY-EIGHT

Rod

"Did you have a good Thanksgiving? Enjoy your week off?" I ask Kevin when he walks into my office first thing Monday morning.

"Yes, I had a great week. Daisy's parents came up from Florida and her sister came in from Savannah, so Tracy and I ate with them. We were at her house for so long I thought we were spending the night there too. You would love the entire family, man. Her parents are the least pretentious people I've ever met, despite their success. Some of her aunts, uncles, and cousins showed up, too. She has an enormous family." Kevin continues rambling about Daisy and her family, ignoring the dirty looks I'm shooting him.

"Great. So happy to hear you won the *who was stuffed more* contest against the turkey."

"How was your week? How's Juliana doing?" He ignores my obvious jab.

I turn away from the computer screen and scrape my hands down my face. "Not so good, for either. We had a rough week. Juliana took a sudden turn for the worse and went back in the hospital. Isabelle had a complete meltdown over her mother's illness. She can't sleep without having terrible nightmares and waking up screaming and crying. She's convinced Juliana will die and leave her. And… I've had to face a hard truth about myself."

"What's that?" His tone is tentative, showing he's unsure of how to react to me being on the verge of a breakdown myself.

"The truth is I can't do it all by myself anymore. Take care of Juliana and be there when she needs me. Be a father to Isabelle, staying up all night to comfort her and convince her we'll get through this together. Keep this company going, meet the customers' expectations, gain more clients, and meet the constant demands. I'm tired—physically and mentally. I need a break.

"Over the past few days, I've rehearsed what I'd say to you when I saw you again. For the record, my speech contained nothing I've said so far. The bottom line is, I want to put a vote before the oversight board to make you interim CEO while I take some much-needed time off to take care of my family and myself. You know I don't doubt your ability, but I wouldn't put this responsibility on you without talking to you first. Technically, I don't have to go this route since it's a privately owned business, but their vote of confidence carries over to our clients."

"I'm speechless, Rod. This wasn't even on my radar as a possibility when I took off last week. I'm sorry. I should've called you to check in. How long are you planning to take off?"

"Three months, give or take a week, starting New Year's Day. Juliana should finish this round of treatment around the end of March, and we'll know what the next steps are by then. With Isabelle's three-week Christmas break coming up soon, this is the perfect time to begin preparing our clients for my upcoming absence. I can call for an emergency board meeting, complete the vote, and spend the next two weeks catching you up on what I've been working on. What do you think?"

"I've never let you down before, Rod. I'm not about to start now. I'm willing to do whatever it takes to help you and those girls, regardless of how long it lasts. A week or a year makes no difference to me."

"Thank you, Kevin. I never doubted you, but hearing you say the words makes me feel so much better. This company has been my entire life since I was a teenager, staying up late to learn programming language on my own. But I said I'd do whatever was best when it became a household name. There's no one else in the world I'd trust more to take over my baby than you."

I call for an early afternoon emergency meeting, even though every board member isn't available on such short notice immediately after the holiday. We only need the majority vote, though, and there are enough around to cover that. After I explain the situation with my family and Kevin's interim role, they unanimously vote him in as interim CEO with full confidence.

For the next solid week, Kevin and I spend as much of our days together as possible to ensure a smooth handoff of my open items. I've introduced him to most of my key contacts and have tried to steer them in his direction when they continue coming to me for assistance. For the most part, the transition is as seamless as I anticipated. But there's always that one client who refuses to deal with anyone else. That one client, in this case, happens to be a vitally important one to our company.

For them, I've still attended every meeting and answered every email, keeping Kevin on copy as an added emphasis. Today, that client is experiencing multiple issues with the integration of our software with their new interface. Downtime for any business is deadly to the bottom line, so we're all-hands-on-deck to find the mismatched data and correct it. My assistant clears my schedule so Kevin and I can work with the team of developers to locate the problem. We roll up our sleeves and return to the trenches where we started, all packed in one room so we can quickly share discoveries.

After hours of combing through data, I glance at my watch and realize it is already time to pick Isabelle up from school. With the bumper-to-bumper Atlanta traffic between my office and her school, there's no way I'll make it there before the staff leaves.

"Kevin, can you give me Daisy's number, please? I'm late leaving work to pick up Isabelle, and I need to ask if she can stay in Daisy's classroom until I get there."

He's torn, but ultimately, he understands there's no other way. He texts her contact information to my phone and I call her as I rush out to my car. She's been coming to my house a few afternoons during the week to help Isa with her work and distract her from Juliana's absence.

"Hello?" Her tone is tentative over the unknown number calling her.

"Daisy, it's Rod. Don't hang up. This is about Isabelle."

"What do you need, Rod?" She's strictly business with me, cutting me no slack.

I explain the situation and make my request. She's silent for a moment, but then she replies. "I'll bring her to your house, so just meet me there. I promised Juliana I'd still work with Isa after school, and that promise is even more important now that Juliana's back in the hospital."

"That's even better. I can't thank you enough. I'll be there as fast as humanly possible in Atlanta rush-hour traffic." I hurry out the door and jump into my car, winding through traffic and cursing the red lights until I finally reach my house.

When I pull into the circular drive, Daisy and Isabelle are already there waiting for me. I meet them at the front door and invite Daisy inside with us.

"Thanks again. You saved my neck."

"Today is one of the days I'd be here to work with Isa, anyway. There's no need for you to leave work early every day. If you update the documentation in the office, she can ride home with Landen and me after school. Technically, she wasn't supposed to leave with me since I wasn't on the approved list." Daisy keeps her tone all business, not giving an inch on her *no Rod's allowed* stance.

"You're right. Consider it done. I'll also give you a spare key so you can come and go as you please, even when my house staff isn't here. I appreciate your help more than I can tell you."

"Will she stay here with Louise while we're out of school?"

"Yes, she will." I don't bother to tell her I've taken off work to spend time with Isa and Juliana starting then.

"I'll come over earlier in the day during the school break so I won't interrupt your evenings."

"Whatever time is best for you works for me. You're not interrupting anything. It's time for an after-school snack. Landen, are you hungry?"

"Yes, I'm starving. Lunch feels like it was forever ago."

"Let's go to the kitchen and see what Louise made for us today. I bet it's something good." Landen takes one hand, Isabelle takes the other, and three of us venture off to find food. When we turn the corner, I catch Daisy smiling after us.

"Louise always has something good for us." Isa seems to be in a better state of mind today than she was last week, and for that I'm grateful.

When Juliana was first admitted into the hospital, daytime wasn't as bad for Isa as nights were. She cried uncontrollably, her entire body shook, and she couldn't release her hold on me. I held her in my arms all night, trying to soothe her fears and reassure us both that Juliana would still be alive in the morning. With the breaking of dawn, we'd call the hospital and Juliana would muster her strength to tell her baby how much she loved her. Juliana asked that we not come to the hospital while she was in the medically required isolation room. With Isa's increasing anxiety issues, seeing each other without being able to comfort became harder on both little ladies with each visit.

Juliana started improving again over the weekend. It was enough to give us hope her immune system will be strong enough to come home for the upcoming holidays. Isa latched on to every improvement and every upturn her mother made. My ardent prayers were fixed on her continued recovery, because her daughter couldn't cope with anything less. To be honest, I wasn't so sure I'd be able to handle anything else myself.

This morning when we called, Juliana's voice sounded much stronger than it had in the past several days. She was eager to be released and come home to her family.

"Mom, come look at what Miss Louise made. It smells so good." Landen yells for Daisy as he approaches the buffet of food.

She walks in, ruffles his hair, and looks at Louise. "You spoil us too much. Next thing you know, we'll be over here every day, demanding to be fed like a bunch of stray cats."

"Wouldn't that just be terrible? I suppose I'll have to be more careful. Oh, I almost forgot to tell you. The homemade doughnuts will be ready in just a few minutes."

"That's it. We're moving in, Miss Louise." Landen beams up at her, his smile contagious.

"Don't think I wouldn't take you, little boy." Louise winks at him, obviously falling more in love with him every day.

There are so many questions I want to ask Daisy about Landen, but the time is never right. Today is certainly not the day to pry into her past. She's barely speaking to me, but at least she acknowledges I'm alive as we gather around the table to eat together. I have to be careful not to upset that delicate balance. One wrong word and I'm dead to her again.

"Mr. Rod, can I ask you a question?" Landen looks up at me, his big blue eyes inquisitive.

"You can call me Rod, and yes, you can ask anything you'd like."

"If you and my mom got married, would that make Isa my little sister?"

Daisy coughs violently, choking on the sip of iced tea that she had just taken, then stands up to step away from the table.

"Um, no, buddy. Isa is my niece, not my daughter. If your mom and I married, that would make Isa your cousin."

"Oh. I already have lots of cousins. I want a little sister, though. Mom said I can have one when storks start dropping babies from the sky again. But I've never even seen a stork in Atlanta."

Louise and I stifle a laugh, not wanting Landen to think we're making fun of him. "Well, maybe a stork will do a fly-by one night and drop a baby off on your doorstep. Stranger things have happened."

Daisy retakes her seat with a shake of her head. "He doesn't need more encouragement in that area, Rod. He has wanted a little sister a long time now."

The idea of someone else granting that wish sets me on edge. Whatever this thing we've found is still there, trying to convince me fate is a real being. It's telling me Daisy and I belong together and drawing me to her with my every breath. Yet I fought that loving feeling with all I had… until I realized I have nothing without her. Now I may have succeeded in pushing her away for good.

After we finish the snacks, Daisy takes Isa and Landen to the playroom to work with them. Landen works on his second-grade homework while Isa works on more drawings and paintings. The creative process helps to get her inner feelings about her mom out on paper so Daisy can help her verbally work through them. That's the hope and goal of the exercise, anyway.

While they're busy with their work, I head to my office and start working on a secret project of my own. If I can't concentrate on the work at my company, at least I can focus my attention on something I enjoy.

After a couple of hours, someone raps lightly on my door before opening it. "Rod? Are you in here?"

"Yeah, come on in. What can I do for you, Daisy?" Anything. Anything at all.

"I wanted to tell you Isabelle just talked to her mom on the phone, and she seems to be coping with everything well, for now anyway. Juliana sounds so much better tonight, and Isa could tell. Your sister is waiting for you to call her, and Isabelle is waiting for her bath. Landen and I are going home now."

"Thank you for all your help today, bringing Isa home and spending time with her. I don't know what we'd do without you." I stand and walk around to the front of my desk. Daisy takes a step backward.

"As long as Jules and Isa need me, I'll be here for them. They're each suffering with something that's unfair to both of them. If I can help carry some of the burden to get them over this hump, then I'm happy to help. That goes for bringing her home after school, too. Just text me to let me know if you need my help again."

"Thank you. I may have to take you up on that occasionally, but I won't make a habit of it. Promise."

"Good night, Rod."

"Sweet dreams, Daisy."

A flashback of our time on the island flickers in her mind, but she pushes it aside before closing the door on her way out.

I hope those memories turn the tide in my favor, and away from the date she just had.

CHAPTER TWENTY-NINE

Daisy

When the kids and I walk into Rod's mansion, the sweet aroma of hot scones baking immediately makes my stomach growl and my mouth water.

"It must be time for afternoon tea again, Princess Isa. Smells like Louise is fattening us up for the holidays." I chuckle and ruffle her hair.

"That means I have to go change. I can't go to tea dressed in these old rags." She drops her book bag and takes off toward her bedroom.

"I'm not dressing up for snacks. I'm just going to eat them." Landen rushes toward the kitchen, leaving me to pick up their belongings out of the hallway.

Rod emerges from his home office with a long face and bloodshot eyes. My heart drops to my feet.

Juliana.

"What is it, Rod? What's happened?"

"Can you come in here and have a seat for a minute?"

"Of course."

He closes the door behind me and absently moves around his desk to his chair, covering his mouth with his hand and largely lost in his thoughts. I drop down in the chair across from him, just in time before my knees give out. Is he about to tell me Juliana has taken a turn for the worse? Have we lost her? My mind swirls with all the possibilities and terrible scenarios while I wait for him to gather his thoughts.

"Juliana asked her oncologist to call me to talk about her treatment. We hung up not five minutes before you walked in, so I haven't had time to digest everything he said yet. I knew this was coming, but the urgency in his voice has increased. She needs a bone marrow transplant because she hasn't reached remission with the cocktail of drugs and radiation.

"A couple of weeks ago, I went in for a cheek swab to see if I'm a match with her tissue type. The results came back, and I'm not a match. From what he explained, that's not uncommon. A family member will match only thirty percent of the time. But I'd hoped we'd be in that lucky category."

"Now what happens?"

"Now, we pray someone on the donor registry will be the best tissue match for her, and that they'll answer when they're called. The problem is, it can take anywhere from several weeks to several months to find a match going that route. It's just really disappointing and I worry about how much more she can take."

"She's strong-willed, Rod, and she's a mother. She will endure whatever she has to not to leave her daughter. She won't give up."

"I know you're right, but she's all… I've spent my entire life protecting her. Taking care of her. Now I feel—" He hesitates for a moment, searching for the word that's on the tip of his tongue.

"Helpless." I understand that word all too well.

After an extended silence and soul-touching stare, he nods. "Helpless." He scrapes his hand over his face and squeezes his eyes shut. "She beat T-Cell Non-Hodgkin's Lymphoma when she was five years old. She was so sick, but she was so brave.

"Our father went to pick up her medicine at the pharmacy one night and never came back. He left a note on the table that basically said he couldn't take the pressure anymore. Every day since then, I've strived never to be our father."

"You took care of her during that time?" He couldn't have been more than fourteen years old.

"Yeah, I did. I slept in a chair beside her bed every night in case Juliana needed me, and so Mom could rest between her multiple jobs. So to come this far only to lose her now is like adding insult to injury. It also makes me hate our father so much more."

The empath in me wants nothing more than to gather him in my arms and hug the pain away, but the realist in me forbids it. I'm keeping my distance from him for a reason. Conversations about Juliana and Isa are fine, but any feelings for him are against the rules. My rules. But these glimpses into his past and his psyche are more telling than anything else I've heard from him.

That he only mentioned his mother in passing, but with such reverence, reveals a lot too. She slept while he watched over the little one, so he felt responsible for her well-being too. His heart is bigger than he shows, but it's guarded inside an impenetrable fortress.

"You know I'll do whatever I can to help. I'll be glad to get tested, organize a drive to test as many as possible, whatever she needs." I almost said, "whatever you need," but caught myself in the nick of time.

"We'll take any help we can get. She needs this transplant to beat the cancer. Everything takes time, so all we can do is keep her going until then. Thanks for letting me bend your ear. I needed a few minutes to process all the information the doctor just threw at me before talking to Isa." He leans back in his chair, his eyes drifting to the window, and he stares off into space.

"Don't tell her anything yet. You don't have enough answers and she shouldn't be left in limbo right now. Juliana will continue treatment until we find a match. Until then, everything stays the same, and that's all Isa needs to know."

"You're right. In a way, I wish I didn't know either. Thank you, Daisy. For everything." The look he's giving me is far too intimate, too grateful for my help and my presence during this grueling time.

"No need to thank me. I'll look into the registry when I get home tonight. We should probably go to the kitchen and help Louise with the kids now." I stand and move to the door before my emotions get the better of me.

He's hurting and I want to comfort him, but I have to keep my distance to protect myself. Intense situations like this one create too much confusion and blur lines I don't intend to cross. One touch, regardless of the innocent intent, and I'd lose all composure. I knew he'd break my heart the moment I met him. My mind tried to warn me, tried to reason with me, but I wouldn't listen, and I've paid the price for my stubbornness.

With my back to him, I twist the doorknob and release a relieved sigh because freedom is only a step away. Then his hand flattens against the door and his chest pushes against my back.

"Wait." His lips graze the shell of my ear. His deep voice sends a wave of goosebumps down my arm. "I don't know how to make up for what I did in Punta Cana. If there was any one thing, hell, even a *hundred* things, that would let me take it all back, I'd gladly do it.

"Before you go, I want you to know something. The reason I left the island without saying anything is because I had a voicemail about Juliana's cancer. When I heard it, I was incapable of doing anything except getting back home to her. I helped raise her, Daisy. She's almost as much my daughter as she is my little sister, and she's all I have left of my family. If my rushed departure hurt you in any way, I sincerely apologize. I simply couldn't think straight."

"Thank you for telling me that, Rod. Don't think you have to apologize for that, though. It's completely understandable, and anyone in the world would've done the same for their siblings. Had I gotten that message about my sister, I would've been on the next plane home, too. Now that I've gotten to know Juliana, I would've come home for her, too. She loves you as much as you love her. I don't know if you realize this, but you're all she has, too."

He rests his forehead to my shoulder, and I feel his body tremble against mine. I squeeze my eyes shut, hold on to the doorknob with all my might, and fight the urge to face him. Then I feel dampness soak through my blouse to my skin and his shoulders begin to shake, and I'm a goner. When I spin around to face him, I catch a glimpse of tears streaming down his face before his arms encircle me, drawing me against him in an embrace so tight I barely can breathe.

My arms instinctively wrap around his neck and I stroke the back of his hair with my fingers, while whispering soothing reassurances. "Everything will be okay, Rod. We won't stop until we've helped her beat this once and for all. You won't lose her, and I won't leave you to face this alone. I'll be right here every step of the way."

We drop to the floor in a heap, his weight pulling me down with him, but my body intuitively reacts as if we're one. While holding on to me, he rearranges us so I'm straddling his lap, his arms are around my waist, and he buries his face in the crook of my neck.

If not for the tears I feel falling onto my skin, I'd dash out of this room in search of safety from the desire screaming inside my mind. But his intense agony is palpable, and as a fellow human being who shares his fears, I can't leave him to suffer through this alone. Though my heart is heavy remembering how we parted, I push that aside and focus on today.

Then I feel his lips on my neck, softly caressing the sensitive skin there and setting my body on fire. His tight grip around me loosens, and he splays his hands on my back, the heat of his hands searing my skin through the thin material of my shirt. He slides them up my back and around to my face, never breaking contact. He leaves kisses along my jawline as he works his way toward my mouth.

I'm holding my breath, as if that'll somehow shield me from the need building inside me.

He stops just short of his lips reaching mine before he

looks up at me. Our eyes lock, and I feel as if I'm staring into a mirror. We're a breath's width away from spontaneously combusting into flames. Desire shines in his blue eyes, along with so many other emotions swirling just beneath the surface.

In his eyes, I see regret for the past, hope for the present, and uncertainty for the future. We have an inability to mutter those three little words, an invisible wall that prevents us from growing too close, and years of creating masks and layering ice around our hearts.

The longing to tear it all down is there. But the need to keep it all intact, to preserve our own sanity, is in control.

All these emotions stretch between us, contained in a single heartbeat.

"I need you, Daisy." His voice is strained, with misery, with heartbreak, and with a deep vulnerability he's completely uncomfortable showing. "I need to feel your warmth, your touch, your love."

"Rod" I don't know what else I meant to say. All I can do is utter his name in response.

I'm not a pushover. I'm not weak. I'm not prone to falling for promises in the dark that'll never be fulfilled in the light.

But something about what this man makes me feel has been so different from anyone else I've ever met. Is it fate? Or destiny? Is the universe pushing us together?

"I've fucking missed you so much. You have no idea how much."

"Oh, God…" Those two words are all I can muster.

Our mouths clash with a heated fervor, unable to get enough of the other. His hands slide under my dress and push my panties to the side. He pushes his finger deep inside me, and I suppress the moan aching to escape. He increases his tempo and my hips rock, keeping time and searching for more. With he adds a second finger, I clamp my teeth down on his shoulder and dig my fingers into his skin, riding the wave of pleasure until it subsides. My hands move to his zipper, desperate to free him.

With his pants out of the way, I position him at my entrance. He holds my face in his hands as I sink lower, taking as much of him inside me as I can. My hips rock front to back, side to side, and grinding in circles, searching for that sweet release. As I move up and down, we sync our movements. He thrusts upward as I descend on him once more. Our sensual frolic turns frantic instantly, and he flips us so that's he's on top and driving relentlessly into me. When we reach the edge, he covers my mouth with his and swallows the cries that would've reverberated throughout his enormous mansion.

He collapses on top of me, his chest heaving for breath from the exertion. He's still inside me, still pulsating after his release, and I have no clue what to expect next. When he eventually pushes up, he avoids making eye contact when he suggests we quietly move to separate bathrooms to clean up before joining the others.

Regret instantly fills me as I realize what just happened. Or, I should say *why* it happened.

His needing me, missing me, wanting to feel me again, none of it had anything to do with *me*. He's using sex to feel some kind of connection to another person outside of his family. The way he keeps everyone else in his life at arm's length is a form of self-preservation. But when they remain disconnected, it only reaffirms the notion he's not lovable.

He just used me as his latest attempt to self-medicate and

escape from his world for a short time. I let him, still trying to see the best in him.

When I emerge from the hall bathroom, I hear his laughter from the kitchen as he teases the kids. I join them, standing back to observe before announcing my presence. He glances over his shoulder when the children notice me, but he doesn't say anything.

He acts as if nothing just happened between us, as if what happened meant nothing to him. That's the hard truth I have to come to terms with sooner rather than later. He's emotionally incapable of having an adult relationship, overcoming his commitment fears, or allowing his true feelings to flow freely. He'll suppress them, he'll deny them, and he'll avoid them at all costs.

Any time I'm around him, I have to do the same and stop being a glutton for punishment.

When they finish eating, I take the kids to the playroom to get away from Rod and to refocus my attention on the time and attention they need from me. After about an hour, the door opens, and Rod slips inside with a sheepish grin on his handsome face. He sits in a child-size chair watching the three of us at work, then he eventually moves to sit on the floor beside me.

While Landen and Isa are busy talking and finger painting, Rod leans over toward me. "Are you mad at me?"

"Nope."

"In this case, that definitely means yes. I'm sorry, Daisy. I just keep screwing up, don't I?"

I cut my eyes to meet his. "What exactly are you sorry for this time, Rod?"

"I'm sorry for not knowing how to deal with what I feel

for you. I'm sorry for not knowing if I should announce to the world, much less to the kids, that you're my girlfriend even if you don't see me as your boyfriend.

"I'm sorry for not knowing if boyfriend and girlfriend are even the right terms to use. That feels too much like the high school bullshit I'd rather forget. So, I'll say it this way instead. I'm yours and you're mine, and I'm sorry for not knowing how or when to convey that fact to the world, or even to my household. I'm sorry for making you think for one second you're not enough. I'm sorry I'm such a screw-up… and I'm sorry this isn't the last time you'll be hurt or mad because of me.

"Most of all, I'm sorry I'm not the man you deserve."

He expects sympathy and understanding right now. Too bad I'm fresh out of both.

"You had a rough childhood, I get it. You had to deal with adult situations when the others your age could be kids. But you overcame every obstacle that was thrown at you to become the successful man you are today. At some point, you have to move past the sins of your father and accept responsibility for your own."

I stand and sling my purse over my shoulder. "It's time to go home, Landen. Put the toys back where they go and tell Isa goodnight."

Then I turn my attention back to Rod. "How much longer do you think it's okay to continue blaming your parents for your actions as an adult? How long would you allow your employees to get away with that bullshit?"

CHAPTER THIRTY

Daisy

"Hey, Daisy. Guess what? I've got the best news." Juliana's excitement is contagious, even over the phone. "I'm going home today. It feels like I've been in this isolation room forever, but my labs are finally good enough for me to come home. I'm being paroled!"

I laugh along with her. "That's the best news I've heard in weeks, Jules. I know a little girl who will be thrilled to have you home again."

"I can't thank you enough for all you've done for her. She raves about you and Landen nonstop every time I talk to her. For what it's worth, so does Rod. He won't stop talking about you, how much Isa loves you, and how you've been such a life-saver for him. I think he's told me everything there is to know about Landen over this past week."

Even though she meant it as a compliment, I can't help but

cringe at her words. Rod knows Landen as he is today, but he doesn't know anything else. When Rod and I were on the island, I never mentioned my son. Maybe that was wrong of me, but I wasn't ready to share that part of my life with him after knowing him for such a short time.

Turns out, my instincts were spot-on, because he sabotaged our relationship before it had a chance to breathe. Whatever he's saying to her about me now may be nice, but I can't believe a single word of it.

Juliana has shared pretty much everything about Isa's father and what happened between them, making me feel somewhat guilty for not reciprocating. But even Tracy doesn't know the full story because I could never bring myself to say the words out loud. Some stories are better kept close to the vest.

"You know I love Isa. Helping you or her is not a burden at all. Do you need a ride home? I have plenty of free time today. My parents flew into Atlanta yesterday and took Landen back to Florida with them for our winter break. He's spending three and a half weeks on a south Florida beach, soaking up the sun and enjoying the warm sand."

"Why didn't you go with him? Are you crazy?"

"It's good for him to spend time with them away from me, and I enjoy having a break from being a responsible adult for a few days. Even though I end up missing him after a couple of days and wish he were here with me. I'll head down just before Christmas. Thankfully, Santa had Landen's gifts shipped to their house so he'll get his presents on Christmas morning."

"Sneaky—I love it. Rod is working in the office today instead of at home, so if you're available to pick me up, that would be great. I know he'll leave if I ask him, but he's already given up so much for me."

"I am ready, willing, and able to come break you out of prison and take you on a whirlwind adventure."

"A whirlwind adventure along the fourteen miles between Emory and Paces Ferry Road?"

"Exactly. We're both far too comfortable at home to go anywhere else. I'm walking out my front door right now. I'll see you in a few minutes."

We disconnect and I drive to Emory, thinking about her fortuitous release from the hospital just before the holidays. Isa's favorite present will be having her mother home again.

When my phone rings again, I half expect it to be Juliana, asking where I am and threatening to walk the rest of the way to meet me. I wouldn't blame her. I'm not a very good patient, either. But it's not who I thought it would be.

"How's my best friend in the entire world?" I ask as a greeting.

"Your BFF in the whole world is wondering why she hasn't heard from her BFF in a week. Do you have an explanation for this abandonment?"

"Do you mean other than being extremely busy at work, completing documentation on twenty students before the end of the quarter, and helping Juliana with Isa after school? Not really."

"Fine. The whole helping Juliana thing is your only saving grace. Work is never an excuse to avoid me, though."

"I'm not avoiding you, yet. Are you and Kevin still driving to Florida with me for Christmas at my parents' house?"

"Try to stop us. You know I'm not going home to my family for the holidays, even though Kevin is still pushing me to introduce him to them. He's not as adamant about it as he was at first, but the underlying tension is still there whenever we get around the subject."

That breaks my heart for her because I know how hard that meeting would be for her, and for him, even if he thinks he can smooth it over.

"Maybe you should try meeting them at a neutral place for the first time. Somewhere public, with a lot of people around, so they're less likely to act foolish."

"I'm not convinced even that would work. If you remember, they weren't too thrilled you were my best friend. I fully expect an all-out war when they find out I'm dating Kevin. For now, spending time with your family will have to do."

I remember exactly how her parents reacted the first time I went home with her after school. They didn't believe she should mingle with anyone outside of their specific race, even as friends. Her siblings were much more welcoming, though.

"If nothing else, you know my family will welcome you both. We'll figure the rest out later." My parents have all but legally adopted her, anyway.

"About family, I have a huge favor to ask of you. Don't be mad at me." Her lengthy pause makes me nervous. That's not like her in the least.

"Spill it, Tracy."

"Rod and Juliana always have Christmas with Kevin and his family. Kevin doesn't want to leave them alone this year, especially with Juliana's health issues. What do you think about inviting them to come with us?"

Now it's my turn to be silent, speechless, shell-shocked.

"Daisy, are you still there?"

"Uh, yeah, I'm here... just processing what you're asking of me."

"Look, I feel terrible for even suggesting it, but Rod and Kevin have been best friends almost as long as we have. If there was any other way, I wouldn't ask. But even I can't leave them here alone while we're all together for the holidays. Is there any way you can put the past behind you and invite him?"

For Tracy to ask, I know it's vitally important to Kevin. Then I pull up to the hospital and the nurse wheels Juliana out to my car. One look at her face and I know what I have to say.

"Invite them. It's fine. I'll talk to you later, okay?"

"Okay. Thank you, Daisy. You're the best."

We disconnect just as the nurse opens the door to help Juliana sit in the front seat. She's lost weight since I last saw her, and she didn't have any extra to spare then.

"Hey, stranger." She smiles as she climbs into my car, and her face lights up as I pull away from the curb. Her signature quiet strength is still there.

"Hey, yourself. It's good to see you again. Were your ears burning? I was just talking about you." I glance over at her with my eyebrows raised.

"Yeah? What about?"

I fill her in on Kevin and Tracy's request, then ask if she'll join us.

"A big family Christmas? I'd love to come, if you're sure you don't mind our intrusion." Her fingers grip mine and appreciation swims in her eyes, along with the unshed tears.

"You could never intrude. My parents love having company, and you know I think the world of you and Isa.

Spending Christmas with you will be a treat for me. Three more won't be a problem."

"I can't wait to tell Isabelle. She'll be so excited."

We talk about our plans the entire ride to Rod's with her growing more excited by the minute. I jokingly tell her I think she's more excited than Isa will be. But then I'm immediately proven wrong when we walk inside and she shares the exciting news. Rod is waiting in the wings, listening while propped up against the doorframe.

The excitement of being home, making Christmas plans, and playing with Isa tuckers her out, so Louise helps her into her pajamas then into the bed to take a nap before dinner. I turn to leave, but Rod's hand on my arm stops me.

"Are you sure you don't mind us going with you? I swear I didn't put Kevin up to asking."

"I know you didn't. Like I told Tracy, it's fine. It's Christmas, there will be plenty of people there to mingle with, and it'll be good for Juliana and Isabelle to get away for a while."

"I'm already imposing as it is, but I have a request regarding the travel arrangements. It's for Juliana's safety." He appears humble, but with her current health status, I have no objection to playing it safe.

"No problem. What do you have in mind?"

"We can take my company's jet. That way, Juliana doesn't have to be around a bunch of people and all their germs. Plus, we can stash the presents in the cargo hold so the kids don't see them."

"That's actually a brilliant idea. Landen's gifts are already at my parents' house, but he'll appreciate having them in the jet on the ride home. I'm sure Isa will too, and the kids will keep each other entertained. Sounds like a plan to me."

"Great. I'll arrange everything. I've already talked to the doctor's office about a home health care nurse accompanying us, just in case. Juliana will definitely fight me over that one, but she has to be reasonable. She hasn't gained enough of her strength back yet, so someone has to keep a close watch on her overall health status."

"If you point out she has to do whatever it takes to stick around for Isa, you won't have to fight her very much on it. She'll agree to it for her." I give him a reassuring smile but keep my distance. Getting too close to Rod is not a mistake I'll make again anytime soon. "Tell Jules to call me if she needs help with Isa between now and when we leave for Florida."

"Thanks, Daisy." He looks like he's about to say something else, so I leave before he has a chance. I don't need another gratitude-induced encounter. Those never end well for me.

On the way home, my phone rings, and I automatically assume it's Juliana, since I didn't get to say goodbye before I left.

"Hello?"

"Hi, Daisy. It's Cam. I was wondering if you'd like to have dinner tonight. It's short notice, I know, but I'm hoping you don't have plans already."

My mind tells me to thank him and make up an excuse for why I can't go. "Sure, that would be great. I'm on my way home now from a friend's house and I'm starving."

"If it's okay, I can pick you up in about an hour."

"That's perfect. I'll see you then."

We disconnect as I pull into my driveway, and I sit in the car alone, asking myself what I'm doing. Dating isn't in my playbook, now or in the future. After the continued fiasco with Rod, it's the last thing that should be on my mind. But Cam feels safe with his lack of angsty drama and complete transparency. Plus, I don't have to question if he actually wants to spend time with me or if I'm just a warm body he's with for the time being.

After I call Landen, change clothes, and freshen my makeup, my doorbell rings. A quick glance at my watch tells me Cam is right on time. He's dependable, consistent, and responsible. If I'm going to subject myself to the horrors of dating, that's exactly what I need, not someone who constantly makes me feel I'm losing control.

When I open the door, I burst out laughing before I can catch myself. Cam, such a handsome man, is wearing the ugliest Christmas sweater I've ever seen. It's a green sweatshirt with large white snowflakes, ropes of lighted garland, and red baubles. The gigantic smile on his face is a dead giveaway wearing it was a conscious decision.

"Aren't you festive?" I finally find my voice after my laughing fit.

"Well, 'tis the season and all. You look beautiful, as always." He extends his elbow. "Are you ready to go?"

I grab my bag and keys off the table and nod. "Where are we going?"

Before we leave, he checks to make sure my door latched and locked. "Can't be too careful."

I know that fact all too well.

Over dinner, we spend hours just chatting and laughing, getting to know each other better on a more personal level as each minute passes. We share a lot of the same interests, are passionate about similar causes, and have compatible personalities. Before I know it, the restaurant is nearly empty as we approach closing time. Cam and I have been at this same table all night.

"Our poor waitress. She hasn't been able to get rid of us." I dig into my bag and double the generous tip Cam left on the table to make up for what she would've earned if we'd left earlier.

The ride back to my house is as friendly and chatty as dinner. Cam walks me to my door, and after an awkward moment of hesitation, he leans in to place a soft kiss on my lips. So soft, it's barely perceptible, and I question if I closed my eyes for nothing.

"Good night, Daisy. I'll talk to you tomorrow."

"Good night, Cam."

As he slides into the front seat of his car, I quickly make my way inside, then lean my back against the door. After a few times of intentionally banging my head against it, I release a long held breath.

I'm almost positive he kissed me, just a peck, nothing more than a male relative would do, and I felt nothing.

Less than nothing, in fact.

One touch from Rod and my entire body lights up like the night sky on the Fourth of July.

It's not fair. I don't want Rod to be the one who sends chills down my spine and keeps me awake at night, longing for his touch. Rod shouldn't get to be the one who captures my heart and mind, ruining me for any other man.

I stomp toward my bedroom, mad at Rod and myself for this predicament. When I dig my cell out of my bag, I realize I didn't even glance at it during dinner or the hours of chitchat afterward. One glance at the screen and my heart drops to my feet.

Missed Calls: 19.

All from Rod Stone.

Fearing something happened to Juliana tonight, I take the risk and call Rod, even though it's technically too late. When he answers, I immediately know he's three sheets to the wind.

"Daisheee, where have you been? Have you been a naughty, naughty girl tonight?" He slurs his words, and he's slightly belligerent.

"Why did you call me nineteen times tonight, Rod? Are Juliana and Isa okay?"

"They're fine. Well, as fine as you can be with cancer. But you didn't ask about me. Don't you care if I'm okay, Daisheeee?"

I pinch the bridge of my nose between my thumb and index finger. I'm not in the mood to deal with drunk Hot Rod tonight. "Rod, it's late. We should really have this conversation tomorrow, if you still want an answer to your question then."

"No. No, no, no, no, no. You've been out with that other guy again, haven't you? Camelot…Cameo…Camaro…whatever the fuck his name is. Did you let him steal you from me?"

"I'm really not having this conversation with you when you're too drunk to remember it tomorrow. I'm hanging up now. Don't call me until you're sober."

"If you hang up on me, I'll just come over there and blow your door down."

The thing is, I'm not entirely sure he wouldn't try, at least in his current state. "Fine. What do you want to know? Have I moved on and forgotten about you?"

"Yeah, that's eshacleee what I want to know, Daisheee."

"There's no *h* in my name, Rod, or in 'exactly' for that

matter. But here's your answer, anyway. Yes, I have, and it is past time you did the same. Punta Cana was fun, but it's over."

"What about last week? That meant nothing to you?" He's so drunk, I'm not even sure he realizes what he's asking me. I expect him to pass out mid-sentence any second now.

"You've got to be shitting me. Look, we talked about it before I left, and all you had were lame excuses for why you always pull away from me. I don't believe for one second you're not strong enough to fix your flaws. I'm not one to chase after you like a lost puppy, waiting for you to throw some scraps of your love and attention my way. I'm a grown woman with a child to raise to be a man, and I'm doing my damnedest to make sure he's an admirable man. If you can't be a worthy example for him, you don't belong in my life. Plain and simple."

"I want you back, Daisy, and I don't want to share you with anyone else. Please give me another chance to prove I'm worth all this trouble." His inebriated confession shocks me.

Thoughts fly through my head as I hesitate to respond. I'm visualizing every conceivable outcome of his request. My heart says yes, give him another chance, live happily ever after, go for what I want.

"No, Rod. I can't do that. I'm sorry. Good night."

CHAPTER THIRTY-ONE

Rod

After a bit of negotiating, threatening, begging, and an extended staring contest that I lost, Juliana finally consented to having a home health care nurse come with us to Florida. Thank God for the dedicated health care professionals who work weekends and holidays. I don't want to imagine what could happen otherwise.

"Did you pack your bag?" Juliana asks Isa, referring to the toys she wants to take with her for the two hours we'll be on the plane before reaching Naples.

"Yes, ma'am. It's already in Uncle Rod's car."

"That's my smart girl. What about you, Rod?"

"Yes, ma'am. All my favorite toys are already in my suitcase too." I wink playfully, and she smiles, despite trying not to.

"We're meeting the nurse, Daisy, Tracy, and Kevin at the airport, right?"

"That's right."

I'm both excited and hesitant to see Daisy, who I haven't talked to since last week, when I called her after I'd had way too many shots of bourbon. She kept her promise to visit Juliana and spend time with Isa over the past week, but she went out of her way to avoid running into me. At my own house. I've continued working at home to help both my girls as much as I can, but there are times I still have to go into the office. My official leave of absence begins after the new year starts.

Kevin is running the business like the professional he's always been, but some clients will only deal with me. It's nothing personal against him. The key contacts find change difficult to navigate when our business relationship was established a decade ago. Our history keeps them attached to me, and as long as I'm available, they won't deal with anyone else. It'll just take time to transition them over to Kevin, but we're working on it together. The more exposure they have to him, the more likely they are to accept his help when I'm away.

With both of us away from the office over the holidays, neither of us can officially take off work, especially since we had an extended vacation only a couple of months ago. We'll tag team and handle issues as they come in, relying on each other's strengths to get the job done while we work remotely. Admittedly, my head hasn't been fully in the game over the last several weeks. Reeling over Juliana and driving myself crazy over Daisy hasn't helped me focus on work as much as I have in the past.

I cringe when I recall what I said to her on the phone that night. With no prelude to the conversation, I dumped my shit on her lap and expected her to make it into something worthwhile. Sober, I know better. Drunk, I let my insecurities get the better of me. She was right to call me on how I'd allow my employees to act while at work, and yet I continued to fuck up my chances with her even after that conversation.

I'm my own worst enemy, sabotaging every chance we have to have any kind of relationship.

"We'd better go so we're not late." Juliana tries to herd me toward the door.

"It's not as if my plane will leave without me."

"That's not what I meant. The others shouldn't have to wait for us, Rod." She rolls her eyes at me, not bothering to hide it.

Juliana and Isa walk out to my car while I take one last look around to make sure we haven't forgotten anything. When I slide behind the wheel, I glance over at my sister and concern immediately grips me. She's already tired after walking from the kitchen into the garage. I've always looked forward to the future, never fearing it, until now. The possibility of losing my sister is too real, and more than I think I can bear.

"You're wasting time staring at me. Start the car and drive us to the airport, peon." She doesn't bother to look at me when she issues her command.

"Yes, ma'am. Whatever you say."

Despite Juliana's attempt to be the first to arrive, we're actually the last. No one seems to mind, though, since they're all talking and laughing. Madeleine, the home health care nurse, is here, already part of the gang as if she's always known them. When we join them, the excitement of Christmas and a beach vacation rolled into one gets the better of us, and we're like one big pack of kids. The private airstrip staff checks in our luggage and informs us we're free to board the plane.

"I'm glad your mom enjoys entertaining large groups. How does she feel about loud and rowdy ones?" My attempt to engage Daisy is obvious, but I don't care as long as it works.

"She's used to that. My entire family will be there at one time or another. There's not much she hasn't seen or heard by now." Daisy's answer is polite, but there's a coolness to it I can't pretend I don't feel.

When we walk out onto the tarmac, I notice Juliana intentionally places herself at the end of the line before we reach the jet. Daisy notices, too, and nonchalantly moves to the back of the line to stand beside Juliana. The captain emerges to verify my identity before contacting the tower for clearance to take off, giving me a chance to watch Daisy and Juliana without being overt.

The two ladies chat continuously as they climb the stairs. Daisy is in front of Juliana, stopping on each step to say something to her as the rest of the troop sit down and buckle in. To anyone else, they're simply engaged in conversation. But I know better. I know Daisy is helping her in the only way she knows how—she's preserving Juliana's dignity by appearing to be the one delaying our departure.

My heart swells inside my chest until I think it'll rupture. She's the most loving and thoughtful person I've ever met.

The captain finishes with my identification just as they buckle into their seats, and the crew instructs us to prepare for takeoff. Luckily, I secure a chair facing Daisy, directly across from her. Isa decides to exercise her freedom, from all the way across the aisle, and sits beside Madeline. By the time we reach cruising altitude, Juliana is fast asleep, but her skin isn't as pale as it was before.

"Stop worrying." Madeleine directs her comment to me while removing the stethoscope from her bag. "Her body's been through a lot, so it'll take time to rebuild her stamina. She's a fighter though, and she'll bounce back quicker than you think."

"Thanks for that vote of confidence. It must be obvious if you recognized the signs in me before I even said a word about it."

"I may have seen the same expression on others' faces a time or two." She chuckles then moves to Juliana's side, listening to her heart and her breathing without waking her. My guess is she became so accustomed to it while in the hospital, she doesn't even feel it now. "All good. Let her sleep as long as she wants. It's good for her."

Madeleine moves back to her seat, leaving Daisy and me without a buffer. Where to start?

"Thank you for letting me come with you. I wouldn't have stopped my sister from coming with Isa if you didn't want me here. But I know it was your kind heart that wouldn't allow that to happen. I promise... I'll try my best not to make you mad in any way."

She smiles. "You couldn't quite promise not to do it at all, could you?"

I can't help but laugh. "No, because I don't want to lie. There's no use in denying it either. I have a knack for saying or doing the wrong thing at the worst possible time. It's a gift, really."

"You should regift it, and I don't usually encourage that behavior." Her laugh at my expense is music to my ears.

"There's no way any of us would leave you behind like that, especially at this time of year. Thank you for trying to behave, but don't change on my account. That never works. Just be yourself and let the chips fall where they may."

"I'm not sure who I am anymore, to be honest with you. With everything that's happened, it's hard to tell right-side up from inside out." That's a brutally honest confession, coming from me.

"You realize those two aren't opposites, right? I mean, you can be both at the same time." She tilts her head to the side and lifts her eyebrows.

"See? This is where I'm at in life. That sums it up fairly well, I think." My self-deprecating chuckle doesn't fool her.

"You're doing the best you can with what you have to work with. None of this is easy for anyone, that's for sure. But you have to stop being so hard on yourself, Rod. Besides, that's my job." She has the cutest smirk. It's a cross between an angel and a true smart-ass.

"Easier said than done, I'm afraid. I've been so good at it for so long, I can't give it up now. What would my super-power be then?"

"Being hard on yourself is not your superpower. Pissing me off is. I think you need to pick one to give up as a New Year's resolution, then you can work on the other one later." I love that sassy mouth. Fuck, how I've missed it.

"Fair enough. In that case, I'm willing to give up my current superpower and develop an entirely new one that doesn't involve making you homicidal when I'm around."

"That would help me a lot, because prison orange is just not my color."

The rest of the plane ride goes by way too fast, with us

talking and laughing like friends do. But I meant every word I said. I'll do my best not to screw this up the way I have every other chance she's given me. Maybe it's the time of year. Maybe she's more sentimental than I realized, letting the holidays fill her with cheer. Or perhaps she's more forgiving than she should be, because I don't think I'd be as compassionate and charitable as she is.

When we reach her parents' house, I'm floored by the amount of festive decorations adorning their yard, the outside of their spacious home, and every palm tree in their yard. Even with the bright Florida sun high in the sky, all the lights are lit, and the animated characters are doing their thing.

Landen rushes out to meet us, thrilled to see his mom again. Then he turns his attention to his friend. "Isa, isn't this awesome? You should see it at night."

Isa stares at the trimmings with her mouth gaping open and her eyes as big as saucers. When I glance at Juliana, I realize she's in awe as much as the children are.

A hit-and-run sledgehammer slams into my gut when the stark realization hits me. In all the years I've raised Juliana and helped with Isabelle, we've never celebrated Christmas like this. I was so focused on providing them with the best of the material things money can buy, I never realized these moments, these memories, are what would've stayed with them forever. All the money and success in the world couldn't buy her expression, or replace the many lost opportunities for a lifetime of reminiscing.

I feel like a complete and utter failure.

Daisy's parents come outside to greet us with warm smiles and open arms. Everyone gets a hug and a kiss. They don't care that we've never met. They don't mind that we're not family. They're both thrilled to invite us into their home and share their lives with us in every way.

"Rod, this is my mom, Chelle, and my dad, Brian." Daisy pulls me out of my past and into the present.

"Yeah, we met just a minute ago when your dad laid one on me. I think he snuck a little tongue in there too, I'm not sure." I'm kidding, we all know that, and a little joke helps break the ice, anyway.

"I did, but just a little. I'll do better next time." Brian chuckles as he claps me on the shoulder, then Daisy moves down the line to finish all the introductions.

Brian grabs suitcases out of the SUV we rented and heads toward the door. Kevin and I follow his lead and head to the back of the vehicle.

"Dude, have you ever met parents like that? They literally didn't think twice before kissing *me* when I first met them, and I'm dating a friend of the family. I've never had anyone's parents embrace me the way they do. Too bad they're Daisy's parents instead of Tracy's."

"Then you've been around the wrong people, my friend. You're the best man I know. I don't know what's up with Tracy's family, but they'd never find a better man for their daughter, even if he fits in better with their skin tone."

His brows draw down and a grim expression covers his face. My poor choice of words didn't help. I meant what I said as a compliment, but I may have unintentionally implied he shouldn't be with Tracy. That's not the message I intended to convey at all.

"Hang on, man. Get that thought out of your head. Tracy isn't like her parents, the same way I'm not like my dad. We can't control who raised us, only what we do with the rest of our life."

He nods, his expression brightening a bit. "It's hard to keep that in mind sometimes. I'm working on it, though. I'll get there, eventually. She hasn't given me any reason to doubt her, other than not taking me home to meet the parents yet."

"Did you ever consider you may not want to meet them? Tracy doesn't even go around her family if she can avoid it. Maybe you should cut her some slack. She's crazy about you."

"Maybe you're right." He tucks a bag under his arm before lifting another one. "Maybe you should take your own advice."

"What are you talking about?"

He nods toward Daisy. "You just said you're not your dad and not to judge Tracy by the people who raised her. Take your balls out of your purse and stop being a scared little bitch."

We walk into Chelle and Brian's house and I'm the one rooted to the floor with my bottom jaw hanging open. The outside decorations are nothing compared to what's on the inside. Every room looks like it's been personally decorated by Santa's elves. Lighted garland is draped along the staircase bannister and curves around the second-floor landing. Every room has a tree decorated with a theme that matches the other decorations adorning every surface.

Juliana and Isa wander from room to room, gushing over the elaborate decorations. "Mommy, is this the real North Pole?"

Chelle laughs heartily and bends to speak to Isa. "I wish, my sweet little girl. But no, we're not that lucky. Brian and I just like to make our home as close to the real thing as possible. We might go a little overboard."

"No, this is not at all overboard. This is perfect." Juliana turns in slow circles, trying to take in every detail.

"Mommy, this present has my name on it!"

"It sure does. There may be a few more around here too. You never know." Brian waggles his brows at Isa, and she giggles uncontrollably.

Without warning, the front door swings open, and a large group of people walks in. Before I can move out of their way, arms squeeze my neck and lips leave warm kisses on my cheeks. The oldest man in the group walks over to Daisy, lifts her off the ground, and twirls her around. She squeals with laughter and wraps her arms around him.

"Uncle Adam, put me down, you lunatic. I'm too heavy for you to lift me like this."

"You don't weigh more than a feather, sweet girl." He gives her a big kiss before putting her down.

She turns to the rest of us, makes introductions of her uncle, aunt, and all the cousins, along with their spouses and kids. I'll never remember all the names, but everyone is as warm and welcoming as her parents. When Daisy gets to my little family, I glance over at my sister and niece. The sheer joy on their faces nearly drives me to my knees. I can't recall ever seeing them this happy before.

They're surrounded by a large, loving family. Enveloped in a multitude of arms, kisses, and love, from complete strangers who have a talent for making them feel like a part of the family from the moment they met. In Juliana's twenty-five years, I've never been able to provide this type of environment.

My house may be the largest and most expensive in the area, but it's cold and unwelcoming.

Even when I have the best of intentions, I fuck up the simplest relationship that has the least bit of emotion tied to it.

Though I've never shirked responsibility or failed to meet their basic needs, I've still somehow turned into my father. I've resented missing out on my own carefree twenties because I had to raise my sister, though I never let her know. My father and I are both nothing more than cold, unfeeling, uncaring, selfish motherfuckers.

I have to get out of this room, out of this house, right this second, because the walls are closing in on me and I can't breathe. While everyone is busy mingling and catching up, they won't notice my absence. Even if they do, I'm the master of making up excuses of why I'm unavailable, emotionally or physically.

As nonchalantly as my racing heart will allow, I move toward the front door until I'm outside in the stifling humidity. I slowly walk around the exterior of the house, keeping my gaze trained on the decorations in case anyone asks, but inside I feel like I can blow at any second. After several minutes of practicing deep breaths, I feel my pulse slowing and my mind clearing.

When I turn around, Daisy's watching me the way one would watch a wild animal that's wounded and needs help. Unsure of how to approach it, but too invested in saving it to turn away, regardless of the damage it can inflict. I've already caused her enough pain and trouble. The last thing I want to do is add to it now.

"What are you doing out here?" I finally ask.

"I could ask you the same thing, but I doubt you'd tell me

the truth. I've seen that look in other's eyes before, Rod, so I have a good idea what's going on with you."

"Oh, yeah? What's that?"

She takes a few steps closer, keeping a leery eye on me while trying to close the gap. "It looks like maybe you're a little overwhelmed by my family. Possibly on the verge of an anxiety attack. So you came outside to get a little air, put a little space between you and the horde of people inside."

"I'm very strong-minded. I don't have panic attacks, Daisy."

"No? Okay. My mistake, then. I thought you might need someone to talk through whatever's bothering you. Problems aren't quite as overwhelming when you let them out, instead of bottling them inside." She raises her brows in question, giving me the chance to save face and talk at the same time.

When I'm silent too long, she nods slowly. "You know where to find me if you change your mind. I won't pressure you."

She turns to walk around the corner of the house, and I can't take my eyes off her. When she makes the turn and is instantly out of sight, I feel as if my heart stops beating altogether.

"Daisy!" I didn't mean to yell that loud. The entire neighborhood probably heard me.

She pops back around the corner and rushes to me. "Everything's all right, Rod. Focus on the sound of my voice and taking the next breath. There's no one around except you and me."

We ease down to the ground and sit in the shade on the isolated side of the house. She rubs my back in long, soothing strokes. Her soft voice reassures me over and over that what

I'm experiencing is nothing to be ashamed of and is perfectly normal.

Nothing about it feels normal, but if I know anything for certain, it's that she's the epitome of all that is good and gentle in this world. I cling to that truth until my heart resumes working. Then I lean my head over on her shoulder, close my eyes, and immerse myself in the love and charity she's giving. I'll stay right here as long as she'll allow.

When I feel like myself again, I speak without lifting my head. "That has never happened to me before. I'm sorry I'm ruining your trip home."

"You haven't ruined anything. Don't even think that. Is the worst over now?"

"Yeah, I'm gaining a little clarity of mind again. Thank you for staying out here with me."

"You're welcome, but for the record, you never have to thank me for that. I've been in your shoes before. I understand all too well how devastating it feels."

"Your family is the best, Daisy. They've welcomed us into their cozy home. Within an hour of meeting them, my family is already part of yours. I've failed Juliana and Isabelle… miserably. I believed the material things were what they wanted, what they needed. But seeing their faces today, I realize I've not only missed the mark, but I wasn't even anywhere near the target.

"I don't know what'll happen in the coming weeks. I can't save my sister. I'm facing raising Isa as my own if Jules can't beat this cancer. She's growing weaker by the day, even though I try to fool myself into thinking she's getting better. All I want is to save my sister."

"Rod, what did I tell you about being too hard on yourself?

Do you know what I see when I look at the three of you? A family who loves each other fiercely and would do anything to ensure everyone is taken care of and loved. Your sister and your niece have never doubted your dedication to them, not for one minute. Apparently, you can't see it, but I see it plain as day. You are everything to them, and they love you with everything they have. If that's not the sign of a man who did everything right, I don't know what is.

"Did either of them have a perfect childhood? Of course not, because that's a fantasy world. It doesn't exist. None of us have had a perfect life. But they've had a wonderful life with you, and they wouldn't trade that for all the cousins and all the aunts and uncles in the world. They'd take you over all that any day and twice on Sunday."

All I can do is nod. I have no words.

"Your sister is fighting for her life with everything she's got. We'll help her with that fight in every way we can. They have tested me to see if I'm a tissue match for her. I'm just waiting for the lab results to come back and the oncologist's office to call me. Let's just take it one day at a time. If I'm not a suitable donor, we'll have bone marrow testing drives until we find one. Don't give up on her. She's not giving up on us."

"You have my word. I'll never give up."

We walk around to the backyard, Daisy playing host and showing me the pool area as we approach the door. More family has arrived in the time we sat outside, and I'm positive our absence was noticed since we weren't around to greet them. But no one mentions it or seems perplexed as we gather in the large dining room, taking our seats to enjoy the delicious feast already on the table.

We're all just one big, happy family.

CHAPTER THIRTY-TWO

Daisy

After a long day of traveling, spending time with family, and talking Rod off the proverbial ledge, I am wiped out, and it's not even late afternoon yet.

"I'm going upstairs to take a nap before dinner. I can barely keep my eyes open. What about you two? I can show you to your room if you want to shower, nap, change clothes, or just chill in front of the television for a while." I look at Juliana and Isa, knowing at least one of them needs to rest.

"That sounds perfect. Lead the way. Come on, Isa. It's naptime, my little love."

"Okay, Mommy, but only because you need it more than I do."

We chuckle at her cuteness as we make our way up the stairs. After getting them squared away in one of the guest rooms, I disappear into my room and fall face-first onto the bed. Just as my eyes close and I feel the warm blanket of sleep overcoming me, my cell rings from inside my purse at the foot of the bed. Since almost everyone I know is here with me, I'm too curious to let it go to voicemail.

When I see the name on the screen, I'm equally scared and excited.

"Hello?"

"Can I speak with Daisy Nash, please?"

"This is Daisy."

"Hi, Daisy. This is Claire with Morgan Oncology Center." She goes through the questions to confirm my identity before continuing with her reason for calling. "We got your tissue type results back from the lab today, and it turns out you are a potential match for Juliana. There are a few more extensive tests we'd have to do to ensure you'd be a complete match, but I'm afraid those tests will have to wait."

"Because of the holidays?" That means the time for a transplant isn't too far away. A few more weeks and we could be well on our way to a bone marrow transplant for Juliana. This could be the cure she's been waiting and praying to receive.

"Um, no, not because of the holidays." Claire hesitates for a moment. "I take it you don't know then. Daisy, you can't donate bone marrow at this time because your pregnancy blood test came back positive."

Read more of Rod & Daisy in All I Need, coming soon! Pre-order your copy today!

~

Dear Reader,

Thank you for taking the time to read this book. This story has been a long time in the making and has been through several revisions, but I'm finally happy with the outcome. Sharing a book with the world is never easy, but I always hope you'll love it as much as I do.

These characters have a lot of depth and intricacies not commonly found in romance books. While the storyline is accurate medically and I do my best to maintain that integrity, I employed some creative liberties to ensure the story flows, and it's easy to read.

With today's technology advancements, procedures change rather quickly, even with transplants. "Bone marrow transplant" is an older term that may not be used as much as it once was. Today, it's more commonly referred to as a hematopoietic stem cell transplantation, but that's a lot to digest, even inside your head. There are also several more steps in the tissue match process that aren't depicted here, because that isn't germane to the story. Siblings aren't a match as often as you'd think, which is why so many people rely on the bone marrow registry to find a match.

I hope you've enjoyed Rod & Daisy so far! There's much more to come in *All I Need*, More surprises. More twists and turns. More love. More tears. More fun. More Hot Rod. :)

Lots of love,

Angel

BOOKS BY A.D. JUSTICE

Steele Security Series

Wicked Games (Book 1)

Wicked Ties (Book 2)

Wicked Nights (Book 3)

Wicked Intentions (Book 4)

Wicked Shadows (Book 5)

Crossing Lines Series

Fine Line

Blurred Line

Hard Line

The Vault Series

Warning Part One

Warning Part Two

Warning Part Three

The Crazy Series

Crazy Maybe (Book 1)

Crazy Baby (Book 2)

Crazy Love (Book 3, Free Short Story)

Dominic Powers Series

Her Dom (Book 1)

Her Dom's Lesson (Book 2)

Covis Realm, Easthaven Crest Series

Cloaked

Deceived

Unveiled

Stand—alone Novels

Saving Grace

Completely Captivated

Intent

Mistletoe Not Required

Immortal Envy

Just One Summer

ABOUT THE AUTHOR

A.D. Justice is the award-winning, *USA Today* bestselling author of several series and stand-alone romance novels in various romance genres, including romantic suspense, contemporary, and paranormal.

When she's not writing, she loves spending time with her alpha male husband in the Northwest Georgia mountains. They're living out their own HEA, frequently on horseback with a dog in tow.

She is also an avid reader of romance novels, a master of procrastination, a chocolate sommelier, a twister of words, and speaks fluent sarcasm. An avid animal lover, she has two horses, three cats, and two very spoiled dogs.

She loves chatting with her readers. You're welcome to stalk her across all social media!

Connect with her online!

Newsletter
Facebook Reader Group
Website

facebook.com/adjusticeauthor
instagram.com/authoradjustice
bookbub.com/authors/a-d-justice
amazon.com/author/adjustice
pinterest.com/adjusticeauthor

ACKNOWLEDGMENTS

First and foremost, I want to thank my Lord and Savior for His continued forgiveness of a sinner.

To my husband: I love you more than words can convey. I'm grateful for all your ideas and being my sounding board.

To my readers: Every story is personal and important to the author, but you are the reason we share our books with the world. Thank you for your time, feedback, and support. Whether you like, love, or hate the book, know that I appreciate you with all my heart.

To the bloggers: None of this would be possible without your help, support, and tireless pimping. I love everyone in this great group of people. I can't name one without naming everyone because you've all been so helpful and are wonderful people.

To my PA/PR Guru: Autumn, thank you for all your help and support. You are so very much appreciated.

To my friends: Chelle Bliss, thank you for your help with the blurb. Okay, fine. Thank you for writing the blurb! :)

T.K. Leigh, thank you for, well, everything, every day!

Michelle Dare, you are simply the best.

I love you ladies with all my heart!

To my editor and proofreader: Karen and Amy, thank you for taking such good care of my words.

www.ingramcontent.com/pod-product-compliance
Lightning Source LLC
Chambersburg PA
CBHW031621100726
47898CB00006B/1885

9 781733 907064